# The Darlings in Love

ALSO BY

# Melissa Kantor

*Confessions of a Not It Girl*
*If I Have a Wicked Stepmother, Where's My Prince?*
*The Breakup Bible*
*Girlfriend Material*
*The Darlings Are Forever*

# The Darlings in Love

## Melissa Kantor

HYPERION
New York

Printed in the United States of America

First Edition

1 3 5 7 9 10 8 6 4 2

V567-9638-5-11305

Designed by Marci Senders

Reinforced binding

Library of Congress Cataloging-in-Publication Data
Kantor, Melissa.
The Darlings in love / Melissa Kantor. — 1st ed.
p. cm.
Sequel to: The Darlings are forever.
Summary: Three fourteen-year-old best friends experience the joys
and heartbreaks of first love.
ISBN-13: 978-1-4231-2369-9
ISBN-10: 1-4231-2369-7
[1. Love—Fiction. 2. High schools—Fiction. 3. Schools—Fiction. 4. Best friends—
Fiction. 5. Friendship—Fiction. 6. New York (N.Y.)—Fiction.] I. Title.
PZ7.K11753Db 2012
[Fic]—dc23 2011016071

*Medea* by Euripides; translated by Alistair Elliot;
published by Oberon Books, December 1996
Oberon Books Ltd., 521 Caledonian Road, London N7 9RH

Visit www.hyperionteens.com

*To Abby Ranger*

*Love is a fire,*
*but whether it is going*
*to warm your heart or*
*burn your house down,*
*you can never tell.*
—Joan Crawford

# Chapter One

NATALYA PULLED HER dark blue winter jacket more tightly around her, shivering in the sharp January wind as she waited for the light to change. She was almost half an hour early for lunch with Victoria and Jane, and she had stupidly planned on watching the chess players in Washington Square Park. She loved seeing the men (they were always men for some reason) curled over their games, totally oblivious to the fact that she was lingering at the periphery of their vision. Focused and silent, they reminded her a little of her dad, who'd emigrated from Russia long before Natalya was born.

But clearly no sane person would be playing chess outside on a day when it made your lungs ache just to breathe. If Natalya could have teleported to Ga Ga Noodle, she would have, but since she couldn't, the shortest way to the Darlings' favorite lunch spot was the hypotenuse across Washington Square Park. She hurried under the shimmering white arch, too cold to linger in appreciation of its majesty as she normally might have.

As she headed west, she saw to her amazement that two people were playing at the southernmost table. Both were so bundled up that it was impossible to tell whether they were old or young, fat or thin, male or female; they just looked like enormous collections of outerwear playing each other. Natalya wondered how they managed to grip the pieces through their thick mittens. Standing on the walkway about twenty feet from where they sat, she felt the painful tingling of her toes from the cold and shook her head, half awed, half bewildered by their commitment to the game.

As she lingered, one of the players reached up and tucked his scarf more firmly around his throat. The gesture made Natalya register the fact that the scarf bore the colors of Thompson Academy, her elite private school's brother school. Natalya was used to seeing guys from Thompson hanging out on the front steps of Gainsford in the afternoons, talking to their friends or sisters or girlfriends, their purple-and-gold team jackets clashing brutally with Gainsford's uniform of red-and-green plaid skirts. She had never understood why, when their schools were coordinated in so many ways, no one had tried to match the Gainsford and Thompson colors.

It was too cold to stand still for another second, and Natalya took a step forward. Her movement caught the attention of the boy with the Thompson scarf, and he glanced her way. Natalya gasped.

It couldn't be. . . .

His chin and forehead were covered, but Natalya was positive she knew exactly who she was looking at. Even as she told herself she was crazy to think she was looking at *him*, her heart began to pound hard against her ribs. *Stop it*, she told herself. It is *not* him. He lived miles away from Washington Square Park, all the way on the Upper East Side. What would he possibly be doing downtown, playing chess outside in subzero weather?

The guy kept looking in her direction, but he didn't call out or wave, and after a few seconds, he turned back to the chessboard in front of him. Natalya bolted for the corner. As she stepped into the street, a bike messenger running the light swerved wildly to avoid crashing into her, but she was already so discombobulated that the near-accident barely registered.

"And you're *sure* it was Colin?" asked Jane, leaning across their table at Ga Ga Noodle, her enormous green eyes growing even larger than usual as Natalya told her story. Even though Jane had been in L.A. with her dad for all of Christmas vacation, she and Natalya hadn't wasted any time on catch-up chitchat.

Best friends know when they have an emergency on their hands.

Natalya had only hung out with Colin Prewitt twice, but that had been enough for her to develop a serious crush on him. A serious crush she'd pretended didn't exist so she could be friends with his cool sister, Morgan, who was the most popular girl in Natalya's grade and who thought her brother Colin was a major dork. Though Natalya had ultimately realized she'd chosen the wrong Prewitt sibling, Colin had made it clear that it was too late for her to change her mind. Remembering his face when she'd blown him off the last time they'd seen each other, Natalya nodded slowly. "I'm sure."

"That's incredible!" said Jane, leaning back in her chair and crossing her arms. "The odds of you two running into each other must be . . . tiny."

"One in eight million," Natalya agreed. "Give or take."

Jane was still sitting in shocked silence when the door opened and Victoria dashed inside calling, "Sorry! Sorry! Sorry!" as she crossed the nearly empty restaurant to their table. Her pink cheeks matched her fuzzy pink earmuffs. With her baby blue coat and straight, beautiful blond hair, she might have stepped out of a J. Crew ad.

"You look so pretty," said Natalya, standing up and hugging Victoria.

"I'm sooo sorry I'm late," said Victoria, squeezing Natalya back, then turning to hug Jane.

"Natalya just saw Colin," Jane announced as Victoria hung her coat over the back of an empty chair.

"Oh my god! What'd he say? What'd *you* say?" Victoria dropped into the chair across the table from Natalya.

Natalya told her what had happened. When she'd finished, there was a long silence broken only by Tom, their usual waiter. "Hello." He was carrying a tray loaded with three virgin piña coladas, the drinks the Darlings had ordered so often they no longer had to ask for them.

"Wow," said Victoria, holding her cherry by the stem and twirling it thoughtfully through her drink. "So neither of you said *anything*?"

"I was just so . . ." Natalya looked down at her hands, as if the word to describe how seeing Colin had made her feel might be written there.

In the silence, Jane studied her friend's face. "Wait a second." She waited for Natalya to look at her before announcing, "You still like him."

"No I don't!" Natalya said automatically. "It's just . . . embarrassing, that's all."

"Yes, you do," Jane countered, still watching her. "You still like him."

"I . . ." Natalya pulled anxiously on her necklace, with its single luminous pearl. Jane and Victoria were wearing matching necklaces, as always. "I don't know, maybe I do," Natalya finally admitted.

"It's okay to like him," Victoria assured her.

Natalya dropped the pearl and plucked angrily at the paper wrapping on her straw. "No, it's really *stupid* if I still like him, considering I e-mailed him twice that I was sorry, and he never e-mailed me back. He's obviously forgotten all about me."

"Yeah, right," Jane snorted. "You're a super cute, genius chick who's practically, you know, a chess grandmaster. Colin meets girls like that every day. *In his dreams*."

"You think?" asked Natalya, perking up. Then her shoulders

slumped. "Whatever. Let's talk about something else." She looked over at Victoria. "How was the swearing-in ceremony?"

"Nat . . . ?" Victoria probed gently.

But Natalya just held up her hand to silence Victoria. "Seriously, it's not worth talking about. I was just really surprised. Forget I even mentioned it. Now . . ." She dropped her straw into her glass and looked across the table at Victoria. "Tell us about D.C."

Victoria took a sip of her drink before answering. "I know this is a big *duh*, but it wasn't until I saw his apartment that I realized now that he's a senator, my dad's going to be living down in D.C. all week for the next six years! And sometimes he'll even stay there on the weekends. He's there now." She shook her head sadly. "My mom's really bummed. I can't imagine if it were Jack and me." Her cheeks flushed at the mention of her boyfriend's name.

"Ooooh, Jack," said Jane, clasping her hands in front of her chest and making her voice mock dreamy. "Jack. Jack. Wherefore art thou, Jack?"

Victoria giggled, then threw her napkin at her friend. "I do *not* sound like that."

Jane dodged the napkin. "Yes, you do. Everyone does. Even my *mom* is starting to sound that way about boring Richard."

"No!" said Victoria, horrified. They all knew what a complete zero Jane's mother's new boyfriend was.

"Yes!" Jane corrected her. "Last night my mom sat me down and was all, 'Honey, I want you to know that Richard is becoming very special to me, and I'm hoping you two will get to know each other better.'" She rolled her eyes. "The man does not *speak*. It's like he's in a coma. How do you get to know someone like that?"

"What does your mom say?" asked Natalya, laughing.

"She says he's *shy*." Jane gave her friend a look of incredulity. "But you know what I say?"

"What?"

"At a certain point, shy becomes clinically dead."

"I always pictured your mom getting together with someone really cool," said Victoria.

"That's because of Nana," Jane explained, referring to her grandmother who had died suddenly in July and whom all three friends had loved. Nana had been the one to name them the Darlings. "All of Nana's boyfriends and husbands were cool. Oh, which reminds me! The invitations for the opening came. And my mom said that the party's going to be super swanky, which means we will all be purchasing *awesome* dresses." She reached into her bag and pulled out a glossy postcard. "Look! Isn't it beautiful?"

Natalya and Victoria huddled over the card, which featured a painting of a young woman in a one-piece bathing suit lying on a deck chair with a drink on the table beside her and an open paperback on her lap. The pale yellow of the woman's suit stood in sharp contrast to the vivid blue of the water and the bright red-and-white stripes of the chair; even in the photograph, it was easy to see how rich and luscious the brushstrokes were, to practically feel the thick texture of the painting's surface.

"I didn't realize Nana was so gorgeous," said Victoria, almost to herself. "I mean, she was really pretty even when she was older," she added quickly.

"No, I know what you mean," Jane said. She craned her neck to look at the painting of her grandmother as a young woman. Beneath it were the words *EDGAR VINYARD: The Elizabeth Rawlings Years. A New Permanent Installation, Barnard College.* "Nana said Edgar painted her more beautiful than she really was because he loved her so much."

Victoria pressed the card to her chest. "Oh my god, that is *so* romantic."

Jane nodded. "He was the love of her life. And he wasn't even famous yet. I mean, not as famous as he got after he died." She sighed. "I don't think Nana ever got over him. In her will she said she left the paintings to Barnard because her years with Edgar and her years at college were some of the happiest of her life."

"I'm seriously going to cry," said Victoria. She looked back at the picture. "I want someone to love me that much."

"Well, the fact that you have a date to the opening is probably a good sign," said Jane.

But Victoria shook her head. "Jack can't come. He's got plans that night."

"Okay, that's a bummer," Jane acknowledged. "But at least you *have* a boyfriend. You're not a spinster like I am."

"Hey, if you're a spinster, then so am I!" Natalya objected.

Victoria waved away her friends' fears. "You can't be a spinster at fourteen!" she assured them, sliding the card back to Jane.

"Maybe not in *this* century," Natalya said. "But definitely back in the day."

"Whatever. I'm over love." Jane brushed away their debate. "It's all in the past for me."

"Is this about Mr. Robbins?" asked Natalya. "Because you can't swear off love just from that."

"Seriously." Victoria gave her friend a meaningful stare. "He was your *teacher*. It's *good* that nothing happened between you two."

Jane stabbed her straw into her drink. "Let's talk about something other than love."

"Yes, please," groaned Natalya.

"Okay," agreed Victoria. "As long as it's not biology." She pressed her palm to her forehead. "I've got a massive test Monday, and I haven't even started studying for it."

"Done," promised Natalya.

"Though in your case, love and biology are kind of the same thing." Jane was referring to Jack's being in Victoria's bio class.

"Well, when you think about it, aren't love and biology *always* the same thing?" asked Natalya.

"Truer words were never spoken," agreed Jane, and in honor of their astute observation, the Darlings clinked their glasses together.

They didn't talk about Colin for the rest of the weekend, and Natalya did her best not to think about him. She'd meant what she'd said: it *was* stupid to like some guy who had clearly forgotten all about you. Still, despite not speaking his name again for the entire time she was with her friends, Natalya found herself taking a detour through Washington Square Park Sunday morning on her way from Jane's to the subway. She told herself it had nothing to do with Colin, that it was a beautiful day and she just felt like taking a walk.

A light rain was falling, and she paused in the exact spot where she'd stood less than twenty-four hours earlier, staring at the row of stone chess tables. They were all empty.

It had been stupid to think he'd be there.

And even if, by some bizarre chance, he *had* been playing chess outside in the rain, what did she think would have happened? That he would have jumped to his feet, told her he forgave her for blowing him off, and announced he'd been secretly dying of love for her for the past three months?

By the time she got off the subway in Brighton Beach, it was pouring, and she arrived home soaked, freezing, and furious with herself. The only thing dumber than choosing Morgan Prewitt over her "dorky" brother Colin was regretting her decision months after she'd made it. Whenever Natalya or her brother, Alex, complained about something that was really their own fault, their father always said, *"Vy sdelali svoi krovat', v nastoyashchyee vremya lezhat v nem."* In other words, Natalya had made her bed.

And now she had to lie in it.

Natalya's mom made her take off her soaking clothes and get into a hot shower as soon as she walked in the door. After she'd put on a pair of sweats and a hoodie and drunk a scalding cup of tea, she went to the new computer her parents had gotten her for Christmas and logged on. She had a major bio lab to finish, and even for someone who liked weird, scary Dr. Clover as much as Natalya did, the task was a daunting one. Still, she gave herself five minutes to check out the pictures of Victoria's dad's swearing-in ceremony, since she'd told Victoria that she wanted to see them.

As soon as she opened her Facebook page, Natalya saw she had a message. But it wasn't from Victoria.

Colin Prewitt sent you a message.

A message. Colin had sent her a message. Her hand was shaking so hard, she could barely force the mouse to navigate so she could read what he'd written. When she did, she found herself staring at a single sentence.

I saw you at Washington Square Park yesterday.

So she'd been right. It *was* Colin. And he *had* seen her standing there when he'd looked up and adjusted his scarf.

But if it was Colin, and he saw her, why hadn't he done something: called her name or said hello? And why the cryptic message: I saw you? Shouldn't he have written I saw you *and* . . . ? Or I saw you *but* . . . ? Like, *I saw you, but I had laryngitis and couldn't call out to you.*

The whole thing was very weird. But was it bad weird? Or was it good weird? What did he mean by writing to her? And how was she supposed to respond?

Her plans to finish her lab report evaporated. Heart pounding, she texted Jane and Victoria to call her immediately.

# Chapter Two

IT WAS A little hard for Jane to have not just her mother, but *both* Victoria and Natalya being all dewy-eyed over guys, given that she was through with love. It was like being allergic to cats and everyone you cared about decided to adopt a kitten.

Still, Jane was excited for Natalya about the message Colin had sent. And she loved the response the three of them had composed yesterday. As soon as first period ended on Monday, she headed into the crowded hallway of The Academy for the Performing Arts, checking for news from Natalya saying Colin had responded to their—well, officially Natalya's—response to him. There was nothing from Natalya. But there *was* a voice mail from her mother.

"Hi, honey, it's me. Listen, Richard and I are having dinner at Panne e Vino at seven. Are you free to join? I'll be seeing patients until six, so just leave me a message." *Ugh*. Panne e Vino was her and her mom's place. Just like Ga Ga Noodle was the Darlings' place. You couldn't just start inviting random guys to your place.

What was her mother's *problem*?

Rather than call her mother, Jane wrote a text to Natalya.

Anything? she typed.

A second later, Natalya's response appeared on her screen. Nyet.

Jane felt a tiny shudder of guilt. Had she given her friend bad advice?

Last night on the phone, Natalya and Victoria had kept trying to phrase a long, intricate response about how sorry Natalya still was and how she'd been thinking about Colin and really regretted not pursuing their friendship. *Blah blah blah*. Each time they launched into a new version of the same e-mail, Jane felt herself growing increasingly irritated. Finally she'd said, "Look, Nat, you've already sent him that message. *Twice*."

"What do you mean?" asked Natalya.

"I *mean*, the last two times you e-mailed him, it was with some long, heartfelt apology, right?"

"Right," agreed Natalya warily.

"So forget it. That conversation is over."

"Aaand . . ." Natalya prompted.

"Aaand," Jane echoed, "this one is . . . lighter."

"Lighter." Natalya's doubt was evident.

Jane had a sudden inspiration. "You've got to answer in kind. He said, 'I saw you.' So now you say, 'I saw you too.'"

Natalya and Victoria laughed.

But Jane didn't.

"You are *not* seriously suggesting I say that," insisted Natalya.

But the more Jane thought about it, the better an idea it seemed to be. "It's perfect. Oh!" She let out a cry of excitement. "And then put your cell number! That is *totally* flirting."

Both Natalya and Victoria started laughing again. "Trust me," Jane assured them. "He'll get what you're doing."

"I don't know if *I* get what I'm doing," Natalya said, clearly unconvinced.

"Maybe she could say, 'I saw you too' *and* something else," offered Victoria.

"Nope," said Jane, shaking her head even though Natalya and Victoria couldn't see her through the phone. "It's got to be just that. That and her cell."

Five minutes later, Natalya, somewhat reluctantly, had sent the message.

And here it was the next morning, and Colin hadn't replied.

Now Jane could feel her own doubts growing about the wisdom of her advice. In the world of romance, she wasn't exactly a gold medalist. More like the Queen of It Seemed Like a Good Idea at the Time. Why had she interfered when Natalya and Victoria were composing their sincere message to Colin? She should have just shut her mouth and let them work their magic. After all, Victoria had a boyfriend. And Natalya had a boy who clearly hadn't forgotten her even though they'd only met twice, both times months ago.

She, on the other hand, was sailing the ocean of love as a first-class passenger on the *Titanic*.

Before she could text Natalya she was sorry and that Natalya should just go ahead and write Colin whatever she wanted, a hand reached out of the mass of people traveling the crowded hallway, grabbed her arm, and pulled her aside so abruptly that she almost dropped her phone.

"Hey!" Her surprise at being touched, combined with her depressing train of thought, made her voice snappish.

"Hey, yourself."

The face she found herself looking into did nothing to alleviate her annoyance.

It was Mark's.

She and Mark had been friendly for about ten minutes at the beginning of the year, just long enough for her to discover that he was the biggest poseur in the school. It was because of Mark's announcing his intention to audition for the major fall production of *A Midsummer Night's Dream* that Jane had decided to audition in the first place. Of course Mark had been too chicken to actually go through with the tryout, which had meant Jane was the only freshman who'd auditioned. She dropped her phone into her bag and looked back at Mark, who was leaning contentedly against the wall of metal lockers.

"Yes?" she asked.

He raised an eyebrow at her and smiled. His expression reminded Jane that she'd once thought Mark was cute. Still, as usual, he undermined his acceptable physical appearance by giving her a self-satisfied grin, one that was clearly intended to inspire her to ask what he was smiling about.

Refusing to be inspired, Jane paused for a long beat, and then, when Mark remained silent, shrugged and started walking toward her next class, which was English. Mark quickly fell into step next to her.

"I've got a proposition for you."

"Okay." They came to a crowded T-junction, and Jane made a left. Mark stayed alongside her. Walking in the opposite direction, Dahlia, a girl who'd been in *Midsummer* with Jane, waved at her. "Want to have lunch?" she called, barely slowing down as they passed each other.

"Sure," Jane shouted back. In the first weeks after the show, Jane had avoided her fellow cast members, scared that her asking Mr. Robbins out for a drink might be something they were all gossiping about behind her back. But as November had become December, and December, January, she'd slowly accepted that no one associated opening night or the show in general with anything but Jane's triumph as the only freshman since Fran Sherman (the biggest star at the Academy) to land a part in a main-stage production.

Nobody but Jane, that is.

"This is one of those opportunities you will *not* be able to say no to," Mark assured her confidently.

"Try me." She glanced over at him. He was wearing his usual

uniform: a long-sleeved T-shirt (today's was light green and said LITTLE SHREDDER), black jeans, and checkerboard Vans. His thick black hair was in a ponytail. Mark wore exactly what all the skater boys at Jane's old school had worn and what all the skater boys at the Academy wore.

The only difference was, she'd never seen him with a skateboard.

"I will. So, in March, there's going to be *A Night to Remember*." He blocked the words out in the air, as if he were drawing a Broadway marquee, then turned to Jane and explained, "An evening of great love scenes."

In light of her recent experience with love, it was impossible not to laugh at Mark's proposal.

"I'm glad you find this funny," he said, misunderstanding her laughter.

Jane wasn't about to explain the real reason she was laughing. Instead, since they'd arrived at her classroom, she said simply, "This is where I get off."

He tilted his head. "You're not seriously saying no. I haven't even done my hard-core pitch yet."

Jane shrugged. "It's shocking, I know. But I will have to live without acting opposite you in 'a great love scene.'" She put air quotes around the last four words.

"Oh, don't bet on *that*." He pointed his finger at her and gave her a knowing look, but when she didn't respond, he dropped his hand and turned serious. "It wouldn't be acting opposite me. I'm going to direct. I'm a fabulous director, by the way."

*God, Mark, cocky much?*

Before Jane could respond to his generous assessment of his own directorial skills, he added, "I want to do a scene from *Medea*."

Despite her feelings about Mark, Jane was suddenly listening. Ever since Nana had taken her to see *Medea* at the Brooklyn Academy of Music when she was in seventh grade, Jane had dreamed of playing Medea, one of the most powerful, vindictive female characters in the history of theater. It was impossible not to be tempted by the part, especially since she'd been too shell-shocked by what had happened with Mr. Robbins to audition for *Chicago*, the current main-stage production. The only acting she'd done since *Midsummer* was in her scene-study class.

Maybe what she needed was a small production, something to get her feet wet.

"You're considering it," Mark concluded, watching her hesitate. Then he gently hip-checked her. "Face it: you can't resist me."

Mark's thinking he was so irresistible made it easy for her to resist him. She shook her head. "Sorry, I can't."

The late bell rang just as Mark opened his mouth as if to argue with her. Then he shut it and nodded, his lips pressed into a line. As Jane swung into her classroom, she remembered to call over her shoulder, "But thanks for asking." She didn't know if he was still standing there or if he'd heard her, and the truth was, he was so arrogant that she didn't really care.

# *Chapter* Three

WITH ITS WALLS covered in black-and-white Ansel Adams landscapes and Richard Avedon portraits, shelves stacked with photography reference books, and double bed blanketed with a soft red comforter, Jack's room was Victoria's favorite place in the world.

Too bad she almost never got to be in it.

Jack's mom taught preschool a few blocks away, so she was usually home in the afternoon. If she wasn't, his father, who played cello with the New York Philharmonic and had morning rehearsals and evening performances, was pretty much guaranteed to be in the apartment from four to six. When he'd been younger, Jack told Victoria, he'd loved that one, and sometimes both, of his parents picked him up from school and spent the afternoon with him. He'd always felt a little bad for kids who had to log after-school hours with babysitters because their moms and dads worked late.

But lately Jack didn't feel bad for those kids.

He envied them.

Jack's parents had made it clear: they did not want Victoria and Jack in Jack's room with the door closed. And Victoria's parents had made it equally clear that if neither of them was home, Victoria and Jack couldn't be at her apartment. Since her dad was basically living in Washington, and her mother worked until six or seven every day, they couldn't be at her apartment in the afternoons *at all*. (The one time they'd tried to take advantage of no one's being there, the doorman had inadvertently ratted them out by cheerfully telling Victoria's mom when she got home from work that she'd "unfortunately just missed" Victoria and her friend Jack.)

All of which made what they were doing right now practically a miracle.

Victoria lay with her head on Jack's stomach, their bodies forming a T across his bed. One of Jack's hands was running lazily through Victoria's hair, and the other was holding hers. The Hastings were spending the afternoon walking along the High Line before getting an early dinner in Chelsea with friends from out of town. When Victoria had turned on her phone that morning, there had been a text from Jack.

who has an apartment all 2 themselves after school? call me & find out.

It had felt like Christmas in January.

"I love Sweden," Victoria said.

"Why?" asked Jack, his voice rumbling gently against the back of her head.

"Isn't that where your parents' friends are from?"

Jack laughed. "They're from Denmark, actually."

Victoria laughed too, then rolled onto her side so she was facing Jack. He curled toward her, his face just inches away. "Denmark, Sweden," she said. "They're kind of the same, right?"

"Close enough," Jack agreed. He kissed her lightly on the nose. She raised her face so his next kiss found her lips. At first their kiss was gentle, but then he put his hands on her face, pulling her toward him, and it became deeper and more intense. Kissing Jack made Victoria feel like she was slipping out of her body and, at the same time, like she was slipping *into* it, really existing inside herself for the first time in her life.

He gently kissed her closed eyes. "I'm hungry, but I don't want to stop kissing you."

"Mmmm," Victoria sighed dreamily. "That reminds me, I brought cookies."

"Oh no," Jack lamented. "The impossible choice. Your delicious kisses versus your delicious cookies."

She laughed as he traced the edge of her ear with his lips. "That tickles."

Victoria's phone buzzed. "Do you want to answer that?" Jack asked.

She didn't, really. She just wanted to be here. With Jack.

Instead of reaching for her phone, she pulled his face back

to hers and started kissing him again. "I'll take that as a no," he mumbled, through their kiss. She slid her arm around his back.

When his phone rang the opening bars of Lost Leaders' "All the Stars," he groaned and pulled reluctantly away from her. "I just have to see if it's my mom. If I don't answer, she'll use her Spidey sense to figure out what we're doing, and she'll race home."

Victoria kissed him once, swiftly, then let him go. He got up and dug his phone out of his bag. "I *knew* it!" he said, holding the screen up toward Victoria so she could read the words THE MOM.

"Hey, Mom," he said. Propped up on her arm, Victoria watched as he sat on the window seat and toyed with the shade pull, appreciating how cute he looked in his jeans and soft gray sweater, the same color as his eyes. Sometimes when she saw Jack in the hallway at school, she couldn't believe he was really hers. It wouldn't have surprised her if their whole relationship turned out to be just a figment of her imagination, something she'd wanted so fiercely she'd believed her own dream. Every time he saw her coming toward him down the hall, and she watched his face break into its slow smile of happy recognition, she felt the same glow of joyous surprise.

It's real, she would think. It's really real.

"When?" Jack asked. "Oh yeah?" He stood up and strolled across the room to where his guitar leaned against the wall, then idly plucked at the strings before picking it up and sitting down in his desk chair. "Okay, Mom, I'm glad you called, but I gotta go." He listened for a second, then said, "At my desk." Something about the way he said it made Victoria's ears prick up. It was like

*22*

he was lying or something, even though he really *was* sitting at his desk.

Jack's mom must have sensed something too, because whatever she said next, Jack responded, "I'm *not* lying," but he grinned and shook his head, mouthing to Victoria, *I'm a terrible liar.* "Yes, Mom, as a matter of fact, she is." He listened for a second. "Yes, Mom, I *am* impressed. . . . Yes, you *should* work for the CIA. . . . Mom, we're not doing anything untoward. I promise you won't have any grandchildren in the immediate future." Victoria felt her face grow bright red, and even Jack blushed at what he'd just said. Despite being halfway across the room from the phone, Victoria could hear his mother's voice grow loud with annoyance. "You're right, Mother, that was a *completely* inappropriate thing to say." He put his hand on his heart. "I sincerely apologize. . . . Yes, I do realize how lucky I am. . . . It's true, you are much more permissive than most mothers." Jack rolled his eyes at Victoria, who smiled sympathetically. "Though, let me point out, not as permissive as some. . . . Sorry, sorry," he added quickly. "No, I don't want you to come right back uptown this second. . . . Okay, Mom. I love you too. . . . Yeah, see you soon . . . Okay. We will. I promise. Bye." He hung up and gave Victoria a sheepish look. "My mom says hi."

Victoria raised an eyebrow. "It sounded like she said a lot more than that."

"As you know, my mother is not one for brevity," he reminded her. It was true: Victoria liked Jack's mom a lot, but she definitely was chatty.

Idly, almost like he didn't realize he was doing it, Jack began picking out a tune. He had never played the guitar for Victoria before; she'd noticed the instrument in the corner and wondered if he played at all, or if the guitar was just something he'd planned on mastering and then given up, the way she had ice skates hanging in her closet, which she'd worn once and never put on again.

But clearly Jack had spent way more time with his guitar than she had with her skates. Victoria watched his agile fingers moving across the strings, then lifted her eyes to his, which were staring at her. She felt the melting feeling she always experienced when Jack looked at her like that.

Still looking into her eyes, he began to sing along to the tune he was playing. Jack's voice was soft but deep and sure, and he let the song unfold slowly and sweetly. The words were about swimming alone under the night sky, and they described a place so still and perfect and beautiful, Victoria wished she could be there.

Suddenly Victoria felt her eyes filling with tears. Everything about this moment was just so perfect. It was as if her whole self—her very soul—was standing on tiptoe with joy. Why did they call it "falling in love"? She didn't feel like she was about to fall. She felt like she was about to fly.

The silence that hung in the room when the song ended felt as significant as the music had. Victoria and Jack stayed perfectly still, staring at each other. Neither of them spoke. They didn't need to. To Victoria, it felt as if somehow they were communicating on a level deeper than language.

Jack spoke first. "I love you, Victoria." His voice was serious, his eyes dark and intense as they bored into hers.

Victoria felt her heart pounding in her chest. Jack put the guitar down, stood up, and walked over to where she lay on the bed. Then he reached his hand down to her.

Victoria let him pull her to her feet, and they stood facing each other.

"I don't want you to—" Jack began, but before he could finish, Victoria blurted, "I love you too." As soon as the words were out of her mouth, Victoria realized she'd been waiting to say them, like they were a present she'd picked out for Jack months ago and had been carrying around with her as she waited for the right moment to give it to him.

He smiled and took her other hand, intertwining his fingers with hers. "I was going to say that I didn't want you to think you had to say it back."

"I know," Victoria whispered. "I said it because I wanted to say it." She stood on her toes and tilted her face to his. As his lips came down to meet hers, she felt the familiar soaring feeling she always felt when Jack kissed her; only now, after what they'd just said to each other, it was stronger. She was taking off. She was leaving the world far below.

She was flying in love.

# Chapter Four

NATALYA HAD COME to dread English.

It had never been her favorite class to begin with, but she hadn't officially loathed it until October, when she'd stopped being friends with Sloane Gainsford, Morgan Prewitt, and Katrina Worthington, the most popular girls in her grade.

Back in October, Natalya had thought maybe she could stay friends with them and still do her own thing, but they had made it abundantly clear that that was never going to happen. Morgan's friends had lunch with Morgan when she told them to, liked the boys Morgan told them to like, and partied how and where Morgan told them to party. You couldn't be a tourist in

Morganland; once you were invited inside its borders, you lived there, or you were exiled forever.

These days, it wasn't like Morgan and her friends made up mean jingles featuring Natalya's name or tried to trip her when she walked by. They just effortlessly managed to make her feel like a complete loser. Once, for example, she'd said hello to them when they were walking down the hallway toward her, and they'd said nothing back, just stared at her as if they had no idea who she was or why she was talking to them. Since then, she'd twice seen Katrina and Morgan roll their eyes at each other when Ms. MacFadden, their English teacher, called on Natalya, and Natalya responded with something particularly stupid.

Today, Ms. MacFadden smiled at the class and said, "Let's start by looking at the scene in Gatsby's house when Daisy finally spends the afternoon there. Natalya?"

Even before she, Morgan, and Katrina were ex-kind-of-friends, Natalya had hated when her English teacher called on her, mostly because she hated the kinds of questions she asked. *How did you feel about last night's reading? What did the character really mean when she said/did/thought that?* Her prompts made Natalya feel as if she should go out and buy a mood ring or a crystal ball. Dr. Clover, her bio teacher, would never ask a student how she *felt* about evolution or what was motivating a leaf she was examining under the microscope. Natalya's math teacher never began class by gently inquiring, "Did everyone enjoy those problems we did for homework last night?"

It was as if English were something other than a class, some weird hybrid of academic inquiry and psychotherapy.

Today, Ms. MacFadden hadn't even asked a question. She'd just said, "Let's start by looking at the scene in Gatsby's house when Daisy finally spends the afternoon there," then Natalya's name with a little rising inflection, like Natalya would be able to read her mind and know exactly what Ms. MacFadden wanted to know.

Natalya considered the scene she had read for homework. Gatsby had his old girlfriend, Daisy, come to his house for the afternoon. He showed her all the stuff he owned, because he'd gotten really rich since the last time she saw him. At one point, Daisy was looking at his shirts, and she started to cry because they were so beautiful. Personally, Natalya couldn't imagine crying over a bunch of shirts, no matter how nice they were, but she didn't think Ms. MacFadden wanted to hear about that.

Instead, Natalya said, "I guess . . . I wasn't sure what the point was of showing her the shirts."

Ms. MacFadden cocked her head to the side. "What do you mean by 'point'?"

Sometimes her teacher's questions made Natalya feel as if she were an idiot, and other times they made her feel as if Ms. MacFadden were the idiot.

This was one of the Ms. MacFadden-is-an-idiot questions.

"Well," Natalya explained carefully, "I mean, he *is* trying to get her to leave her husband and marry him." Natalya felt she was pointing out the obvious, but maybe her observation was breaking new ground for Ms. MacFadden. "Shouldn't he have a plan or something?"

"You mean he should introduce her to a divorce lawyer?" The

teacher's eyebrows were raised in amusement. From the side of the table where Morgan and Katrina were sitting, Natalya heard a snicker.

"No!" Natalya said firmly. Was Ms. MacFadden willfully misunderstanding her? "He doesn't have to be *that* obvious about it," she continued more calmly. "I just think that since she's mad at her husband, and, you know, she seems to be into Gatsby right now, he should press his advantage." Her phone buzzed, and her heart leaped at the possibility that it could be a text from Colin.

Ms. MacFadden's face lit up with understanding. "Are you saying that all's fair in love and war?"

Natalya was too flustered by the thought that Colin might have texted her to have any idea what she'd been saying to Ms. MacFadden. All she wanted was to end the conversation and see who'd just sent her a message. "I guess so," she answered.

Ms. MacFadden gave Natalya one of the enthusiastic grins she usually reserved for girls like Morgan and Katrina, students who'd spent the summer reading *Pride and Prejudice* and got teary-eyed when they talked about Anna Karenina's tragic end. "That's a wonderful insight."

It was the first time all year her teacher had liked something Natalya had said, and Natalya wasn't even sure she'd said it. Still smiling, Ms. MacFadden called on a girl whose arm had shot to the ceiling the second Ms. MacFadden called on Natalya. "Yes, Amy?"

Amy took a deep, significant breath. "I just feel like Gatsby feels like Daisy feels . . ." Natalya tuned out Amy's feelings about feelings and, without looking down, began inching her phone out of her bag just as Ms. MacFadden cried, "Oh, Amy, I love that idea."

As she gave a tiny, private eye-roll, Alison Jones, who sat directly across the table, gave her a knowing grin. Natalya really liked Alison, who, despite being as beautiful as Morgan Prewitt, as rich as Morgan Prewitt (Natalya and Jordan had gone to Alison's palatial penthouse in December for a major bio-study session), and as Old New York as Morgan Prewitt, was exactly as nice and friendly as Morgan was scary and snobbish. Privately, Natalya thought of Alison as the anti-Morgan. She smiled back and glanced down at her lap to check her phone.

One new message from Jane.

i m sorry if i gave u bad advice. u should just write colin that u want to be friends. or whatever. i m retarded when it comes to guys. sorry. your darling j.

Reading Jane's message, Natalya wondered if maybe Ms. MacFadden was right. Maybe Natalya *had* been saying "all's fair in love and war." Not that she was in love with Colin, but still. She liked him. So she was working with her friends to come up with a strategy to seduce him. Well, not *seduce* him, she quickly corrected herself. But it was too late. Just thinking the word *seducing* made Natalya unable to repress a snort of embarrassed laughter at herself. Luckily it was disguised by the bell.

"Don't forget your compare-and-contrast paragraphs on Daisy and Myrtle!" Ms. MacFadden reminded the class as they began shoving books into their bags.

At her announcement, a few girls hastily reached for their assignment pads, but Natalya had already written the paper.

Walking into the hallway, she typed a response to Jane.

u r not retarded. colin is retarded. the e-mail u sent him was really cool. i mean the e-mail i sent him. we sent him. whatever. xoxo your darling n

"Hey," said Alison, coming up beside her. They fell into step together as Alison asked, "Do you ever feel like Ms. MacFadden feels that English class should feel like a group therapy session?"

"Definitely," agreed Natalya, laughing at how perfectly Alison had echoed both her own thoughts about Ms. MacFadden and Amy's flaky commentary on the book. Her phone buzzed, and Natalya was about to look down to see what Jane had replied when Jordan, coming down the hallway toward Natalya and Alison, called to them without slowing down, "See you at lunch?"

"Totally," agreed Alison.

"Definitely," said Natalya, flipping her phone open.

"See you," Alison called to Natalya as she let the crowd of girls sweep her off to her next class.

Normally, Natalya might have taken a moment to be internally grateful that she'd made friends like Jordan and Alison. At the very least, she would definitely have said *something* in response to Alison's leaving, even if it was simply "Bye."

But checking her phone seemed to have taken from Natalya the power of speech.

ok. now that we've both seen each other, r we ever going 2 finish that game of chess we started? colin

# Chapter Five

AT LUNCH JANE listened to Dahlia talk about rehearsals for *Chicago* with more than a little envy. Jane missed being in a cast. She missed hanging out in the theater, having lines and blocking to memorize. The massive amount of schoolwork she'd been spending her afternoons on lately was a sorry substitute for the hours spent rehearsing *Midsummer* in the fall.

"You're coming opening night, right?" asked Dahlia, sweeping her sandwich wrapping and empty potato chip bag onto her tray.

"Of course! You think I'd miss it?" Jane dropped her fork into the empty container that had held her Caesar salad, and stood up. As she did, Mark suddenly materialized at her side.

"We have to stop meeting like this," he said, giving her a suave smile.

"Hi, Mark."

Mark waved at Dahlia. "Hello," he said. "I'm Mark."

"Dahlia," said Dahlia. Jane could tell from the way Dahlia looked at him that she thought Mark was cute.

*Just wait until he starts talking. Then he's not so cute.* She hoped Dahlia was receiving her telepathic communication, but Dahlia misinterpreted the look Jane gave her.

"Well, I've got to get going." She hurriedly grabbed her tray and backed away from the table. "See you, Jane."

"See you." As her friend practically sprinted away, Jane rolled her eyes at Dahlia's fantasy that Jane was desperate for alone time with Mark.

"Tell me you're finding my stalking you endearing," Mark suggested.

"What gave me away?" Jane pressed her hand to her mouth in mock embarrassment.

"Oh, I've got your number." Mark gave Jane a knowing wink, then beckoned to someone standing behind her.

"I have someone I want you to meet," he said.

"Is it the person you've gotten to take my history test for me next period?" Jane asked. "Because that would earn you mad points."

Mark snapped his fingers regretfully. "Not quite." Still looking just past her shoulder, he continued, "It's the person I want you to act opposite in that scene I told you about." Nodding at whoever was behind her, Mark said, "Jane Sterling, meet Simon

Booth. He's a sophomore here at ye olde Academy. Simon, Jane Sterling. Who needs no introduction."

"I wasn't kidding when I said—" Jane began.

But before she could finish her sentence, she found herself shaking hands with the handsomest boy she had ever seen in her life. With his square jaw, perfect aquiline nose, shiny blond hair, creamy skin, and vivid blue eyes, Simon wasn't just handsome. Looking up at him, Jane felt simultaneously thrilled and calm, the way she felt when she stood on the porch of her father's house in L.A. at sunset and looked out over the city and to the Pacific Ocean beyond. He was . . .

Perfect.

"Hi, Jane," he said. His voice was deep, his smile toothpaste-commercial bright. Had Mark found him in a catalogue or something? "I'm Simon."

Though she prided herself on having something to say in absolutely any situation, now Jane barely managed to stutter a monosyllabic response. "H-h-hi." Simon's handshake was firm but not crushing. For an insane second, Jane wanted to keep holding his hand, but then she made herself let go.

Mark seemed to sense the effect Simon was having on Jane, because he didn't speak for a moment, just let her bask in the beauty of her potential costar. Then he said simply, "Si, I'm hoping you can convince Jane to be in that scene from *Medea*."

"It would be an honor to act opposite you. I loved you in *Midsummer*." Simon's smile was slightly abashed, as if despite the fact that he was gorgeous and a sophomore, he was a little awed to be in Jane's presence.

Jane didn't think she'd ever gotten such a genuine compliment. *It would be an honor to act opposite you.* She was so taken aback by his sincerity, she almost forgot to say, "Thanks."

"I've never had the guts to try out for a main-stage production, and I'm a *sophomore*." He shook his head as if amazed anew by Jane's courage, then realized his words could be misconstrued, and added quickly, "I don't mean I would have gotten a part if I *had* tried out."

"Now's no time for modesty, dude," Mark insisted. "This is the big sell here." He put his hand on Simon's shoulder. "Simon is a gifted actor. He was one half of a brilliant *Happy Days* in the fall."

Simon blushed. "Brilliant's a bit of an exaggeration. It's a great play. Have you read it?"

Jane shook her head. She hadn't even heard of it.

"Don't feel bad; neither had I until the audition." Again that warm, gentle smile. "Then I went on a total Beckett orgy. He's . . . amazing. I feel like it totally changed the way I think about theater. If you want, I'll lend you my copy of the play."

"Hey!" Mark snapped his fingers sharply, as if he'd just gotten an inspired idea. "I know! You can lend it to her *at rehearsal.*"

Simon rolled his eyes as Jane laughed. "Mark, enough, okay?"

"Enough?" Mark yelped. "Simon, you're supposed to be working *for* me."

Shaking his head more with amusement than frustration, Simon said, "He really is a good director. I couldn't have done *Happy Days* without him."

"Oh yeah!" Mark pumped his fist in the air. "I told you I was great."

Jane raised her eyebrow at him. "I believe the word Simon used was *good*, Mark, not *great*." Another word Simon had used was *orgy*, but Jane knew better than to linger on that.

"Hmmmm." Mark stroked his nonexistent beard as he considered her point. "You're right. I believe the word I used before was *fabulous*, not great, wasn't it?"

Before Jane could respond, Simon interrupted. "Mark, you're your own worst enemy here." He turned to Jane. "Seriously, I'll lend you the play even if you don't do the scene. But I think it would be really fun to work with someone who's as gutsy and talented as you clearly are." While he spoke, Simon kept looking at her with his blue, blue eyes, as lovely and endless as a summer sky.

Jane hesitated. Mark was annoying, there was no doubt about it. But she was going to have to get back onstage at *some point*. She did go to the Academy for the *Performing* Arts, after all. Besides, Simon seemed so nice. And so smart. And so . . . gorgeous. She wanted to borrow his Beckett plays and hear how they had changed his ideas about theater. She wanted to spend time with him.

If she said no to Mark, was any of that going to happen?

"Yeah, I guess. Okay," she said casually, though the decision felt anything but casual.

When Simon's face split into a smile, it was like the sun coming out; Jane couldn't not smile back. "Are you sure?" he asked. "We're not bullying you into this, are we?" He reached out and put his hand on her shoulder, a part of her anatomy of which Jane had never been particularly aware, but in which her entire being suddenly felt concentrated.

"Oh, she loves when I bully her," Mark assured Simon. He glanced at Jane, who was looking at Simon, who was still holding her shoulder. Then Mark took out his phone. "Jane, as soon as you regain the power of speech, you feel like giving me your number?"

Without taking her eyes off Simon, Jane asked Mark, "If we're going to work together, do you think you can try not to be the most annoying person in the universe?"

Mark pretended to consider her question. "Mmmm, probably not."

Simon suggested they all exchange numbers. Jane entered Mark's number more or less unconsciously, but when she typed SIMON, she savored every letter, almost as if she were writing something holy.

*Simon.*

"Okay," said Mark, flipping his phone shut and nodding happily. "Mission accomplished." He stepped away. "See you later, Jane."

Simon hesitated briefly. "I guess I'll see you at rehearsal."

"I guess so."

Was it Jane's imagination or did Simon follow Mark a little . . . reluctantly? She watched the two of them walk away, noticing how perfectly Simon's rib cage tapered down to his waist. He was wearing a dark red T-shirt that was tight but not *too* tight, with a pair of faded jeans. The way he looked made her think of a poem her English teacher had them memorize right before Christmas break. She couldn't remember the whole poem anymore, but her favorite part had stayed with her. It was: "A thing of beauty is a joy forever."

Simon was *definitely* a thing of beauty.

As she watched his perfect back disappear into the crowded cafeteria, Jane's phone buzzed.

colin wrote back!!! colin wrote back!!! he wants 2 finish r game of chess!!! u r a genius!!!!

So her advice to Natalya *hadn't* been bad. It had worked, and now Natalya had a date to play chess with Colin. Rereading Natalya's text, the memory of Simon's smile still fresh in her mind, Jane couldn't help thinking that maybe she wasn't on board the *Titanic* after all.

Maybe she was the captain of the Love Boat.

# Chapter Six

TWENTY MINUTES LATER, Natalya had a free period. Like the conscientious student she was, she sat with her notebook open and a pen in her hand, ready to get down to work. The work she was ready to get down to, however, had nothing to do with school.

"Okay," she said into her cell, which was wedged between her shoulder and her chin. "What do I write back?" Despite its being a damp, overcast day, she was sitting outside on the steps of Gainsford, the only place at school she'd been able to find privacy.

"Sorry," answered Jane. "You're on your own."

Natalya was sure she'd misunderstood. "What? Jane, what are you talking about?"

"You're ready to text Colin back on your own."

"No!" Natalya shook her head frantically. "Not ready. Definitely not ready. Janey, I need you!"

Jane was laughing. "Nat, listen to you. Of course you don't need me. He *already* likes you, remember? You guys have a whole . . . *frisson* that totally predates me. You just needed a little help getting back on your feet. But if you keep relying on me, I'll become a crutch."

"Yes! I need a crutch." Natalya lowered her voice to a whisper even though she was the only one around. "Please. I'm begging you. You *have* to tell me what my next move is."

"I give you my blessing. Just be yourself. It worked before."

"Jane. Jane! JANE!" Natalya didn't even care that she was shouting.

But Jane was gone. Natalya thought about calling her back, but she knew her friend. If Jane said she wasn't going to help Natalya, she wasn't going to help her. She typed an angry text into her phone and sent it off. i'll get u 4 this.

Immediately, Jane replied: u mean u'll thank me 4 this.

Natalya growled at the message, then stared at her phone for what felt like eons. *Be yourself.* That was what Jane had said. *Be yourself.* It should have been the simplest thing in the world, but Natalya found herself turning the two words over and over in her brain as if they were incomprehensible hieroglyphics. Surely Jane didn't mean for Natalya to respond, yes, colin, we r going 2 b finishing that game of chess and we'd better do it sooner rather than later bc ur all i think about.

At the thought of sending that text, Natalya laughed out

loud. A girl she didn't know was walking up the steps, and she gave Natalya a bewildered look.

*What, you've never seen a person sitting outside in the freezing cold and laughing maniacally to herself before?*

She waited until the girl had disappeared through the main doors, then took a deep breath and grasped her phone firmly. She was being kind of absurd. Colin had asked her a simple question: r we going 2 finish that game of chess? She did, in fact, want to finish the game he was talking about. Ergo, the answer was yes.

Ergo. Had Morgan really thought Colin was too big a dork for Natalya to talk to? Clearly she didn't know Natalya used the word *ergo* when trying to negotiate her way through a flirtation.

To: Colin Prewitt

yes.

The second she hit SEND, she regretted it. What if he didn't remember what he'd written and had no idea what she was saying yes *to*? What if he thought she was weird for just sending a single word? Should she write a second text elaborating on her first?

She opened her phone to explain what she'd meant by yes, but as the text materialized in her brain, she knew she could never send it. the yes i just sent u referred 2 your question about whether we will finish our chess game. by yes, i mean: yes we will.

She could not send him that text.

She could not send him *any* text.

She'd made her move, taken her hand off her piece, and now she had to wait and see what countermove Colin would make. She sat for a minute, shivering against the cold gray day, then looked down at her phone like maybe it would have received a response from Colin without notifying her.

Not surprisingly, there was no new text.

There was no text in History, either. Or Greek. And Algebra came and went without any word from Colin. Which Natalya knew because she checked her phone approximately fifty times during each class. This, she was able to factor, equaled a frequency exceeding once per minute.

By the end of the day, as she packed up her bag with the books she needed, she promised herself she'd stop checking. This was getting insane. What if it took him days to get back to her? She was going to give herself some kind of repetitive stress disorder from reaching into her bag so often.

Now that school was over, she switched her phone to loud and dropped it in her bag. She would not even *think* about it unless it buzzed or rang. Then she said good-bye to Jordan and Alison at their lockers and made her way down the front steps. Just as she passed the spot where she'd sent Colin the "yes" she'd been worrying about ever since, her phone gave a piercing ding. Frantically, she dug around in her bag. Her fingers grasped at half a dozen things that weren't her phone (her pencil case, her makeup bag, her assignment book) before they finally wrapped around her beloved cell.

n, i respect your brevity. will meet u 2morrow nite @ 7 @ the site where we played last time. c.

Not caring who heard, Natalya gave a fierce squeal of joy, then skipped down the last few steps, dialing the Darlings as she went.

# Chapter Seven

WEDNESDAY AFTER SCHOOL when the door marked Black Box B closed behind Jane, she found herself standing in the darkest place she'd ever been. It was as if the pitch black were pressing in on her, making it hard to breathe. She took a hesitant step forward, fully expecting to slam her shin into a chair or her face into a wall, but she didn't hit anything. She took another step.

"Careful you don't trip."

Jane let out a small cry of surprise. She'd thought she was alone in the darkened room.

"Sorry." Suddenly a row of hanging lights came on, and she

saw Mark, who was standing by a wall of switches. He had a pen tucked behind his ear.

"You scared the *crap* out of me." Jane pressed her hand to her pounding chest.

Mark didn't seem to have heard Jane's complaint, or else he'd heard it and didn't care. He circled the room, examining the effect of the lights he'd just flipped on.

Jane looked around also. Black Box B was, as its name suggested, a square room painted black. Glancing up, she saw that the black walls only extended about fifteen feet above her head, and that beyond and behind them were regular white walls, as if a black box had been constructed inside a larger white box.

"The point is to have a performance space you can set up any way you want to," said Mark, answering her unasked question as he crossed back to the wall of switches. He flipped something off and something else on, and now warm light bathed the entire center of the room in a soft pinkish glow. He nodded briefly at the effect, then continued. "They're doing the love scenes in the round, but they've set this theater up in all kinds of ways. Did you see *The Balcony* last semester?"

Jane shook her head.

Mark shrugged. "No biggie. It was just kind of cool, how they used the space." He crossed the room, grabbed two chairs by their backs, and pulled them over to the other side of the room.

"Would you like help?" It felt almost awkward to be having a normal exchange with Mark, one in which neither of them was trying to insult or one-up the other.

"No thanks."

"Okay," said Jane, and she dropped to sit cross-legged on the floor. She was impressed by how focused he was. For once, he was too busy to be posturing.

When the door opened and Simon walked in, Jane turned to look at him over her shoulder. "Hey," he called softly.

"Hey," she answered.

She'd thought she remembered what he looked like, how perfect he was, but either she'd forgotten, or else, in his navy blue V-neck sweater and black jeans that hung low on his hips, he looked even more impossibly beautiful than he had the day before.

"Hey, Mark!"

Attending to his chairs, Mark grunted in response.

Smiling the same gentle smile Jane remembered from their first meeting, Simon took a few steps toward Jane and looked down at her. "I'm kinda nervous."

"Really?" She wondered if he was nervous because of her, because she'd been in the big fall production. But that was a stupid idea. It wasn't like she was a celebrity or something.

"Well, sure." He dropped his bag. "Mind if I join you?"

She shook her head, and he sat down, so close to her, their knees were almost touching. "Don't you get nervous before the first rehearsal?"

Jane considered his question. She was a little nervous about acting opposite someone as handsome as Simon, but not only was that not something she was going to admit, it also wasn't what he was asking. She thought back to how she'd felt the afternoon of her first rehearsal for *Midsummer*. "I don't know. I think I'm more the get-excited type than the get-nervous type."

"Oh, that's way better," said Simon. "I wish I were the get-excited type."

Normally Jane might have made a suggestive joke about what he'd just said, but lately she worried that maybe she didn't have the best judgment about what to say and when to say it. It made her feel weird and tongue-tied. Not around the Darlings. And not around someone like Mark, who she didn't care about, but definitely around someone as cute and nice as Simon.

Rather than risk saying the wrong thing, Jane toyed with the pearl at her throat.

"That's pretty," said Simon, noticing the necklace.

"Thanks. It belonged to my grandmother."

Simon reached out to touch the pearl, then hesitated. "Do you mind?"

Jane shook her head, and he very gently took it between his thumb and index finger. His fingers were long and tapered, and he managed to examine the pearl without yanking the chain against her neck.

"Beautiful," he said, letting the pearl drop and looking at Jane. "Are you close to her?"

Even though Nana had been dead for more than six months, Jane still missed her, still found herself looking forward to Tuesdays, which had been the day Nana always picked her, Natalya, and Victoria up from One Room and took them on adventures around New York.

"I was. She died last summer," Jane answered simply.

"Oh," said Simon. "I'm really sorry."

"Thanks." Jane could feel her throat growing tight, the way it did whenever she tried to talk about Nana.

Simon looked away, giving her a moment of privacy. "My grandmother died two years ago," he said, eyes on the opposite wall. "We were really close. I still think about her a lot."

The sadness in his voice made Jane feel strangely close to him, even though they didn't really know each other at all.

"*Okay!*"

Jane jumped when Mark's voice boomed across the theater. It was as if she'd been asleep or in a trance or something. Simon seemed as if he, too, had forgotten about Mark's presence.

"So," Mark said, crossing toward them and rubbing his hands together, "like I said, it's a night of love scenes, and we're doing a scene from *Medea*."

"Yeah, I was going to ask you about that." Simon ran his hands through his hair.

Mark smiled as if he had been hoping Simon would say what he'd just said. "What were you going to ask?"

Simon held out one hand in front of himself. "Medea." He held out the other hand like it was the second tray in a set of scales. "Love scene." Then he mimed trying to balance them. "Does not compute."

Now that she thought about it, Simon was right. Jane had been so focused on Simon and Mark and all the pros and cons of working with them that she hadn't realized how bizarre it was that Mark wanted to use a scene from *Medea*—a play about a woman who murders her own children because their father has betrayed her by falling in love with someone else—in an evening of love scenes.

An evening of *hate* scenes, maybe. But such a thing probably didn't even exist.

"Okay, let's think about *An Evening of Love Scenes*, shall we?" asked Mark. He looked into the empty space on the floor in front of him and moved his hands as if they were circling a crystal ball. "Wait. Wait. I'm seeing. Yes, it's a scene from *The Importance of Being Earnest*. And . . . here's a scene from *Much Ado About Nothing*. And I . . . my god, can it be? Not one but *two* versions of the balcony scene from *Romeo and Juliet*."

Jane laughed. Mark looked up and smiled at her and Simon. "Call me a cynic, but, yawn."

"Oh, no one would ever call you cynical," said Simon. "Self-important, maybe. But never cynical."

Mark and Simon both cracked up. Jane was surprised by how well they seemed to know each other. When she and Mark had been . . . well, not friends, exactly, but friend*ly*, at the beginning of the school year, he'd acted like he knew a whole bunch of upperclassmen when really he'd just known one random sophomore. Simon was a sophomore but not the one Mark knew. So apparently Mark had become good friends with at least one cool upperclassman in the past few months. Which was kind of a mystery. Why would someone as cool as Simon be friends with someone as annoying as Mark?

"No, seriously," Simon said as their laughter faded. "What are you thinking?"

Putting his hands on his knees, Mark leaned toward Jane and Simon. "You both know the backstory, right?"

"Not *that* well," Simon admitted.

Mark turned to her. "Jane?"

Jane had done about ten million different units on Greek mythology at her old school, and she easily launched into the story of Jason and Medea. "Medea helps Jason steal the Golden Fleece. Then she kills her brother to prevent her father from catching them when they escape. They flee to Corinth, have a couple of kids, then Jason leaves her for another woman, and she murders their children to get back at him."

"Wow!" Simon whistled, whether because of the grim plot line, or Jane's perfect recall of it, she wasn't sure.

Mark looked at Jane and narrowed his eyes. "You're neglecting a crucial detail. *Why* does Medea help Jason steal the fleece in the first place?"

"She's in love with him," Jane answered confidently.

"But *why* is she in love with him?"

Okay, how much longer was this catechizing going to last? "She's in love with him because Aphrodite put a spell on her when—"

"*Aha!*" Mark exclaimed, clapping his hands once.

Was she dense or was Mark hopelessly opaque? One quick glance at Simon's bewildered expression gave Jane her answer. "Aha, what?" she asked.

"*Aphrodite put a spell on her,*" Mark repeated slowly, an excited gleam in his eye. "A spell that, in everything I've read about the play, *is never lifted.*"

Suddenly, as she sensed what Mark was driving at, Jane felt a tingle of excitement. "Wait, are you saying—" she began, but then her phone buzzed. Out of habit, she grabbed it and checked the screen.

i m trying out a new recipe for next cooking class @ the community center. do u want 2 be guinea pig w/jack later? ur darling v.

Did she want to spend the afternoon eating Victoria's delicious desserts? Um, survey says . . . *duh!* Jane was about to type her response when Mark said, "I'm sorry, is our rehearsal getting in the way of your social life?"

She snapped her head up and was about to respond with something snarky when she realized he was right. Remembering Mr. Robbins generally made her feel like a complete moron, and she tried to avoid having any thoughts of him whatsoever, but she'd never forgotten the key word he always used when he talked about acting: serious. It wasn't about being good or bad, talented or untalented. It was about being serious or not being serious.

Mr. Robbins wasn't here now (thankfully), but if he had been, what would he have said about Jane's reading and replying to her friend's text while her fellow cast member and her director waited for her to finish?

Jane slid her phone back into her bag. "Sorry," she muttered. She couldn't look at Simon.

Mark opened his mouth, his expression annoyed, but before he could say anything, Simon interrupted, "You were saying . . ."

For a second Mark seemed torn between self-importantly telling Jane off for texting during his rehearsal and self-importantly sharing his theory about one of the greatest plays ever written.

The latter won.

Stretching his legs in front of him and leaning back on his elbows, Mark asked, "Has either of you ever been in love?"

Jane was completely taken aback. Mark's question was the last thing she'd been expecting.

Neither she nor Simon answered him for a minute.

"I've been very deep in *like*," Simon said finally, his eyes down and his voice quiet. Then he looked up at Mark. "Does that count?"

Jane felt a wave of relief that he hadn't said *Yes, actually, right now I'm completely in love with my girlfriend. I'll be meeting up with her after rehearsal.*

Mark frowned. "Sorry. I don't think so." He turned to Jane. "Lady Jane?"

What was Jane supposed to do with both Mark and Simon staring at her, waiting for her to answer? *Well, in the fall, I thought I was in love with Mr. Robbins. You might know him—head of the drama department?*

Two words: No. Way.

"Have *you*?" she shot back at Mark.

"I have," answered Mark casually. "Once. And, like Medea, I had my heart stomped on."

"Ouch," said Simon, grimacing.

Jane said nothing. She had no trouble imagining someone dumping Mark. Her problem was trying to imagine who would go out with him in the first place.

"Yeah, well, I'm heavily medicated now, so I can talk about

it," said Mark. "Kidding," he added. "My point is that even in the real world, when someone dumps you, you still love that person. Maybe just for a little while, maybe forever." He hesitated briefly, then shrugged. "This play isn't about the real world. It's about a woman who had a *spell* put on her. Eros shot her in the heart with one of his nasty little arrows." He moved his eyes as if watching an arrow sail over his head, then land in Jane's heart. "*Boom!* She's *got to* love Jason *forever*; it's beyond her control."

"But, I mean . . ." Simon seemed hesitant to contradict Mark, but finally he said, "She kills his kids. I mean, *their* kids."

Mark nodded and drew a long breath through his teeth. "Yeah, well, love sucks." He got to his feet and crossed to where his backpack was sitting on the floor. "Let me grab you guys a couple of scripts, and we can do a quick read-through."

While Mark rummaged through his messy-looking bag, Jane started to feel impatient and excited. She wanted to read the play again, to see what it would sound like with Mark's theory influencing her.

There was a light pressure against her shoulder. She turned her head slightly and saw that while she'd been lost in thought, Simon had slid close enough to her that his shoulder was pressed against hers.

"Hey," he said quietly.

"Hey, yourself," she responded, equally quietly.

"Listen, I'm sorry if I bummed you out by making you think about your grandmother before," he apologized.

Jane shook her head. She'd almost forgotten about talking

about Nana with Simon. "It's okay. I like thinking about her. I mean, it makes me sad, but I don't want to forget her."

"I know what you mean." Simon hesitated, then seemed to decide to tell her something. "This may sound really weird, but sometimes when I meet someone, I imagine introducing that person to her. You know, like I try to figure out if she'd like them or not."

*Don't ask. Don't ask. Don't ask.*

But as much as Jane wanted to be someone who held her tongue, she couldn't resist. "Well?" she asked, and her voice was just the slightest bit flirtatious.

"What?" asked Simon, clearly bewildered by her question.

Jane mock-rolled her eyes, like she couldn't believe how dense he was being. "Would she have liked me?"

Simon burst out laughing. "Oh, *that's* what you meant." Still laughing, he put his arm around her and gave her a squeeze. "Sorry, I totally did not see where you were going with that." He cocked his head and studied Jane, as if he were looking at her not through his own eyes but through someone else's. Then he gave a brief, definitive nod. "She would *absolutely* have liked you."

"Found one!" Mark called, his head practically inside his bag.

"What about yours?" asked Simon. "Would she have liked me?" He'd taken his arm from around Jane's shoulders, but because of the way he was leaning back on his hands, their upper arms were pressed against each other. Jane liked how it felt.

Looking down at their legs, which were stretched out in front of them, she tried to imagine introducing Nana to Simon. She pictured ringing the buzzer of Nana's apartment, Nana coming to the door and seeing how handsome Simon was. Sometimes when they'd had a cute waiter at a restaurant, Nana would say to Jane, "Now that is a *very* nice-looking boy!" and Jane would shriek, "Nana!" And they would both laugh.

Jane glanced up and realized Simon was studying her face, which she knew had grown downcast. "I made you sad again by asking that, didn't I?" he asked.

She shook her head, sorry her expression had given him the wrong idea. "It's actually kind of nice to think about. It makes it almost like she's still alive."

"See?" asked Simon, smiling at her. "I told you."

Jane smiled back at him.

"Okay, guys," said Mark, crossing over to where they were sitting, and joining them. "I finally found the other one. Here you go. Let's open to page nineteen."

As Jane turned to the page, she said to Simon, without looking up at him, "The answer is yes, by the way."

"What answer is yes?" asked Mark absently, flicking through his script.

Jane explained to the top of Mark's head. "Yes, my grandmother would have liked Simon."

"Oh," said Mark, looking up, clearly more confused than he'd been before she'd answered him. He shrugged. "Well, with that face, who wouldn't like Simon?"

"Oh, Mark," said Simon, feigning embarrassment.

They all laughed briefly. Then Mark, his voice more businesslike than Jane had ever heard it, asked, "Are we ready?"

Jane felt a wave of exhilaration. Nothing, nothing could equal the excitement of the first read-through of a script. She took a deep breath and looked down at the page in front of her. "Ready."

"Ready," agreed Simon.

"Okay, then. Let's take it from the top," said Mark.

And with Mark's first words of direction, the rehearsal officially began.

# Chapter Eight

NATALYA CHECKED THE TIME. Seven o'clock. She opened her phone and scrolled back through her texts until she got to the one Colin had sent her. She reread it. He said he'd meet her where they played last time, and she had known right away that he meant the Web site where she'd first challenged him to a game back in October. She was there now, her computer screen showing the game they'd started in the fall, as if minutes, as opposed to months, had passed.

She checked the time on her computer. One minute after seven.

It was a tight game. The screen showed it was Colin's turn

to move, and Natalya cocked her head, trying to predict what he might do. He could use his rook to attack a pawn she'd left vulnerable, but that would mean leaving his knight unprotected. If he *didn't* move his rook in the next couple of moves, he would risk slowly getting trapped behind a phalanx of his own pieces. . . .

Her phone buzzing in her hand startled her; as usual, facing a chessboard had pulled her from the real world. She checked to see who'd texted her. Jane.

has ur date started yet?

it's not a date. it's a game, she texted back.

To which Jane responded, keep telling yourself that.

Natalya rolled her eyes and shut her phone, going back to studying the board in front of her. When the computer gave a tiny *ping* and a window opened in the lower right-hand corner, it took Natalya a second to snap out of her deep contemplation of the game and realize this had to be Colin signing in. She wished Jane hadn't called it a date. The word made her think of ringing doorbells and introducing boys to her parents and all kinds of things that freaked her out.

She said a private prayer of thanks to the god of computers that if this *was* a date with Colin, at least it was a virtual one. Then she read what he'd written.

Cbprewitt@thompson: sorry im late.

Npetrova@gainsford: that's ok. I was looking at the board.

Cbprewitt@thompson: scared of how good a player I m?

Npetrova@gainsford: more scared 4 u than OF u.

Cbprewitt@thompson: I m looking @ this game and thinking I can take u in seven moves.

Natalya examined the pieces in front of her, mentally sliding them around in imaginary moves and countermoves. She prided herself on being able to think a few moves ahead, but only grandmasters could think *that* far ahead. Was Colin really able to envision the game seven moves in the future? Hmm . . .

Npetrova@gainsford: u r totally bluffing.

Cbprewitt@thompson: TOTALLY!

She giggled and typed,

TOTALLY BUSTED!

Cbprewitt@thompson: I had u going there, didn't I?

Npetrova@gainsford: 4 a minute.

Cbprewitt@thompson: I have to make u squirm a little after u blew me off for your bff.

The allusion to Morgan *did* make Natalya squirm, and for the first time since she and Colin had started IMing, she wished she could ask the Darlings what to say. She closed her eyes briefly, imagined they were standing in front of her. Instantly, she heard Victoria telling her to apologize again, Jane telling her she'd apologized enough already. She opened her eyes.

Maybe it was just as well that she was alone.

Npetrova@gainsford: morgan's not my bff.

Cbprewitt@thompson: can I please ask WHAT you see in her? I mean, u strike me as an intelligent, self-actualized person. y would u hang out with the human equivalent of an X-Acto blade?

Natalya bit her lip. She wasn't sure what an X-Acto blade was, but she got Colin's point. Still, what was she supposed to say? *I'm not as self-actualized as I seem? I'm just a scholarship girl and your sister dazzled me?*

Finally, she typed:

we're not really friends anymore.

Cbprewitt@thompson: not to be pedantic, but would you say: a) we're not REALLY friends anymore or b) we're REALLY not friends anymore.

Natalya had Ms. MacFadden to thank for the recent addition of *pedantic* (concerned with formal book learning and narrow rules) to her vocabulary. Apparently English class wasn't a *total* waste of time after all.

Npetrova@gainsford: I'm going to go with b. We r not friends.

Seeing what she'd just typed made Natalya laugh. She had often wished the social world of Gainsford could be a little more like the academic one, and by inviting her to define her relationship with Morgan in multiple choice terms, Colin had just made it so.

Cbprewitt@thompson: well then I guess the best Prewitt won. Which may be a harbinger of the game we're about to play.

Ms. MacFadden hadn't taught them *harbinger*. Natalya quickly reread his sentence, biting her lip in concentration. *A harbinger of the game we're about to play.*

Aha! He was saying he was going to beat her at chess.

Cbprewitt@thompson: ok, your silence indicates u r clearly scared.

*No, my silence indicates I am clearly a dork who is using this conversation as an opportunity to improve my vocabulary.*

Npetrova@gainsford: I m looking @ the board. I m seeing nothing 2 scare me. I m seeing victory.

Cbprewitt@thompson: well, aren't we confident?

Now that they were focused on the game, Natalya felt her anxiety about vocabulary and Morgan and apologies slipping away. All she felt was the excitement of the game she was about to dive back into. So the response she typed was completely true.

Npetrova@gainsford: yes we r confident.

Cbprewitt@thompson: on that note, let the games begin.

Npetrova@gainsford: not to b pedantic, but u mean let the games CONTINUE, right?

Cbprewitt@thompson: touché.

# Chapter Nine

THE HALLS OF Morningside were always chaotic during period changes, but the chaos that reigned after the last class of the day always felt to Victoria more like a volcanic eruption or an earthquake than dismissal. The bell rang, and within seconds, every student in the building had stampeded to his or her locker. Pouring out of History with the rest of her class, she felt like a tiny pebble being carried along by a raging river.

"Hey, you!"

She saw Jack at the same second as he said hello and slipped his arm around her shoulders, and she walked with him to the side of the hallway where her locker was. It was so nice when he came to find her at the end of the day, as though he hated that they'd been separated as much as she had. They kissed, and someone hollered, "Get a room!" Jack pulled away smiling and gently rubbed his forehead against Victoria's.

"Does he think we don't *want* to get a room?" asked Jack.

"Seriously," agreed Victoria, remembering how amazing it had been to have his room all to themselves the other day.

"So . . ." Jack linked his fingers through hers. "What are you doing right now?"

Victoria glanced at the clock across the hallway. She had almost forty minutes before she had to be at a community center uptown, where she, Maeve, and Georgia were going to be teaching a class of fourth graders from a local public school how to make zucchini bread from scratch. She slipped her hand up Jack's neck and toyed with his hair. "I have a few minutes," she said. "Want to go to Rick's and get hot chocolate?"

Instead of answering her, Jack asked his own question. "Want to come to a recording session?"

"A recording session?" Victoria had seen recording sessions in movies. She loved montages where some unknown band or singer recorded a best-selling single that climbed to the top of the charts. Excited, she asked, "Who's recording something?"

"The Frightened Pirates," said Jack, referring to his friend Rajiv's band. "His uncle's this mega record producer and he got Rajiv some time at a studio where his label records a lot."

"Oh." Victoria always felt a tiny bit uneasy around Jack's friends Rajiv and Lily, who sang in Rajiv's band. Jack, Rajiv, and Lily had gone to elementary school together, and they had tons of private jokes and references Victoria didn't get. Sometimes when the four of them were sitting together at lunch, she felt like a foreign exchange student.

"Wouldn't I be in the way?"

"Are you kidding? They'll be totally psyched if you come." Jack was always saying Lily and Rajiv thought Victoria was awesome, but since Victoria was pretty sure she'd never said one interesting thing in their presence, she found Jack's claims a *little* hard to believe.

Rather than express her doubts, Victoria admitted, "I've never been to a recording session."

Jack grinned, and his voice, when he spoke, was animated. "It's great! I mean, sometimes it's a little like watching paint dry, which is not so great. But you really get to hear music in a whole new way, and if it's with a good producer, they make all these choices about how to lay a track down and it's just . . ." He shook his head, seeming to search for words, then smiled down at her sheepishly. "Do I just sound like an enormous dork or what?"

Victoria laughed, shook her head, and kissed him lightly on the lips. There was nothing better than listening to Jack talk about music, any kind of music. His body grew buoyant with enthusiasm, and he radiated a contagious pleasure.

"It sounds amazing," she said. "Maybe I could come for a little while."

"Awesome!" Jack lifted her off the ground in a bear hug. "I've gotta go grab my stuff and call my mom. Meet you out front in five?" He was already walking down the hall.

"Oh, hey!" She suddenly remembered to ask, "Where is it?"

"Chelsea!" He spun around to shout the word through the thinning crowd, then turned back in the direction he'd been walking.

*Chelsea*. Damn. Victoria dropped back against her locker. She could barely *get* to Chelsea in the time she had, much less listen to several songs be recorded and get back uptown. She looked up at the clock longingly, like maybe it would agree to stop time for the next several hours. As if in answer to her plea, the long hand clicked forward a minute.

"Who's ready to teach some grubby kids about the pleasures of organic produce?" called a voice. Victoria turned and saw Georgia and Maeve walking toward her. She knew it was Georgia who'd just yelled the question—Maeve was about as likely to shout something down a crowded hallway as Victoria was.

"Um, me?" Victoria's tone was gloomy.

"Um, me?" Georgia echoed, incredulous. "How about, *I am!*" She yelled the last two words, tossing her long brown hair as she did, and Victoria gave her a wan smile.

"What's wrong?" asked Maeve quietly.

Victoria shook her head and turned to face her locker. "Nothing." She spun her lock around and yanked it open. She'd have to work quickly so she could have a few minutes to break the news to Jack that she couldn't join him.

"I'm *sooo* not getting a nothing's-wrong vibe from you, girl," said Georgia.

Victoria jerked her biology book angrily from her locker and shoved her history textbook into the slot it had occupied. "I just *never* get to see my boyfriend, that's all. He invited me to go with him to something, and I can't go." She checked to make sure she had all the books she needed, then slammed her locker shut, as annoyed with herself for whining as she was at the universe for separating her and Jack.

"Oh, man, that sucks," said Georgia.

"Yeah, I'm really sorry," agreed Maeve.

"Maybe, like, is there some way you could, you know, get out of the thing you're supposed to be doing?" Georgia suggested.

Victoria hadn't plotted her complaining as a means to trick Maeve and Georgia into letting her out of cooking class, but it suddenly occurred to her that that was exactly what had just happened. Slightly shocked at the unexpected twist the conversation had taken, she turned from her locker slowly. Both girls stood studying her, sympathetic expressions on their faces.

It was clear they had no idea what she was about to ask, and she felt a little guilty. Would they think they'd been set up? That she'd complained with the expectation that they'd offer to let her out of going to the community center with them?

But she honestly hadn't. She'd just been feeling sorry for herself, and they'd asked why, and she'd told them. Still, when Victoria spoke, she was hesitant. "Well . . . I mean, I don't know if I can get out of it," she said slowly. "It's kind of up to you guys."

Less than five minutes later, she was standing in front of the school, feeling like someone who'd been given a get-out-of-jail-free pass. No sooner had she told Maeve and Georgia about the recording session than both girls had urged her to go, promising that they'd be fine without her and wouldn't even consider for one second taking her away from an afternoon with Jack.

"You'll make it up to us," promised Georgia.

"Yeah," agreed Maeve. "When it's write-up time." She was referring to the project report the three girls had planned to submit as a group to get their community service credit, a report that included a lengthy essay on the "impact of their work."

"Oh my god!" promised Victoria, so happy she could have danced a jig right there in the hallway. "I will so totally do the entire report for us."

"We'll hold you to that," said Georgia, before hugging Victoria and heading down the hall with Maeve.

Victoria couldn't believe her incredible luck. Instead of taking a dozen nine-year-olds on a tour of the farmer's market and then bringing them back to the community center loaded down with zucchini, guiding them through the process of measuring out flour and baking soda, she was going to be with Jack. Kissing Jack. Holding Jack. Talking to Jack about music, his favorite subject. She was practically levitating with excitement.

She pushed her way onto the sidewalk, not even minding the crowd, so happy that she felt as if she were sailing above her fellow students. Her phone rang, and she saw it was her sister, Emily, a freshman at Princeton. Despite being a straight-A student, Emily had a wild streak, and Victoria knew Emily would be psyched to hear about her plans to hang out with Jack at a cool recording session. Sometimes she dodged Emily's calls, since hearing about her sister's fabulous life could make her feel like a total loser, but today she picked up.

"Hi!" she practically chirped.

"Hey," said Emily. "Mom just told me you're off to do that farm-to-table community service thing, and I realized I totally spaced on asking how the first meeting went." Before Victoria could answer, Emily added, "Your students will be happy to hear I eschewed the french fries in the dining hall and had soup made from *locally grown* squash for lunch!"

"I'll be sure and pass your story on to the junk food–obsessed children of New York City," promised Victoria, surveying the crowded sidewalk for Jack.

"Please do," said Emily. "So tell me everything. How'd it go? Are you psyched to go back?"

Jack pushed open the front door and stood for a minute, scanning the groups of students massed on the steps and sidewalk. Instead of answering her sister, Victoria waved to him. He smiled, waved back, then stopped to talk to a guy in their bio class who called him over.

"Hello?" asked Emily irritably.

"Sorry," said Victoria, focusing back on the conversation. "What was your question?"

"The moment's passed," said Emily. "What's up in general?"

"Wellll . . ." Victoria smiled wickedly. "Who's spending the afternoon listening to a really cool band's recording session in Chelsea?"

"Um, someone other than you?" offered Emily.

"Nope. Try again."

"I'm lost. Mom just told me you were cooking with those kids." Emily rarely sounded confused, but she was clearly confused now.

"My boyfriend invited me to go hear his friends who are in a band record their new CD." The words tumbled breathlessly out of her. "And Georgia and Maeve said they'd totally cover for me."

"Wait, you're bailing on the kids *and* you're dumping the work on your friends? How uncool is that?" asked Emily.

Since they'd been getting along better, Victoria had forgotten how annoying her older sister could be, but this conversation was definitely reminding her. "God, Emily, you sound like Mom sometimes, you know that?"

"And you sound like one of those girls who never utters a sentence without the words 'my boyfriend' in it."

"I am *not* one of those girls."

Emily made her voice high and girlish. "My boyfriend's in a band. My boyfriend invited me to hear him record. Do I like that? I don't know. Let me go ask my boyfriend."

"I do *not* sound like that." No one could make Victoria's blood boil like her sister.

"How do you know what you sound like?" Emily demanded.

"You think *you* don't sound that way when *you* have a boyfriend?" Victoria made her voice as breathy as Emily's had been. "Oh, I just *loooove* foreign films now that I'm going out with James. Oh, did I say foreign films? I meant the World Cup. Oh, did I say James? I meant Bill."

"You're hilarious," said Emily, not laughing. "And let me just point out that even if I happened to date some guys who introduced me to new things, I did not drop *all* of my responsibilities the second they offered me a Scooby snack."

"I am *not* dropping all of my responsibilities, and an afternoon with Jack is not a Scooby snack!"

Emily snorted.

Jack finished his conversation, high-fived his friend, and jumped down the steps, making his way toward Victoria. His cheeks were flushed from the cold, and he looked even more adorable than usual. When he got to where she was standing, he gave a low bow.

"Madam," he said. "Your chariot awaits."

"I gotta go," Victoria said into the phone.

"Yeah, I'm sure you do," said Emily.

As she hit END CALL, Victoria took a second to wonder if it counted as hanging up on someone if the person had simultaneously hung up on you. Then Jack cocked his head, slipped his arm around Victoria's waist, and squinted at her. "You know I don't really have a chariot, right?"

She shrugged, put her arm around his waist, and grinned back at him. "I figured as much."

He kissed her lightly on the top of her head, and they turned south, toward the subway. Still keeping her arm around Jack, she dropped her phone into her bag and, with it, put away all thoughts of Emily and their conversation.

# Chapter Ten

NATALYA WAS NORMALLY glad to have a double period of Bio, but Friday she had trouble focusing on what Dr. Clover was lecturing about. She was fuzzy. Distracted. She'd felt this way ever since her chess game on Wednesday night. This morning she'd stood in front of her closet for several minutes trying to decide what to wear, before remembering that Gainsford had a uniform, one she'd been wearing every day for the past six months. So what to wear wasn't exactly a *choice*.

u r 2 good 4 me!

That was what Colin had written after she'd beaten him. u r 2 good 4 me!

Was it a compliment? Did he mean he didn't want to play chess with her again? Should she have tried to play less well so he could beat her? She twisted her pearl necklace around her index finger. It was almost like there were *two* chess games being played—the one with their pieces on the board, and the one with their sentences on the screen. She'd won the first one, but she'd spent the rest of the night and all day yesterday and today turning his sentence over and over in her mind, a little afraid it was just another way of saying *checkmate*. The fact that she hadn't heard from him since they'd played only served to convince her that her fears were well-founded, not paranoid.

She glanced down at her phone, which she had taken to holding on her lap, but of course if there'd been a new text, she would have felt it buzz. She shook her head, impatient with her phone and herself. She had to stop. More than forty minutes of the double period had passed, and she had barely any sense of what they were studying. Dropping her necklace, she turned the phone to silent, then put her left hand on the lab table, like touching the cool stone surface would keep her anchored in the present.

Dr. Clover, all four and a half feet of her, stood at the board, using a piece of chalk in its metal holder to point at a dizzying array of lower- and uppercase $R$'s, $G$'s, $P$'s, and $W$'s, linked one to the other with arrows, lines, and brackets. At various spots on the board, the letters were interspersed with phrases ("true-breeding," "contrasting traits," "tall v. dwarf") and individual words ("hybrid," "recessive").

"As I've explained," Dr. Clover concluded, "if you cross two heterozygous plants, one-third will be homozygous recessive, one-third will be homozygous dominant, and one-third will be heterozygous. That is why recessive genes can resurface even several generations later. In other words, it explains why two brown-eyed parents can have a blue-eyed child. In theory, those parents could each have one gene for blue eyes inherited from *their* parents, the child's grandparents. If they had three children, one could be homozygous brown-eyed, with two brown genes, one could be heterozygous brown-eyed, with one blue gene and one brown gene, and one could be homozygous blue-eyed." She wrote a frantic combination of capital and lowercase Bs as she spoke.

Natalya copied down *homozygous blue-eyed* as a quiet groan from her lab partner made her turn her head. Catching Natalya's glance, Jordan rolled her eyes. She reached out her arm and wrote on the corner of Natalya's paper, I GIVE UP. Natalya laughed, then wrote, COPY MINE, and slid her notebook over to Jordan just as Dr. Clover lowered the lights and pulled a white screen down over the board. Then she turned on her computer and projected a dozen Punnett squares onto the screen. Above them were the words "Mendel's Peas."

These must have been reproductions of Gregor Mendel's original experiments, scientific proof of the principles of reproduction that one man had discovered more than a hundred years before Natalya was born. Natalya squinted at the images, feeling a sense of calm descend upon her—something she hadn't felt since before she'd seen Colin in Washington Square Park last week. She watched recessive genes hide behind dominant ones for generations, then reemerge when they met up with the same recessive trait. The diagrams were as predictable and orderly as a chessboard on which a game was about to begin. She could have studied them forever.

"Now, who can tell me what's wrong with Mendel's experiment?" asked Dr. Clover.

There was silence in the room. Natalya stared harder at the screen in front of her. If Ms. MacFadden's questions made her want to disappear, Dr. Clover's made something in Natalya's chest rise up with excitement, like each query she put to the class was a direct challenge to Natalya, one she was desperate to meet.

Still, Natalya couldn't find anything wrong with these experiments. Mendel's work was beautiful. It was perfect.

The silence grew. Though everyone was looking at the front of the room, Natalya sensed that all eyes were somehow on her, as if the class was holding its collective breath, waiting for her to answer Dr. Clover's question.

"Anyone?" Was it her imagination or did Dr. Clover's eyes linger on Natalya a bit longer than they did on anyone else.

A hand went up at the front of the room, and Dr. Clover called on Alison Jones. Alison was the only girl in the grade besides Natalya who didn't hate biology, and once, when both their lab partners had coincidentally been absent, they'd partnered. Natalya had been impressed by how much Alison knew about evolutionary biology, by how comfortably she'd used the microscope (unlike most of the other kids in the class, who didn't understand that you were supposed to look into it normally, not scrunch up your entire face and mash your eyes against the top). Alison had explained that her mom was a microbiologist and that she'd practically grown up in her lab looking at slides.

"Yes, Alison?" said Dr. Clover. Natalya felt a small slap of disappointment that Alison was able to answer the question when she wasn't. "There's nothing wrong with the experiments, Dr. Clover," said Alison confidently. "They're perfect."

Now Natalya was doubly annoyed with herself. *She'd* thought the experiments were perfect too, only she hadn't wanted to say that when Dr. Clover had clearly been saying the experiments *weren't* perfect. But apparently Dr. Clover *hadn't* been saying that. Natalya felt a tiny bit of her irritation with herself spill over and become irritation with Dr. Clover for asking what had turned out to be a trick question—and with Alison for being able to answer it.

"Yes," agreed Dr. Clover, nodding at the image as if seeing it anew. "They *are* perfect." She swiveled her head around to look back at the class. "Anyone else?"

And suddenly, as if it had been telepathically communicated from Dr. Clover's brain to hers, Natalya knew the answer. Her hand shot into the air so fast she thought she heard something in her shoulder pop.

"Natalya?"

"They're *too* perfect!" Natalya said. "Exactly one-third of the offspring are heterozygous, one-third are homozygous recessive, one-third are homozygous dominant. He has one-hundred-percent accuracy. That's impossible in a scientific experiment." Natalya's heart pounded with joy at her discovery.

Dr. Clover seemed to have a rule against smiling, but Natalya thought she saw the slightest gleam of pleasure in her teacher's face as she said, "That is correct, Natalya." Flipping on the lights, Dr. Clover added, "An interesting footnote in the history of genetics is that it is generally believed that once Mendel discovered the general principles of inheritance, he either fudged some of his results or suppressed data that contradicted his theories." Dr. Clover leaned on her podium and looked out at the class. "Biology, like life itself, is many impressive things. But it is never perfect."

Right at that second the bell rang, and though Dr. Clover did not seem impressed by the excellence of her timing, the class sat silently for a moment, something that never happened with the last period of the week. It took Dr. Clover's breaking the spell of her own words to snap the students back to an awareness of the fact that school was over until Monday. "Read chapter eight in the textbook, do questions one through four on page two twenty-five. Type your answers, please." And with that, she pivoted on one foot and left the room.

"Oh my god, you're a *genius*," said Jordan, sliding Natalya's notebook across the table to her.

Natalya wanted to hug Jordan. She wanted to hug Dr. Clover. But instead, she said simply, "You should see me in English class."

Jordan rolled her eyes at Natalya's modesty as Alison came over to their table.

"Nice!" She high-fived Natalya. "I totally thought I had that one." Natalya was impressed that Alison didn't seem to mind Natalya's getting the question right.

"I thought you had it too," admitted Natalya, shoving her textbook and notebook into her bag.

Jordan shook her head, amazed. "How am I—Miss Faints-at-the-Sight-of-Blood—friends with the biggest bio geeks in the universe?"

Alison shrugged. "Just lucky, I guess." She and Natalya shared a conspiratorial grin as the girls headed into the hallway.

"Please don't tell me you're crushed out on Clover too, okay? I can handle anything but that," said Jordan. It was an ongoing joke that Natalya actually *liked* Dr. Clover, the most universally loathed and feared teacher at Gainsford.

"You know," said Alison, cocking her head to the side, "I think she's kind of growing on me."

Jordan groaned as Natalya and Alison laughed. "You're killing me." She turned to Natalya. "You coming to the game on Saturday?"

"I can't; I've got plans." Natalya, Victoria, and Jane were meeting at Act Two, their favorite vintage clothing store, to buy *fabulous* dresses to wear to the art opening at Barnard.

"Bummer," said Jordan.

"Speaking of plans!" Alison snapped her fingers. "What's your e-mail? I've been meaning to send you an invitation to my birthday party."

"Really? Thanks!" Natalya was surprised. She'd known she and Alison were have-lunch-and-study-together-sometimes-because-we're-both-friends-with-Jordan friends. But she hadn't thought they were invite-each-other-to-your-birthday-party friends.

It was nice to stroll through the emptying building with Alison and Jordan. Even if the three of them weren't friends the way the Darlings were, they were still friends, and Alison's invitation was like a tiny promise that they were about to become better friends. When Alison and Jordan peeled off to go to soccer practice, Natalya got the sense that they were honestly bummed they wouldn't see her at Saturday's game. She wondered, if they hadn't had to play soccer, would they have wanted to come to Act Two with her, Jane, and Victoria?

Something told her they would have.

As Natalya made her way to the front door, she thought about Alison's party. The day she and Jordan had gone over to Alison's, the three girls had been driven in a town car by a chauffeur who called Alison *Miss Jones*. Alison hadn't been snobbish about it, but she hadn't seemed to find the experience weird or remarkable either. Which meant that her birthday party was pretty much guaranteed to be way more fabulous than the birthday parties Natalya's friends at her old school had thrown, the ones where everyone had gone bowling or to Chuck E. Cheese.

She'd have to get Alison a present. The thought made Natalya bite her lip nervously. What could she possibly get for Alison that Alison couldn't afford to get for herself?

She took out her phone to call Victoria and Jane. One of them would definitely have an idea.

But when she opened her cell, there was a text waiting for her that made her forget all about Alison's gift.

i m ready 4 a rematch if u r. in person? wash sq park, tmrw, 12:00. b there or b square. colin.

Square. Square. Natalya saw the Punnett squares Dr. Clover had drawn on the board, again heard her biology teacher speak her final words of the day's lesson. Words that Colin's text had just proven to be one hundred percent wrong.

Racing to the front door of the building so she could tell Jane and Victoria this latest development, Natalya laughed out loud at her imagined correction of Dr. Clover.

*Maybe biology isn't perfect, Dr. Clover.*

*But my life definitely is.*

# Chapter
# Eleven

FRIDAY AFTER SCHOOL, as Jane pushed open the door to her apartment, she could hear her mother talking. At first she thought maybe her mom was on the phone, but then she heard her say, "Would you like another glass?" and her heart sank. You didn't invite people you were on the phone with to have another glass of wine.

Richard was there.

"Hello!" her mother called, her voice cheerful. "Is that you, honey?"

"Yes, Mom," Jane answered, thinking, *Who else would it be?*

She stepped into the living room. Her mother and Richard were sitting on the sofa, each holding a wineglass. She and her mom were supposed to be going to an eight o'clock showing of *Auntie Mame* at the Film Forum. Had her mother forgotten and made a plan with her beloved Richard?

"Hi, Mom. Hi, Richard."

Richard smiled, said nothing, and gave an awkward wave.

"Hi, sweetheart!" Her mother's words tumbled out in a nervous rush. "Richard's plans got canceled, and so I invited him over for a drink."

*Of course you did.*

Jane shrugged. "Okay." Just because she and her mom had plans later didn't mean her mother couldn't have a drink with Richard *now*.

Her mother was perched on the edge of the sofa, not speaking, still looking up at Jane with the weird, nervous expression that she always seemed to have when Richard was around.

Finally Jane said, "Um, I guess I'll get some homework done until it's time to go." She actually didn't have that much work due Monday, but Mark had reserved the black box for rehearsal Tuesday afternoon, and he'd asked Simon and Natalya if they thought they could be off book by then. That meant a ton of dialogue to memorize. She'd been planning to ask her mother to run lines with her before the movie, but clearly that wasn't going to happen.

"Well, see you later," Jane called over her shoulder as she turned to walk down the hallway to her room.

She'd only gone about five feet when her mother cleared her

throat and said, "Honey, can you believe it—Richard's never seen *Auntie Mame*."

*Auntie Mame* was one of Jane's favorite movies, and not just because Nana had been the one to bring the Darlings to see it one rainy Tuesday afternoon years ago. There was something about the crazy, adventurous character of Auntie Mame that had reminded Jane of Nana even then, and now that Nana was gone, Jane had imagined tonight as a chance to remember what it felt like to be with her. She'd pictured sitting with her mom after the movie and reminiscing about Nana, bringing her back to life with their shared memories.

Jane was glad her back was to the sofa because there was no universe in which she could have disguised the scowl that crossed her face after her mother basically asked her to invite silent, dour Richard to come to the movies with them. Although nobody but Jane knew it, one of the better performances of her life was the calm, one-word response she gave her mom, still keeping her back to the grown-ups. "Oh?"

"He said it sounds like a wonderful movie," said her mother, her voice full of enthusiasm.

*He said that? Really? A whole sentence? Why am I so not believing you?*

"I was telling Richard all about Nana," Jane's mother continued. "But I know he'd love to hear more."

Richard didn't say anything. For all Jane knew, he'd left the room while her back was turned.

"My mother was *quite* a character," said Jane's mom, laughing. "She had Jane and her friends drinking piña coladas from the time they were teeny tiny little things. Virgin piña coladas," she added quickly.

Listening to her mother laugh about Nana and their special drink made Jane feel awful. How was that any business of *Richard*'s? No doubt he was picturing Nana as some kooky, unstable old lady, when really she'd been nothing like that. She'd been wise and loving, and she'd always taken Jane and her friends seriously. Jane thought of her last dinner with her grandmother, how Nana had raised her glass and smiled at Jane.

"To my beautiful granddaughter on her birthday. Here's to you, darling. May you always do what you're scared of doing."

Suddenly, out of nowhere, Jane's eyes filled with tears, and she headed into the hallway without excusing herself.

If Richard didn't have to talk, neither did she.

She'd missed a call, and as she was walking down the hall to her room, Jane dialed voice mail. It was Natalya. "You have *got* to call me back. Colin wants to play chess tomorrow. I mean *in-person* chess. I mean play chess in person. I am *having a complete wardrobe crisis!!!!!*" Jane listened to the message, then threw herself on her bed, staring at the box of invitations to the art opening that she'd promised her mother she would address. Natalya had a date with Colin. Victoria was madly in love with Jack. Her grandmother had been a muse to one of the great painters of the twentieth century. Even her own mother clearly wanted to be alone with Richard instead of headed to the movies with her daughter.

Jane had never felt like such a complete loser in her life.

There was a knock, and a second later her mom pushed open the door.

"Hi." She hesitated at the threshold. "Do you mind if I come in?"

Jane shrugged. Clearly her mother was going to do whatever she wanted whether or not Jane minded.

Her mom sat on the bed next to Jane. She looked pretty in her gray pencil skirt and navy blue turtleneck sweater, but even the flattering outfit annoyed Jane. What were the odds she'd gotten dressed up to go to the movies with her daughter and not because she was going to be seeing Richard?

*Um, how about a million to one?*

Her mother took Jane's hand in hers. "I didn't mean to imply that I wanted Richard to come with us to the movies."

Jane was about to tell her mother what an enormous lie that was, but just then her phone buzzed. She glanced down.

SIMON, read the screen.

*Simon!*

Simon was texting her. She whipped her phone open.

tell me u haven't memorized ur lines yet.

Quickly, Jane texted back.

i haven't memorized my lines.

"Jane? Can you put your phone down for a minute and talk to me?"

Her phone buzzed an immediate response. "Just a sec, Mom." She read Simon's response.

have i told u lately that i love u?

"Jane?"

Even though she knew Simon was just quoting the song, she couldn't suppress a shiver of excitement as she read his words. Suddenly, she had an idea.

"Just a sec, Mom." She typed her text fast, not giving herself a chance to change her mind. what r u doing now?

She was so focused on her phone that when her mother placed her hand on her arm, Jane was actually startled to be reminded that someone was sitting on the bed with her. "Jane, I'm saying I'm sorry if I made it seem like I expected Richard to join us for the movie, okay?"

Her phone buzzed again, and Jane looked down. not memorizing my lines. i m in deep trouble.

Suddenly Jane realized something. Her mother was planning on being out of the apartment for the rest of the evening. True, she was planning on being out of the apartment *with Jane*. But if Jane were suddenly *unavailable*, her mother had Plan B sitting on the sofa waiting for her.

She made her decision instantly and typed another text. want 2 come over and memorize 2gether @ my house?

"Jane, I promise to leave you alone as soon as you acknowledge you understand the words that I am speaking to you. Can you do that?" Gently, her mother took Jane's chin in her hand and lifted her face. "Hello. This is your mother speaking. I am not a phone. Can you hear me?"

Giddy with the text she'd just sent, Jane laughed. "Yes, I hear you, Mom. I hear you."

"And you understand that I am not saying Richard has to come with us to the movie, is that correct?" Her mother was still holding her chin, as if she were positive the second she released her daughter, Jane was going to forget she was in the room again.

"Yes, yes!" Jane said impatiently. Her phone buzzed once more, and she held it up and turned her head slightly so she could read it.

just tell me where you live, babe.

Oh my god. *Oh my god.*

Oh my god. Simon was coming over!

"Jane, I am going to throw that phone out the window."

"Sorry, Mom," said Jane, leaping to her feet and crossing the room to her closet. She was wearing old frayed jeans and an ancient gray sweater with a stain at the waist. Totally acceptable for attending the movies with your mother. Totally *un*acceptable for rehearsing a scene with the hottest guy on the planet. "Um, Mom, the thing is, that was the guy who I'm doing that scene with for school, and it turns out he's free to rehearse, and we're supposed to be off book on Tuesday, so it would be kind of huge if we could work on it, so if it's okay with you I'm just going to bag on the movie okay?"

"What?" asked her mom.

Jane's phone buzzed again. She grabbed it. and by 'tell me where u live,' i meant i don't know your address. Laughing, she typed her address. She could practically hear the hum of an electric current as it ran through her body.

"Jane, I don't understand. You mean you want to rehearse your scene instead of going to the movies with me?"

Jane was so not imagining that there was relief in her mother's voice. Normally she might have been hurt, but instead she just thought, That's right, Mom. I want to rehearse with Simon, and you want to go out with Richard. Everybody wins.

Turning briefly to look at her mother, she said simply, "It's fine, Mom. I'm sure."

Her mother stood up and smoothed her skirt. For a second, she seemed almost at a loss for what to do. "Oh. Well. I guess . . . I guess I'll ask Richard if he wants to see the movie with me."

"Great," said Jane, barely listening. She stepped into her closet and was soon buried deep inside her eclectic wardrobe.

"Maybe he and I will get dinner or something now," her mom said, after another long pause. Her voice was muffled by the clothes hanging on either side of Jane.

"Sure," Jane called. "Whatever." She pushed aside a long black beaded dress that even she knew would be overkill. Still, she didn't want to wear just anything. She needed to look casual, as if she'd just been hanging out at home when she got Simon's text, and hadn't even bothered to change her clothes. At the same time, she had to look *super* cute. She thought about Simon's perfectly fitting T-shirt and the excellent sweater he'd been wearing at rehearsal. He definitely knew about clothes, and Jane had the feeling he'd notice if she were wearing a good outfit.

And she *totally* wanted him to notice.

Pushing aside the ugly turquoise dress she'd worn to her cousin's bat mitzvah the year before, she found herself staring at a short-sleeved, red cashmere sweater just back from the dry cleaner. She loved the sweater—it was soft and feminine, snug but not *too* snug. Not snug like, *Hi, I'm a total slut.* Snug like, *Oh, is this sweater totally hugging my curves? I hadn't even noticed.* The fact that it had just been cleaned struck her as a sign. She grabbed the hanger and stepped out of her closet.

To Jane's surprise, her mother was still standing in the middle of her room.

Was she *never* going to leave?

"Well, it looks like I'll see you when I get home."

"Yeah," said Jane. She should have asked Simon where *he* lived. What if he rang the bell before she had a chance to shower and change? She had better move fast.

Her mom came over to where Jane was standing and gave her a hug.

"Okay. Well, bye, Mom. Have fun."

"You too, honey," said her mom, letting Jane go and walking across the room. At the door, she paused, and it was all Jane could do not to scream, *Would you please go already?!* She forced herself to smile.

"See you later," her mother said again.

"See you later," Jane echoed.

It seemed like it would never happen, but to Jane's enormous relief, her mother finally, miraculously, left. And Jane, laughing out loud to herself at how fast her evening had gone from awful to awesome, headed into her bathroom to take the fastest shower in the history of romance.

# Chapter
## Twelve

BEHIND THE ANONYMOUS-LOOKING white door in the former factory where it was located, Penguin Studios looked exactly like the recording studios Victoria had seen in movies. The space was tiny, with barely enough room for a few chairs and a small table overloaded with a microwave, half a dozen mugs, and a coffeepot, none of which seemed to have been washed since the invention of the CD.

The room was dominated by an enormous console that, with its dozens of meters, buttons, switches, lights, and screens, looked complex enough to land a spaceship. Above it was a window into a small room that held only an old-fashioned microphone and a music stand. Lily was in there, half sitting, half leaning on a metal stool, her thick brown hair in a loose ponytail, the silver hoops in her ears gleaming in the fluorescent light. She wore a short denim jacket and a pair of perfectly faded jeans.

Sitting at the console in a rolling chair was a man about Victoria's dad's age. He had a baseball hat on backward over his salt-and-pepper ponytail, and he was chewing on an unlit cigar. When Victoria and Jack walked in, Rajiv and the man were in the middle of a conversation about how much reverb Rajiv wanted for the song "Love It or Leave It." A boy who looked like he was in high school, but who Victoria didn't recognize from Morningside, sat on the floor holding a pair of drumsticks and nodding his head as Rajiv spoke.

"Hey, everyone," said Jack, waving to the room at large.

"Hey, man," they answered. From the sound booth, Lily called hello.

Jack introduced Victoria to the boy with the drumsticks (Sam, from Jack, Lily, and Rajiv's old school) and RJ, the man with the baseball hat. RJ grunted at Jack, and he actually called Victoria "doll," as in, "Hey, doll, you want a coffee or anything?"

"Oh. No thanks," said Victoria, glancing at the dirty table. She hadn't realized people still called girls that.

Jack was immediately drawn into the reverb conversation. RJ was worried that too much would make Lily sound like someone named Enya, while Rajiv kept saying he didn't want Lily sounding too twangy. Victoria slipped to a corner of the small space and sat on a chair that was backed up against the wall.

"Dude, she's not going to sound like Dolly Parton," Jack said to Rajiv, placing a reassuring hand on Rajiv's shoulder.

The conversation lasted a long time. Victoria tried to follow along, but it was hard when she had absolutely no idea what they were talking about. At one point, she realized Sam had been silent as long as she had. So she wasn't the only one who was completely lost in the maze of technical and musical references Rajiv, RJ, and Jack were making. But then Jack said, "Lucinda Williams meets Billie Holiday," and Sam cracked up along with everyone else. Right at that second, Jack looked toward where Victoria was sitting, and she quickly splashed a smile across her face. He smiled back.

"Okay, then," RJ said finally. He spun his chair so he was facing the glass wall behind which Lily was standing. "You ready, honey?"

"Ready as I'll ever be, baby." Lily tossed her head confidently. Clearly it was no big deal to her to be standing in a recording studio, everything hanging on her doing a good job, trading casual endearments with a professional record producer. Victoria tried to imagine being in Lily's place, and the thought was so panic-inducing, she realized she was gripping the bottom of the chair with her hands, as if at any second she could be pulled off and forced to sing a solo.

"Let's take it from the top," RJ said, and Rajiv counted Lily in.

The song was about an amusement park that's been torn down to make room for an apartment complex. It's the night before her high school graduation, and the singer is walking along the streets where the rides used to be, describing all the times she went to the park—with her family when she was little, then with her friends, then, later, with a boyfriend who dumped her for some other girl. She's trying to remember where everything was (the Ferris wheel, the roller coaster) and exactly what it looked and smelled and sounded like, but she's also trying to make sense of the relationships she had with the people she went there with, to figure out where all the people ended up or why she isn't close to them anymore. The song was heartbreakingly sad, but there was something defiant in it, like even though so many bad things had happened to the girl, she was still standing tall. Lily had a sweet, pure voice, and she held the song's final high note perfectly. Victoria could feel the sound deep in her chest.

As soon as the song was over, RJ said through the mike, "Got it."

"That was great, Lily!" Victoria was grinning from ear to ear. She couldn't believe what an incredible voice Lily had.

"Thanks!" Lily smiled at Victoria's compliment but then immediately asked, "RJ?" It was clear whose compliment she was waiting for.

Victoria thought Lily had sung the song perfectly, so she was surprised when RJ asked, "Can you open up a little on those high notes?" He turned a small dial to the right, simultaneously moving his cigar to the other side of his mouth.

"Yeah." Rajiv leaned forward. "Try not to sound quite so much like an Alison Krauss wannabe. Think you can manage that, honey?"

Everyone in the room laughed, including Jack. Lily laughed too, then flipped Rajiv the finger. RJ hit a couple of buttons on his computer and said, "Ready when you are." Lily began to sing again.

Victoria wondered who Alison Krauss was. She wished Rajiv and Lily, with their piercings and their talent, their references to musicians she'd never heard of, weren't quite so . . . cool. The thought immediately made her feel guilty. What if Jack complained about Jane and Natalya?

Jack had come over to stand beside Victoria when Lily started singing, and to make up for her disloyal thought about his friends, Victoria stood up and whispered in his ear, "Lily's got a great voice."

Jack nodded, but then he leaned forward slightly, as if trying to get out of the range of Victoria's voice. It made her feel even stupider than her compliment to Lily had. Obviously he was trying to listen to the song. Why was Victoria bothering him with her lame comments?

She sat down slowly, wondering if Jack was sorry he'd asked her to come.

Lily's voice slid gently over the last words of the song, and there was a moment of silence in the studio.

"Girl's got some pipes on her," RJ grunted, half to himself.

"Well?" called Lily from the booth.

Rajiv leaned forward and flipped a switch on the console. "RJ said it kind of sucked, but it's probably the best you can do."

"Ha-ha," answered Lily. She shaded her eyes and squinted through the glass that separated her from the rest of the group. "Jack?"

Jack nodded. "It sounded great. That's just what I was hearing in my head when I wrote it."

Victoria swung her head around to look at Jack. "You

wrote that song?" She hadn't meant to sound accusatory, but her surprise gave a slight bite to her question.

"Jack's our secret weapon." Rajiv turned and high-fived Jack. "If he weren't such a crap guitar player, maybe we'd let him play with us."

"What? Jack's an awesome guitar player!" Victoria said, realizing too late that she sounded like she was Jack's mother or something.

"Dude, I'm just messing with him," said Rajiv. He winked at Victoria, and, feeling like a loser for having taken him seriously, she gave him a small smile back.

Lily left the recording booth and joined Jack, RJ, Sam, and Victoria in the console room, and Rajiv took her place on the other side of the glass. He tuned up briefly, then began to play. The song was both recognizable as the one Lily had sang, and also different; where Lily had gone high, Rajiv went low, where she had held a single note, he played a complicated chord. Victoria hadn't thought the song could sound more heartbreaking than it had when Lily sang it, but as Rajiv's fingers moved along the neck of the guitar, it was so beautiful that she felt her eyes grow damp.

Clearly Victoria was the only one who'd been moved to tears, because as soon as Rajiv was done, Jack, RJ, and Lily practically fell over one another offering up things Rajiv needed to change for the next take. If a group of people had criticized something Victoria baked as thoroughly as this group critiqued Rajiv's playing, Victoria would never have stepped foot in the kitchen again. But Rajiv just nodded, asked a few questions, and then, when everyone was done talking, told RJ he was ready to take it from the top.

This time Victoria tried to listen with a cooler head, to hear some of the problems everyone else had noticed the first time— the missed note, the mistimed beat, the rushed finale. But again Rajiv's playing sounded beautiful to her, and she found herself getting as lost in the song as she had before. By the fourth time Rajiv started from the beginning, Victoria had given up on being a music critic and just let herself appreciate what she was hearing.

When they'd all decided Rajiv had completed a take that "wasn't bad," Sam headed into the booth. Victoria tried to focus, but listening to the drums without any melody made her completely lose the thread of the tune, and once that happened, all she heard was noise. Every once in a while, Jack would look over at her, and every time, Victoria made sure to smile back at him. But secretly she was bored. Deadly bored. So bored that at five o'clock, when Sam stopped playing, apologized, and said, "You know what, let's just take it from the top again," she wanted to scream. Instead, she reached into her bag and checked her phone. Three missed texts and a voice mail.

For a second she panicked. Was it her parents? Had Emily told them about her bailing on the community service center? Stomach tight, she checked the texts. She breathed easier when she saw they were all from Natalya.

3:25

colin wants 2 play chess in person 2morrow! nothing to wear!! call me!!!!

3:45

is it weird if i wear my uniform to meet colin?

4:10

help! help! help!

Victoria bit back a giggle, then checked her messages. "Oh my god!" Natalya's recorded voice wailed. "Why are you not texting me back? I am having a heart attack! What am I going to wear? What am I going to talk about? Do you hear me? Why are you not texting me back in my hour of need? You think those kids need you to help them appreciate organic produce. But really *I need you to tell me what to do!!!*" Natalya's voice got louder with each sentence, and suddenly Victoria, who had been smiling to herself as she listened, realized the room around her had gone completely silent.

She looked up.

Every eye in the studio was on her. Slowly, she closed her phone and put it on her lap. "Sorry," she said quietly. She glanced over at Jack. He was smiling at her, but it was a slightly tense smile, like he knew he had to support her but he was kind of embarrassed by what she'd just done.

"Sorry," she whispered again.

She wanted to go into the hallway to call Natalya, but she felt obligated to stay where she was, as if she'd done something naughty and deserved a time-out. As soon as Jack turned back to watch Sam, Victoria quietly typed, i will call u as soon as i can. don't panic. She hit send, cringing at the sound of the button being depressed. Had anyone else heard the distinctive *click*? But they were all looking at Sam. She dropped her phone into her bag, then sat silently, literally twiddling her thumbs as she waited for the song to be over.

When Sam was finally (miraculously!) done, Victoria nodded

her head, clapped a couple of times, then bent down to gather her bag, sure the session was over. Really it hadn't been that bad, she told herself. When you thought about it, it was kind of cool that now she knew how CDs got recorded.

"Okay, guys," said RJ.

Victoria stood up. She had the strap of her bag over her shoulder, but nobody had made a move to gather up the backpacks, coats, sweaters, and scarves that littered the floor and chairs of the console room. Jack cracked his knuckles. Rajiv, who had his feet up on the arm of Jack's chair, uncrossed his ankles, then recrossed them, with the opposite foot on top.

Sam came into the room as RJ finished his sentence. "Let's hear what we've got."

Victoria sat down reluctantly, expecting the rest of the session to be as boring as Sam's drumming, but she couldn't have been more wrong. As RJ played different versions of the instruments together—drums and guitar, drums and vocals, vocals and guitar—the song filled out and grew in complexity. What had already been lovely became rich and layered, the steady progress of the drums pulling the lyrical notes of the guitar ahead, and above it all, Lily's pure voice hovering, almost taking off and leaving the world behind until the other instruments brought her back to earth.

"Yeah!" said Rajiv as the last quivering note died out. It was the sixth or seventh time RJ had played the song all the way through, but the first time he had done so with this particular set of takes.

"Right on!" agreed Lily, and Jack and Sam applauded.

"You think?" asked RJ. His voice was gruff, but there might have been the hint of a smile behind his cigar.

Jack nodded.

RJ squinted at the screen of his laptop, typed something brief, then announced. "That's a wrap."

Everyone clapped and hooted. Sam and Jack high-fived, and Lily jumped up and down, waving her arms in the air. "Oh, baby!" Rajiv exclaimed. People made a point of slapping Victoria five or hugging her, but she felt self-conscious about having done nothing to help create the exquisite music she'd just heard. Less than nothing, really, if you thought about how she'd interrupted the session listening to Natalya's message. She wished she'd contributed in some way; if only she'd known about the recording session in advance, she could have at least made cookies for everyone.

Rajiv rubbed his hands together and announced, "I'm starved. Who wants to grab dinner?"

Jack turned to Victoria. "You hungry?"

Victoria hesitated. It was Friday night. Her mom would probably let her go out for dinner with Jack.

Dinner with Jack. She would have loved to have dinner with Jack. But she knew she wasn't the one he really wanted to have dinner with.

"I should probably get home."

Jack pushed up from his seat. "I'll take you."

"That's okay," said Victoria automatically. "You guys deserve to go out after all your hard work."

Jack walked over to where she was standing, put his arm

around her, and whispered in her ear, "Are you sure?"

Victoria was sure she didn't want to be the kind of girlfriend who kept her boyfriend from celebrating with his friends. She kissed him lightly on the cheek. "I'm sure," she whispered.

In the elevator, everyone talked about how great the session had been, how good a producer RJ was, how awesome it was going to be when the album was finished. Victoria tried to listen carefully. This was Jack's world, and she wanted to be a part of it.

"So," asked Jack, "did you have fun?" They were standing on the sidewalk outside the building. Lily, Sam, and Rajiv had just headed to a Mexican place around the corner. Jack had promised to be there in a minute, but right now his arms were around Victoria's waist.

"I did," said Victoria.

"Tell the truth," Jack ordered, hugging her. "You were a little bored."

For a second, Victoria panicked. She'd tried so hard to look interested the whole time, but still he'd guessed. Was he disappointed? Should she deny it?

Remembering his comparing a recording session to watching paint dry, she pressed her forehead against his chest. "A little," she admitted, her voice soft.

"Me too." As he nuzzled her neck gently, Victoria felt almost shaky with relief. So she hadn't been the only one who was bored. "But it's all worth it in the end, isn't it? Those guys are so talented." His voice, when he described his friends, was awed.

"I'll make cookies next time!" Victoria announced abruptly.

"What?" Smiling slightly at her non sequitur, Jack pressed his forehead against hers.

"I should have made you guys cookies or something. You know, to contribute."

Jack twined his fingers through hers. "You contributed just by being there."

*But I didn't say anything smart about the music, and then I was listening to that message from Natalya, and your friends are so much cooler and more talented than I am!* The wail of inadequacy in Victoria's head was so insistent, she was surprised Jack couldn't hear it.

They kissed, a long, deep kiss that ended when Jack finally pulled away with a groan. "I could kiss you forever, but I should meet those guys." She let him go, and he stepped into the street and put his hand out, and an instant later, a cab pulled over to the curb. Jack kissed her again, then she slipped into the car, he shut the door, and she pulled away from him and down the block.

As she settled into the back of the car, she pictured Jack joining Lily and Rajiv and Sam. They'd spend the meal talking about the recording session, maybe branch off into other bands, music in general. She knew Jack had been sincere when he'd invited her to join them, but she wondered if he'd thought about how little she would have contributed to the conversation.

Tonight, she vowed, she'd listen to the mix CD he'd made her for Christmas again, only this time she'd take *notes* on it. And next time she was out with him and his friends, she'd make sure to reference some of the songs on it at least once. Hurtling uptown, she wondered if it was weird that going out with her boyfriend and his friends felt a little like a test she had to study for.

# Chapter
# Thirteen

SATURDAY MORNING WHEN Natalya pushed open the door of
Act Two, Victoria was already there, standing in front of a rack of
dresses. She looked up as the bell tinkled Natalya's arrival.

"Let me see!" Victoria demanded, not even bothering to say
hello.

Natalya knew what her friend meant, and she immediately
unzipped her coat and spun around so Victoria could check out
the outfit they'd spent nearly an hour putting together on the
phone the night before.

Victoria applauded Natalya's slim black jeans, low black
boots, and fuzzy red long-sleeved zip-front sweater, undone to

reveal a gray tank top underneath. "Perfect!"

"But you know what I realized? Colin won't even *see* this. It's *freezing*. I'll be buttoned up to here." Natalya put her hand to her throat.

Victoria gave her a sly look. "Not when you go for coffee after."

Without responding, Natalya moved to stand next to Victoria. But she was too distracted to actually see any of the dresses she absently slid along the rack. "Vicks?"

"Mmmm?" Victoria pulled out a dark green velvet dress and cocked her head at it, then held it up to Natalya. "This would look great on you."

Ignoring the dress, Natalya said, "I'm nervous."

"Oh, Nat!" Victoria threw her arms around Natalya, accidentally clonking her in the head with the hanger she was holding.

"Ouch!" Natalya complained, rubbing the back of her head. But she was laughing.

Victoria laughed too. "I just wanted to get your mind off your date."

Natalya stopped laughing. "Do you really think it's a date?" she asked quietly.

"What do you mean?" asked Victoria. She had the feeling Natalya wasn't just asking a simple yes-or-no question.

"I don't know." Natalya ducked her head, letting her hair fall across her face. "I just . . . I don't think I'm the kind of girl guys think of. You know, like that." Even when she was done speaking, she didn't look up.

Victoria hugged the green dress to herself, as if it were

Natalya. "You mean the kind of girl a guy would ask on a date?" she interpreted.

Still not looking up, Natalya nodded.

"Well . . ." Victoria began. Rather than stare at the top of Natalya's lowered head, she studied the dress she was holding. The bodice was green velvet, so dark it was almost black, and the skirt was an equally dark silk. She fussed briefly with the thin strap holding it on the hanger as she composed her answer. "You're a girl," she said. "And Colin asked you to meet him somewhere, just the two of you, right?" She glanced over at her friend, who gave another brief nod.

"I mean," Victoria concluded, "if that's not a date, what is?"

Slowly, Natalya lifted her head. Her eyes were ever so slightly sparkly. "You think so? You really think . . . You really think Colin likes me?" She spoke the last three words so quietly, they were almost inaudible.

In lieu of an answer, Victoria gave Natalya a huge grin. Natalya grinned back. Then her face grew worried, and she bit nervously at her lower lip. "I really like him, Vicks," she confessed.

"I know." Victoria nodded. "He seems like the perfect guy for you."

Suddenly Natalya shook her entire body, like a dog emerging from the ocean. "Let's talk about something else. I'm losing it."

"Okay," Victoria agreed, her voice cheery. "Let's talk about how awesome this dress is going to look on you." She held the dress up against Natalya. As she'd thought it would, the dark green brought out the creaminess of Natalya's skin and the reddish highlights in her hair.

"I don't know." Natalya cocked her head and toyed doubtfully with the dress, turning it back and forth. "Strapless?"

Victoria had the feeling the dress would speak for itself, so she just told Natalya to go into the fitting room and try it on.

"Okay," said Natalya, but she sounded like she was more interested in placating Victoria than in believing her.

While Natalya was behind the black curtain that separated the fitting room of Act Two from the rest of the store, Victoria idly examined the other dresses hanging on the rack. She hesitated at one, a pale pink silk skirt with a dark pink bodice. It was soft and feminine, and she loved the way the silk felt against her skin. Jack would freak when he saw her in it.

She dropped the dress back onto the hanger.

Because Jack wouldn't see her in it. He'd be at Rajiv's birthday party the night of the opening. For a second, Victoria was irritated that he wouldn't be at the opening with her, but immediately she felt bad. Rajiv was Jack's oldest friend, and his parents were taking him, Jack, Lily, and Sam out for dinner. Would Victoria have bailed on Jane's birthday dinner to go to an event with Jack?

Of course not.

She picked up the dress again. Just because Jack wouldn't be at the opening didn't mean she couldn't look pretty. And who knew, maybe there'd be some event that he *would* be at that she could wear the dress to. Maybe the Frightened Pirates' album would win a Grammy, and she and Jack would go to the awards ceremony together. She touched the silky fabric of the dress, imagining Jack accepting the award, turning to look out over the audience. *Without the love of my girlfriend, I could never have won this award. She's everything to me, and I owe everything to . . .*

Natalya stuck her head between the curtains. "I can't wear this," she hissed.

Victoria snapped out of her reverie. "Let me see."

Natalya shook her head from side to side frantically. "I'm practically naked!" she whispered.

"Let me *see!*" Victoria repeated.

Natalya shook her head again, even more violently, and before Victoria could try to convince her to change her mind, the door to Act Two flew open and Jane stood on the threshold of the store.

"Oh. My. God," she announced. Behind the counter holding antique and costume jewelry sat Act Two's only employee, a skinny twenty-something girl with a nose ring. She didn't even raise an eyebrow at Jane's dramatic entrance, just continued to read *The Plague* and sip her liter container of Fresca.

"Where have you *been?*" cried Natalya and Victoria simultaneously.

But instead of answering, Jane repeated herself. "Oh. My. God." She walked to where they were huddled at the back of the store, then stared meaningfully at her friends. "Okay, what was I doing last night? Three guesses."

"Um, seeing a movie with your mom," offered Victoria. It was what Jane had told them she was doing, but Victoria couldn't see how such an evening would translate into a dramatic Q and A.

"Nope. Natalya?"

Natalya stepped out of the dressing area, too intrigued by Jane's mysterious question to worry about her naked back.

"Wow, sister, you look hot!" Jane cried. Victoria turned around to see Natalya, then clapped with excitement. Jane was right: the low-cut dress was sexy and flattering, emphasizing Natalya's small waist. And the color looked just as beautiful against her skin as Victoria had predicted. Wearing the dress, Natalya *definitely* looked like the kind of girl a guy would ask out on a date.

"Um, just so you know? You're buying that dress!" Jane informed her. Natalya opened her mouth to protest, but Jane held up her hand. "Save it, darling. Now . . . drumroll, please." She gave her friends a flirtatious, knowing grin. "Who spent last night one on one with the hottest guy in the tri-state area?"

Both Victoria and Natalya shrieked. Jane grabbed their hands and jumped up and down, shrieking also.

"Oh my god! Oh my god!" they all yelled.

Even nose-ringed Fresca girl couldn't ignore three girls jumping around and screeching at the back of her store. "Everything okay?" she called.

"Fine!" Jane called back before collapsing into hysterical giggles. She stepped toward a rack of dresses and pretended to be evaluating them. "Just looking at some clothes for an art opening we're going to."

Victoria and Natalya moved swiftly to her side. "Spill it." Victoria hissed.

"Now," Natalya added.

Jane turned to face them and launched into the story of her evening.

By the time Simon had gotten to her apartment, she was showered and changed, and her mother and Richard had left for a pre-movie dinner. When Simon walked in the door, he looked more gorgeous than ever: untucked white linen shirt, pair of Levis, and green-and-blue Adidas Sambas. Very old school. His hair was wet and hanging in his face a little, and when he said hello, he pushed it off his forehead.

"It was so *sexy!*" Jane explained, demonstrating the gesture.

"Then what happened?" Victoria demanded.

Jane continued. "Okay, so he pulls his script out and he goes, 'Work first, play later?' And I go, 'Totally,' and then we went into the den and we started reading the scene. We weren't *blocking* it, but we were kind of moving around in character."

"I have no idea what that means, and I don't even care," said Victoria, gesturing for Jane to keep telling.

"And it turns out he's a *really* good actor." Jane paused, trying to find the words to refine her description of his talents. "He's . . . it's like he gets into the character through these tiny gestures. Like, Jason's a warrior, so he had this way of standing . . ." Jane tried to imitate Simon's Jason stance, then shook her head. "Whatever. The point is, when you act opposite someone who's good, it makes *you* better, so *I'm* acting really well." She smiled at her friends. "If I do say so myself."

"Say it!" laughed Natalya.

"Say anything," urged Victoria. "Just get *on* with the story."

Jane laughed with excitement. "So we run through it a bunch of times, and then it's like, okay, we can't do the scene *again*, so what should we do?" She gave Natalya and Victoria a significant look. "So we were like, let's see what's on TV, and we go into the den and *The Philadelphia Story*'s on, and we're both like, 'Oh my god, I love this movie!'"

"Which one is *The Philadelphia Story*?" asked Natalya.

"It's the one where—" Jane began, but Victoria interrupted her.

"It's the one where nobody cares what happened because they want to get back to the story of the *night*!"

Even Jane was impressed by Victoria's eagerness. With a nod of appreciation, she returned to her narrative.

"Okay, so we sit down on the couch next to each other, and we're *really close*, and after a few minutes I'm like, 'Hey, you want a back rub?'"

"Oh my *god*," Natalya breathed.

"I *know*," said Jane, nodding to acknowledge her own awe some boldness. "And he goes, 'Sure,' so I got up on the back of the couch and started rubbing his shoulders.

"Meanwhile, he has the *best* back," she informed them, holding her hands roughly shoulder-width apart to illustrate it. "Really strong and muscular." Closing her eyes at the memory of touching Simon, she continued.

"So I rubbed his back for a while, and then I go, 'My turn,' and we switched. He gave a *really* good back rub too. Not too soft, not too hard."

Victoria nodded to show that she knew what Jane meant. "I can imagine," Natalya assured her friends, and Jane continued.

"Then after a while he stops, and we're just watching the movie, and we're sitting, like, *really* close and . . ." She hesitated.

"And . . . ?" Natalya prompted.

Jane made a face. "This is the only bad part."

Natalya and Victoria looked at her anxiously but didn't say anything. Jane toyed with her necklace as she continued.

"Okay, then he goes, 'Look, I have to tell you something.' And I said"—she batted her eyelashes flirtatiously—"'Is it that you think I'm fabulous?'"

Even though Natalya and Victoria laughed, Jane didn't crack a smile. "So then he goes, 'I *do* think you're fabulous, but that's not what I have to tell you.'" For the first time since she'd gotten to Act Two, Jane hesitated.

"Oh my god, what'd he say?" asked Victoria nervously.

Jane sighed. "He said, 'Remember when I said I was seriously in like with someone?' and I said, 'Yeah.' And *he* said . . ." Again Jane paused, but this time neither Natalya nor Victoria spoke. After a second, Jane finished Simon's sentence. "'The person I was seriously in like with was a guy.'"

There was a long silence.

A *really* long silence.

Finally, Natalya said, "I don't get it. Are you saying . . . I mean, is Simon gay?"

"No!" Jane snapped. Then she quickly added, "Sorry. It's . . . no. He's *not* gay. He just, you know, he had a crush on a guy once. Which is kind of cool, when you think about it."

"You mean because . . ." Victoria began, but she didn't finish her sentence.

Jane finished it for her. "*Because* it means he's, you know, totally open-minded and not homophobic or anything."

"That's true," Victoria agreed. "That's a good point."

"And he just *thought* he liked the guy," Jane explained. She looked from Natalya to Victoria.

"Oh!" Natalya said suddenly. "Remember when you liked Oscar Warner?"

Jane groaned at the memory. "Eeeew. He kept wanting to hold hands at that stupid Batman movie we went to. I was so grossed out." She shook her hand frantically as if she could still feel Oscar's sweaty palm against it. "Why are we even talking about him?"

"Because he is the *perfect* example!" explained Victoria. "You can *think* you like someone until he's grabbing you with his sweaty hands, and then . . ." She scissored her hands in front of her. "No, thank you, mister."

Now that she understood the point of her friend's story, Jane looked relieved. "Exactly. I think Simon's thing was like that." She shrugged. "Nothing ever even happened between them. He just kind of wanted me to know. You know, about his history. And I told him what happened with Mr. Robbins."

Natalya gasped.

"You did?" Victoria was amazed. Jane hadn't even told her *mom* about Mr. Robbins, and she and her mother were super close.

Jane nodded. "It was totally the right thing to do. I mean, he'd told me such a big secret. It didn't feel right not telling one back. He was really cool about it too. He said it wasn't a big deal and I shouldn't be embarrassed. He said it probably happened to Mr. Robbins all the time."

"I never thought of that," said Natalya, considering what Simon had said. "It makes sense, though."

Victoria agreed. "Especially since he's so young and cute and flirtatious and everything."

Jane nodded. "Totally." Then she smiled. "Anyway, then we just . . . hung out and kind of channel surfed. And you know, he, like, had his arm around me, and for a while he had his head in my lap." She sighed contentedly at the memory. "Basically," she concluded, stretching her arms up over her head, "it was the perfect night."

"Wow," said Victoria.

Suddenly, Natalya thought of something. "Did you kiss?"

"Mmmhmmm." Jane smiled and shivered slightly. "When he left." She closed her eyes and tilted her face up ever so slightly. "Really, really gently." She sighed again. "It was amazing."

"That is so romantic," Victoria said dreamily.

"I know," agreed Jane. She giggled. "Now *you* may have an awesome dress"—she pointed at Natalya—"but Vicks and I still have to pick out equally awesome dresses for the opening, because I totally invited Simon to be my date!"

"You *what*?" asked Victoria.

"You *did*?" cried Natalya.

"Yes." Jane took Natalya firmly by the shoulders. "Which is why you have *got* to ask Colin to be your date *today*." She stared deeply into Natalya's eyes, then added, "Sorry I never got back to you about what to wear, by the way."

Natalya blanched. "I can't ask him to be my date. I mean, how would I do that?"

Jane gave Natalya a look that said, *Are you for real?* "How about, 'Hey, Colin, it's been great playing chess with you. Do you want to come to this cool art opening?'"

"Ha-ha," said Natalya, not laughing.

"It'll be easy," Jane promised. "You'll just lead the conversation around to the opening. You know, blah, blah, blah Barnard, blah, blah, blah art. Except make the whole night sound amazing—which it will be—and he'll basically ask you to ask him."

"Guys, I'm not the, you know, leading-the-conversation-around-to-it type." Natalya's face was turning pale. "Besides, it's not like he's my boyfriend. We're just friends."

"Oh, please!" Jane snorted.

Remembering their earlier conversation, Victoria put a sympathetic arm around Natalya. "If it feels right, you'll ask him. But don't worry about it or anything. Just have fun."

Jane opened her mouth to say something, but Victoria gave her a stern look, and Jane held up her hands in mock defeat. "Okay, okay." Half to herself, she mumbled, "If you want him to already have plans that night like Jack does, there's nothing I can do about it."

"I heard that!" growled Natalya.

"Jane." There was a warning in Victoria's voice.

Jane crossed her arms and leveled a look at Natalya and Victoria. "Can I just say one thing?"

"No!" said Victoria.

"Fine," said Natalya at the same time.

Jane chose to hear Natalya. "Was I right about the text?"

Natalya nodded reluctantly.

"And I'm right about this. Trust me." She clapped her hands together for punctuation.

"Trusting you is what got me into this mess," said Natalya, smiling ruefully as she remembered the original e-mail she'd sent to Colin at Jane's urging.

Jane laughed. "Just put your life in my hands, okay, darling? I promise, everything will work out perfectly." She slipped her arm around Natalya's waist and squeezed her, and the three friends went to pick out two more awesome dresses.

# Chapter
# Fourteen

CONSIDERING IT WAS once again freezing out, Natalya wasn't exactly surprised that Washington Square Park was practically deserted. As she picked her way carefully around ice patches, she wondered why neither she nor Colin had suggested meeting indoors for their rematch. What if he'd woken up this morning, gotten dressed, stepped outside, and decided it was way too cold to head downtown and spend a couple of hours freezing his butt off with only Natalya for company?

Just as she was about to check her phone to see if Colin had sent her a text asking to reschedule (or, even worse, simply canceling), she saw, from across the park, that he was already there, waiting for her, the collar of his coat up, a black wool cap pulled down over his ears. The sight of him made her feel all wiggly, like a marionette being worked by an uncoordinated puppeteer.

He was here. He hadn't canceled.

It was a freezing cold day, and he was sitting outside.

Waiting for her.

Without Natalya's calling to him, he looked up as if he'd sensed her coming, and she felt another flush of warmth at the smile that split his face when he saw her.

"I can't believe I agreed to meet you here!" he yelled, over the dozen yards between them.

The sound of his voice made her feel more normal, less freaked out. Laughing, she called back, "Hey, *who* agreed to meet *who*?"

She made her way over to the table, and he shook his head sadly at her. "It's who agreed to meet *whom*," he corrected her. "You know, considering how much it costs, that Gainsford place really gives you a crap education."

Still laughing, she answered, "It's not costing me anything. I'm on scholarship."

As soon as the words were out of her mouth, Natalya wished them back in. Why had she revealed that? She'd never told anyone connected to Gainsford that she was there on a full scholarship. Not even Jordan knew.

She sat down at the stone table without meeting his eyes, shocked at what a stupid move she'd just made.

Colin didn't answer, and she was sure he was embarrassed. Was he going to apologize? That would be the worst. *Wow,*

*Natalya, I didn't know you were poor. I'm really sorry.*

"Full scholarship, you say?" he asked.

Hesitantly, she raised her eyes. Then she gave a slight jerky nod.

Colin cocked his head to the side and gave her a wicked smile. "Well, in that case, I guess you're getting your money's worth."

Natalya burst out laughing. Colin did too, but then he said, "I don't know what we're laughing about."

*Everything,* Natalya wanted to say, but she just shook her head. "I don't know. Just . . . how crazy it is to be sitting here in the freezing cold."

Colin arched an eyebrow at her. "It sounds almost like you're scared to play me."

"I just meant we should have met *inside* somewhere," Natalya explained, reaching out with the arm of her parka and wiping off the light dusting of snow that coated the table. "Besides, *I* beat *you* last time we played. Why would I be scared of a rematch?"

"Because," explained Colin, wiping off the other half of the board with his own sleeve, "you know you got lucky and you don't want to risk the humiliation of my defeating you. Which"— he reached into his pockets, then held both of his gloved fists toward her, inviting her to tap either white or black—"is about to happen."

An hour later, Colin spoke the word Natalya hated to hear more than anything in the world.

"Checkmate." Colin did not even try to hide the triumph in his voice. They both knew he'd played a brilliant game. Natalya, on the other hand, had made a couple of foolish moves from which she'd never recovered.

"You don't have to gloat." She sat back against the bench and glared at Colin. Natalya's father, who had taught her chess, had always warned her against being a sore loser, but she could never entirely hide the prickle of irritation she felt at being defeated, especially when she'd played so badly.

"Who's gloating?" asked Colin, but the smile that spread wider and wider across his face seemed to have a life of its own.

"You are."

"Am not."

"Are too."

Colin raised an eyebrow at her. "Well, you're pouting."

"Am not."

"Are too."

"Am not." By now they were both smiling.

Colin began collecting the pieces from the table, then noticed something. "Hey. It's snowing."

It really was. The stone table they'd been playing on was covered with a light speckling of fresh snow, and when Natalya looked at her arm, she realized she was too.

"We should probably go," Colin said.

Natalya stood up as her heart inexplicably sank. Did he mean *we should probably go our own ways,* or did he mean *we should probably go somewhere together?*

But he didn't follow up his "we should probably go" with, "well, bye," so Natalya thought it would be okay to walk with him. They left the park, and when Colin crossed Fourth Street and headed north on Fifth Avenue, so did Natalya. Picking her way carefully along the sidewalk, which was narrow and uneven with badly shoveled snow, Natalya wondered if at any second Colin was going to ask her why she was following him. She couldn't help wishing her father were right: that life really *was* like chess, that it came in a box with the rules clearly printed on the inside cover, illustrated with attractive, helpful diagrams in black and white, that your opponent's motivations were clear and obvious, and that you could always tell who was winning.

"Just so you know," Colin said, interrupting her fantasy of a world as transparent as a chess game, "I do not think less of you for having lost to me."

Natalya laughed. It was snowing harder now, the flakes falling thick and fast around them. Something about the snow made her feel protected, like even though she and Colin were walking side by side, there was a veil between them. A veil behind which she could dare to be the type of person who might bring the conversation around to a certain art opening.

"Do you like art?" she asked, realizing once the question was out of her mouth how random it sounded.

"Do I like art?" Colin repeated thoughtfully. "Not performance art."

"How about painting art?"

Though they weren't facing each other, Natalya could see out of the corner of her eye that his mouth was turning up into a grin. "And by painting art, you mean paintings, right?"

She frowned and pressed her index finger to her lips as if deep in thought. "What was that word you liked so much . . . ? Oh, right, pedantic!"

He laughed, and Natalya could practically hear the comment Jane would make when Natalya retold the story. *You guys have a private joke! He is sooooo into you.*

"*Anyway*," Natalya continued, giving a mock long-suffering sigh. Thinking of Jane's encouragement gave her confidence. "I'm going to an art opening in a few weeks—a *painting* opening— and I was wondering if you want to go."

"Sounds great," said Colin casually, like there was nothing weird about Natalya's asking him out.

*Score for Jane!*

They'd reached the corner of Fifth Avenue and Eighth Street, and Colin turned to face her. "Well, this has been awesome." He pointed his thumb over his shoulder. "But I gotta take off. So when's this painting-art event of yours?"

Too excited that he was coming to the opening to mind that their afternoon together was suddenly over, Natalya told him the date of the show.

He winced. "Damn, I can't come. I've got a birthday party that night."

Natalya's happiness evaporated, and she felt overwhelmed by embarrassment. How stupid had she been to ask him in the first place? He'd probably just been too taken aback by the invitation to think of a lie right away for why he couldn't go. Then he'd come up with the birthday party excuse and given it to her.

It was her embarrassment that made her ask, "Whose

birthday party?" As soon as the words were out of her mouth, she heard how accusatory they sounded, and she was even more embarrassed.

Colin's expression indicated he also thought it was a little weird that she was grilling him, but he answered simply, "Alison Jones."

"Wait, Alison Jones? Gainsford's Alison Jones?" Natalya blurted out, amazed by the coincidence. When she'd gotten Alison's invitation yesterday, she'd been bummed to see that her birthday party was on the same night as Nana's opening. But now she was glad about the conflict. If the Alison Jones he was talking about was the same one Natalya knew, that meant Colin really *did* have a birthday party the night of the opening. Which meant he really *had* wanted to go with her.

Colin nodded that it was, in fact, Gainsford's Alison Jones, and Natalya, relieved beyond words that Colin had been telling the truth, said excitedly, "I know her! She's in my class." Still amazed and relieved by the coincidence, Natalya shook her head and said to herself, "That is so crazy." Then she looked at Colin. "So, how do you know Alison, anyway?"

As Natalya uttered the word *anyway*, the light changed. Colin answered her question while stepping into the street. "She's my . . . well, she's kind of my girlfriend."

# Chapter
# Fifteen

IT WAS HARD for Jane and Victoria to focus on the Valentine's Day cards displayed at Possibilities when both of them were wondering what was happening with Natalya and Colin.

"This place is enough to make anyone boycott Valentine's Day," observed Jane, glancing around at the wall-to-wall hearts, flowers, and scented red candles.

"Never!" objected Victoria. She glanced at her phone, which hadn't rung. "Do you think she's asked him about coming to the opening yet?"

Jane checked her phone, but she was looking at the time. "I

bet they're still playing. I think chess games last, like, centuries."

Victoria rolled her eyes at a card with a photograph of a man and woman wearing matching his-and-her string-bikini underwear. "These cards are so gross."

"Get a blank one," suggested Jane. "Then you can write your own message inside. That's what I'm doing for Simon."

"You're getting Simon a Valentine's Day card?" Victoria couldn't hide the surprise in her voice.

Jane couldn't not hear it. She whipped her head around to face Victoria. "You think that's a bad idea?"

"No," Victoria answered quickly. "I mean, I don't know. Seriously." She smiled reassuringly. "Don't listen to me. I've never even met him."

Tracing her finger along a row of cards without looking at them, Jane said, "Maybe you're right. Maybe it *is* weird." She'd been so psyched about hooking up with Simon. But what if he just thought of her as a fun person to spend the evening with but nothing more than that? Suddenly she was ashamed of what she'd almost done. "I guess I should wait, shouldn't I?"

Quickly, Victoria put her arms around Jane. "No! I didn't mean that. I just meant . . . I don't know." She hugged her. "I'm sorry I said anything."

Jane was a little sorry too, but all she said was, "That's okay." This was all so complicated. Last night when they were together, telling Simon her thoughts and feelings had seemed totally cool. But now, standing in the world's cheesiest card store, she wasn't so sure. "You're probably right."

"It's just . . ." Victoria shrugged. "Maybe you want to know for sure how he feels about you before you put yourself out there like that."

Suddenly, both their phones buzzed, and they reached for them, like secret agents expecting an assignment.

"Nat," Jane guessed.

"Nat," Victoria echoed.

Simultaneously, they flipped open their phones.

"Noooo!" Victoria wailed as soon as she'd read the message.

"No way!" cried Jane, staring, outraged at the words on her screen.

colin has a girlfriend. not me.

"Ga Ga Noodle?" asked Victoria, still shaking her head in disbelief.

"Totally," agreed Jane, and she quickly typed the words into her phone and sent them to Natalya.

# Chapter
## Sixteen

"I FEEL LIKE *such* an idiot," Natalya cried, jabbing at a shrimp with her chopstick. Why did it have to be Alison Jones? *Alison Jones*. The friendliest, prettiest, most perfect girl in her grade; the girl who was becoming her kind-of friend; the girl it was impossible to hate because she was so damn *nice*?!

"Don't say that!" Victoria chided her. "You're not an idiot."

"Seriously. He should have told you," agreed Jane.

Natalya shook her head. "I think he thought I knew."

"How could you *know*?" Jane's voice was indignant.

"I don't know." In her head, Natalya replayed the conversation leading up to his revelation. "But he was so . . . matter of fact about it." She repeated Colin's exact words, trying to keep her voice as inflectionless as his had been. "'She's kind of my girlfriend.'"

"What does that even *mean*?" demanded Jane, repeating the words with a doubtful tone. "She's *kind of* my girlfriend? Is that like, I'm *kind of* a sleazeball?"

"Jane!" wailed Natalya.

"I'm serious." Jane surveyed the Darlings. "Tell me. What does it mean to *kind of* have a girlfriend?"

Natalya dropped her forehead against her palm. "This is starting to feel like English class."

Shaking her head, Victoria said, "He's been flirting with you all this time."

"No," Natalya protested. "I think . . . I must have just misunderstood him." She thought of her fantasy that life came with clear instructions. Now it turned out she needed instructions and an *interpreter*. "I guess he was just being friendly."

"Friendly!" Victoria slapped the table, enraged. "Friendly?! Colin was *totally* flirting, and that makes him so . . . so . . . yucky."

Jane laughed at the contrast between Victoria's fury and her choice of epithet, but then her face grew serious. "I agree. I mean, his first e-mail? 'I saw you.' That's like, Flirting 101."

Suddenly Natalya had an awful thought. Could it be that Colin *had* been flirting with her, only now that he knew she was at Gainsford on scholarship, he didn't like her anymore?

But that was impossible. It wasn't like he'd asked Alison out *after* learning Natalya was on scholarship.

Unless he'd been planning on breaking up with Alison, and

then, when he'd heard Natalya was poor, he'd changed his mind.

Was that crazy? She looked at her friends, wishing she could share her fear with them, but she knew exactly what they'd say. *It's not like you're* poor. *And anyway, if Colin cares that much about money, he's totally not worthy of you.*

But Natalya wasn't just thinking about money. What separated her from a girl like Alison Jones wasn't simply wealth. Girls like Alison and Morgan Prewitt were the product of generations of interbreeding that had created a rich, beautiful, confident race. They were girls who didn't need instructions, because for them, life really *was* a magical chess game, one they won every single time.

How could Colin choose some random scholarship girl over that?

*Why* would Colin choose some random scholarship girl over that?

Natalya pressed her lips together, overwhelmed by the impossibility of explaining why Colin might have changed his mind about her since his first flirtatious e-mail.

"What did you say when he told you?" asked Victoria gently.

"You should have hit him with your purse!" Jane mimed the gesture as she spoke.

Victoria giggled, but Natalya didn't even crack a smile. "I just . . . I pretended it was all totally normal and cool. Like, oh yeah, small world, we both know Alison Jones, gotta go, see you around." She slumped down in her chair. "Then I waited till he was out of sight, and I texted you guys."

Jane's phone buzzed. She glanced at the screen, then put the phone away without saying what it had said or who it had been from. But while she could hide her phone, she couldn't hide the smile on her face.

"What?" asked Natalya.

"Who was that from?" asked Victoria.

"No one," said Jane quickly. "It's not important."

"Jane!" Natalya warned. "Do *not* start hiding things from me."

"Trust me," said Jane. She reached over and briefly squeezed Natalya's forearm with her hand. "This is not a text you need to hear right now."

"No, I want to hear it," Natalya promised her. "I'm your friend. If it made you smile like that, I want to know what it said."

Jane hesitated, then blurted out. "It's from Simon. He said he had a great time last night and he can't wait to see me on Monday."

"Oh, Jane! I'm so happy for you." For Natalya's sake, Victoria tried to remain subdued.

"I'm so happy for you too." Natalya picked up a knife and mimed stabbing herself in the heart. "So happy I might have to *kill myself.*"

"Stop!" said Victoria, taking the knife from Natalya. "Don't say that. We're going to get you a boyfriend."

"Yeah!" agreed Jane. "A *better* boyfriend."

Natalya shook her head and stared off sadly into the middle distance. She thought about all the dorky things she'd written or said to Colin, how he hadn't seemed to mind, how he'd seemed to like her anyway. *Like* like her.

But he hadn't *like* liked her. And if a guy she had as much in common with and as much fun with as she did with Colin didn't *like* like her, how could *any* guy *like* like her?

"Don't get that look on your face," Jane warned.

"What look?" asked Natalya.

"You know. That I'm-never-going-to-have-a-boyfriend look," Jane interpreted.

Jane knew her too well. Natalya's frown shifted to a sad smile. But even though her expression changed, her thoughts didn't.

# Chapter
## Seventeen

JANE HAD COME to really hate the word *subtextual*. Which might have had something to do with the fact that Mark used it about fifteen thousand times per rehearsal.

*Medea and Jason's love is* subtextual.

*Remember, you can't show your love for Jason, Jane. It's* subtextual.

*Let's keep that passion* subtextual, *okay, guys?*

Mark had explained at the first rehearsal that subtextual meant below the level of the text. It was what was *beneath* the words on the page. What an actor was *feeling* but not *saying*.

Sometimes, when she and Simon were alone, they made jokes about it. In the library at lunch on Friday he'd said to her,

"You're doing your math homework, but what's the subtext? That you want to go across the street and get me a cappuccino?"

"Oh, is *that* the subtext?" Jane had responded. "I thought it was that you wanted to write my English essay for me."

The problem was, what was funny out of rehearsal was far less amusing *in* rehearsal. Every time Jane asked Mark how she should deliver a line, he gave pretty much the same response. *Think about the subtext* or *Think about what Medea's* really *feeling.*

Jane found herself longing for Mr. Robbins's clear, concrete direction. *You're angry, so yell. Let's see a little fear on that face of yours. According to the words on the page, you're sad, but I don't hear any sadness in your voice.*

The performance was still weeks away, but Jane was already getting nervous about making an idiot of herself onstage. She'd never realized before how much she relied on her directors to help her understand a part, but now that she was being given totally useless instructions, she appreciated too late what she'd taken for granted in the past: an actor, no matter how talented, couldn't do it alone.

"It'll be okay," Simon told her. They were in the black box waiting for Mark, who'd texted that he was stopping by the prop shop on his way to rehearsal. "Mark's just feeling his way. We've got to trust him."

Jane shook her head and looked over at Simon sitting on the floor a few feet away from her. "No, *you've* got to trust him. *I've* got to tell him that he's wasting our time."

"Okay, how about this?" Simon cocked his head and gave

her an irresistible smile. "I'll trust Mark and you trust me?"

It was impossible not to smile back at Simon. "Fine," she acquiesced. "But it'll cost you." She scooted over to him on her butt.

"Oh yeah?"

"Yeah," she said, and kissed him.

Jane didn't exactly have a lot of experience with kissing guys. She'd had a boyfriend for three nights at performing arts camp two summers ago, and they'd fooled around a little. Kissing him had been okay, but it had been nothing like kissing Simon.

Simon's lips were always soft against hers, and he didn't keep trying to get to second base every minute like her camp boyfriend had. Also, with camp boy she'd sometimes gotten the feeling that when they were kissing he kind of had no idea who she was, as if she could have been any girl (or even just two lips with a pair of boobs attached to them). But lots of times when she and Simon were making out, he'd pause between kisses to tell her something or ask her something or to make a little private joke; it was as if he enjoyed talking to her as much as he enjoyed kissing her.

Being with Simon was the most amazing feeling in the world.

After they'd kissed for a long minute, Simon pulled away and pressed his forehead to hers. "We should stop before Mark walks in and starts teasing us mercilessly."

"You're probably right." Reluctantly, she moved away from him after stealing one last kiss. A second later the door to the theater opened, and Mark entered. "Sorry, that took longer than I thought it would."

"No worries," said Simon as he and Jane exchanged a private smile. Jane felt her whole body glowing with the warmth of their connection.

"Okay!" said Mark. He crossed the room and handed Simon a sword. *"Poof!* You're a great hero."

Simon took the sword and danced it from one hand to the other. "I feel more heroic already."

"Jane, I'm still working on what your prop will be."

"Oh, I'm sure we'll find something in the subtext," answered Jane.

"What?" asked Mark, distractedly.

Simon shot her a warning look.

"Nothing," Jane answered. "I was just—making a joke."

"Oh," said Mark. "Got it." But he didn't laugh. There was something so . . . uptight about Mark sometimes. It was almost like he knew he wasn't doing a very good job. But if that were true, why did he give his directions with so much confidence, as if every word he was uttering was some golden nugget of directorial genius?

"Now!" Mark rubbed his hands together and walked over to the wall to adjust the lights, talking to her over his shoulder. "I want to take it from 'It was not that. No, you thought it was not respectable as you got on in years to have a foreign wife.'" He flipped several switches, then turned to look at the effect. Nodding at his work, he finished his instructions to his actors. "And remember what I told you last time, Jane. You're *furious*, but you're not furious. Because the subtext is L-O-V-E with a capital L. Got it?"

"So am I yelling at him?" asked Jane. "Do you want me to yell these lines?"

"You're yelling, but you're not *really* yelling," was Mark's answer.

You're yelling or you're not yelling, thought Jane. It's kind of an either-or situation. But as she walked past him, Simon whispered, "Trust me, baby." Then he gave her a secret smile and a wink.

Jane kept her mouth shut. Because maybe the scene was a disaster. And maybe she was working under the worst director in the history of theater.

But Simon was winking at her. And that was better than a standing ovation.

# *Chapter*
# Eighteen

TUESDAY MORNING, VICTORIA could barely contain her excitement as she walked into school holding a box of Valentine cookies she'd baked the previous night. It wasn't just that she was excited to give Jack the cookies. She was excited to give him the news.

That morning her mom, who had a strict no-going-out-on-weeknights policy when it came to Victoria and Jack, had sat down at the breakfast table and slid a small box of chocolate hearts toward her daughter.

"Be my Valentine?" her mom joked.

Victoria had laughed before leaning over and giving her mom a hug and a kiss. "Sure, Mom."

"Thanks for your card," her mother said.

"You're welcome." Standing up and walking her empty cereal bowl over to the dishwasher, Victoria added, "Nice flowers."

Her mom smiled at the elaborate bouquet in the middle of the kitchen table. "Who knew all I had to do to get such beautiful flowers from your father was live in a different city from him?" She laughed at her own joke. And then, out of nowhere, she asked, "So, who's the nicest mother in the world?"

"Um . . ." Victoria pressed her finger to her temple. "Could it be you?"

Her mother pretended to consider Victoria's guess. "Hmm . . . it could be. Because even without your *asking*, I spoke to your father about Valentine's Day, and we decided if you want to go out for dinner with Jack tonight you can."

Victoria practically flew across the room to hug her mother. "Seriously? Are you totally serious?" She let go and spun around joyfully.

Her mother nodded, then mimicked Victoria's vocabulary. "Totally."

Victoria did a little dance as she exited the kitchen, barely listening to her mother remind her she had to be home by eight thirty because it was a school night and blah blah blah blah blah. "Okay, Mom," she kept calling over her shoulder. "Yeah. Okay. No problem. I'll remember."

She grabbed her phone to text Jack, but then she hesitated.

It would be so much cooler to tell him in person, when she gave him the cookies. She would put her arms around him and say something sexy like, "Got any plans later, babe?" Or maybe *he'd* give her an opening by saying something like, "I wish we could go out tonight." She shivered slightly, imagining the kiss he'd give her when he learned that she was free to go out on a school night, then slipped her phone back into her bag. Oh yeah. It was *way* better to announce good news like this in person.

On the way to school, totally wrapped up in her fantasies of their evening together, she had to remind herself that it wasn't as if Jack would have planned anything for them to do. How could he have, since he wouldn't have had any way of knowing she'd be allowed to go out? Still, how romantic would it be to go out for dinner with Jack on Valentine's Day, even if they just went somewhere boring like The Cottage?

Sometimes lately, Victoria felt almost like she was competing with Lily and Rajiv and even Sam and RJ for Jack's attention. It wasn't anything specific Jack said or did that made her feel that way, but ever since she'd been at the recording session and witnessed firsthand their working together, she couldn't help comparing his relationship with his friends to his relationship with her. He and his friends made exquisite music together. When he talked about how talented Lily and Rajiv were, it was clear that there was no one he respected more. Compared to them, what was Victoria? Just his tin-eared girlfriend.

But today she didn't have to worry about any of that. Today was different from all other days. It was as if Hallmark had understood how important it was for couples to have time alone together and had carved one day out of the calendar that was just for people in love.

And now, thanks to her parents, they were going to be able to really celebrate it.

She practically skipped the seven blocks to school, stopping only once to read a text Jane sent her.

richard can't go 2 hamlet w/me and mom 2nite. want 2 come or should i ask my adorable boyfriend?

Victoria giggled. ask simon, she texted back.

When she found Jack waiting for her at her locker, she threw her arms around him and gave him a passionate kiss.

"Wow!" he said, when she finally pulled away. "What did I do to deserve this?"

"Nothing," she said, smiling up at him flirtatiously. "You were just your usual wonderful self."

She took a step back from him, reached into her bag, and pulled out the red box of cookies wrapped with a white bow. "Voilà. Happy Valentine's Day."

"Oh!" he said. "Thank you." Jack suddenly looked uncomfortable. "Thanks," he repeated, adding, "I mean, happy Valentine's Day to you, too." He fumbled with the tape on the box before opening it. "These are really pretty."

As Jack admired the cookies, Victoria started to get a funny feeling in the pit of her stomach. He took a cookie out and held it toward her. "Want one?" he asked.

But the sinking feeling made the thought of eating a cookie distinctly unpleasant, even if it was a cookie she'd spent the previous night baking and icing with romantic messages like *Be mine* and *I ♥ Jack*. And when Jack bit into the cookie without reaching into his bag to retrieve anything for her, the bad feeling only intensified.

"I'm sorry I didn't get you anything," he said, wiping a few stray crumbs from his top lip. "I guess Valentine's Day wasn't really on my radar."

It wasn't on his radar? How could Valentine's Day not be on someone's radar? Even though she was especially excited for it this year because of Jack, Victoria had always loved Valentine's Day. She'd spent two days baking cookies not just for her boyfriend, but for Natalya and Jane, too. She'd even sent a box to Emily, forgiving her for having been so annoying about the recording session.

She swallowed deeply, then managed to force a smile to her lips. "That's okay."

Jack looked at her and immediately registered the sadness on her face. He tucked the box of cookies under his arm and took her face in his hands. "Oh, Vicks, I'm really sorry. I should have realized it was important to you." He kissed her lightly on the nose. "I'll make it up to you next year, okay?"

"Sure." Then Victoria took a deep breath. "My mom said . . ." But everything was so different from how she'd imagined it, she suddenly couldn't remember how she'd planned to tell him what her mother had said. In her fantasy, she'd whispered the invitation to him in between long kisses, but now she just blurted out, "We can go out for dinner tonight."

"Oh!" Jack looked surprised. "That's so cool." He hesitated, then added, "The thing is, I'm supposed to see Lost Leaders with Rajiv and Lily. Would you want to come to that? Or . . . well, it's kind of a late show." His voice grew enthusiastic. "But it's going to be really amazing. I'd love to hear them with you."

Jack hadn't gotten her anything for Valentine's Day. Jack didn't want to go out for a romantic dinner with her. Victoria could feel tears threatening at the corners of her eyes, but then she shook her head, completely annoyed with herself.

After all, what was the big deal? Valentine's Day was just a stupid commercial holiday. Jack was not the kind of guy to get worked up about something just because Hallmark told him he should.

Wasn't that one of the things she loved about him?

"Um, maybe I could ask my parents about the show. What time is it?" Victoria's mom *had* given her permission to go out for dinner. Maybe that permission would be transferable to a concert.

"Nine." He made a face. "I figured your parents would say no, that's why I didn't ask you to come with us." Eagerly, he continued, "I've been begging for this for weeks, and I finally broke my folks." He snapped his fingers. "Do you want my mom to call your mom? As you know, my mom can be *very* persuasive." They both laughed, thinking of what Jack's mom was like.

Despite her laughter, Victoria wasn't exactly happy. Nine o'clock was late. Her parents would never in a million years let her go out at nine on a school night, no matter how persuasive Jack's mother tried to be.

With Victoria's luck, one phone call with her mom, and

Jack's parents would be the ones changing their minds.

Her phone vibrated, and she automatically checked the screen. SIMON COMING 2 HAMLET. HE SO CLEARLY LUVS ME!

Jane.

*Hamlet.*

Victoria's heart began to pound unnaturally fast. She didn't know anything about *Hamlet*, but Jane's school's production of *A Midsummer Night's Dream* had been almost three hours long.

What were the odds *Hamlet* would be over before eleven o'clock?

But did she dare? The last time she'd lied to her parents, she'd not only gotten caught, she'd gotten her photo splashed on the front page of one of the New York daily newspapers. She was *crazy* to risk that happening again. There would be other concerts.

Yeah, other concerts that she wouldn't be allowed to go to, either.

Why did her parents have to be so strict? Jack's parents were letting him go. Rajiv's parents were letting him go. Lily's parents were letting her go. Only Victoria's parents were so unreasonable that they never let her do anything. No wonder they'd named her Victoria. It was like they thought they were still living in the Victorian era.

The Victorian era reminded her of England. Which reminded her of Shakespeare.

Hadn't Shakespeare been alive at the same time as Queen *Victoria*?

Or was it Elizabeth?

Regardless, this was clearly a sign.

Victoria looked up at Jack, a defiant light in her eyes. "I'll go."

Jack lifted her up in an enormous bear hug. "Seriously? You seriously want to go?"

"Of course I want to go!" Victoria kissed Jack on the lips, hard, a little disconcerted by his question. Had he sensed that she didn't have fun at the recording session? Was that why he didn't believe that she wanted to go to a concert with him?

When they came up for air, he asked, "And you really think your parents will let you? Do you want my mom to call yours?"

This time, Victoria hesitated. Should she tell Jack the truth, that they would never in a million *years* let her go hear some band late on a school night?

But what if Jack told her to just forget the whole thing, said he'd go to the concert without her, that he'd see her tomorrow? If he spent all his time having fun with his friends, maybe he'd start to wonder if he needed a girlfriend at all.

She answered confidently. "Yeah, they'll let me."

Putting her down, Jack pumped his fist in the air. "Awesome!" He kissed her again. "Pick you up at eight?"

Oh, she was *so* not going to be at her house at eight o'clock tonight. "No, I should just meet you there," she said. "I might be coming from Jane's house."

"Done. I'll text you the address."

As Victoria watched Jack make his way through the crowded hallway, she thought about the Valentine's Day she'd fantasized. Jack ringing her bell at six, maybe with a small bouquet of flowers. A romantic dinner for two at a local restaurant. Home by eight thirty with her mother's blessing.

Instead she was planning to lie to her parents and risk getting grounded for life, all so she could spend the night with Jack and his two best friends at a concert she didn't particularly want to go to.

She looked back at her phone and reread Jane's text. he so clearly luvs me! Well, it wasn't like Jack *didn't* love her. He just had different ways of showing it.

Rather than linger on how, exactly, Jack showed his love for her, Victoria composed a response to Jane's text.

i m in serious need of help. r u free after school?

# Chapter
# Nineteen

"**ARE YOU GOING** to tell me what this is about or am I going to have to beat it out of you with this?" Jane demanded, holding a small embroidered pillow toward Victoria in a threatening manner.

It was late afternoon, and they were sitting on Jane's bed. Earlier, all Victoria would tell Jane on the phone was that she wanted to come over after school, and she'd explain everything in person. Then, when Victoria had gotten there, she'd refused to be distracted from admiring Simon's roses.

"They're *sooo* beautiful," she said for the thousandth time. She leaned forward and inhaled the scent of the enormous bouquet of roses sitting in its elaborate, cut-glass vase. The petals were a deep, rich red, and their aroma permeated Jane's bedroom.

"Okay, fine, they're beautiful! You can compliment him on his good taste when you meet him Saturday night," wailed Jane. She'd already informed her friend that Simon and the Darlings were going to see *Casablanca* at the Paris theater on Saturday. Now she grabbed Victoria's shoulders and pulled her around so they were facing each other. "Are you going to tell me what's going on or *what?*"

Victoria began fussing with the royal blue piping on a decorative throw pillow Jane had inherited from Nana. "Um, I kind of need you to cover for me."

"*Ohmygod!*" Jane leaped to her knees and bounced up and down on the bed. "What happened?" She let out a squeal. "This is *sooo* romantic."

"Then you'll do it?" asked Victoria anxiously.

"What? Of course I'll do it."

Victoria could have cried with relief. She slumped back, pressing the pillow to her chest. "It's totally not going to happen, but if my mom asks, I was at *Hamlet* with you tonight."

Victoria could pretty much count the number of times she'd been allowed to be out late on a school night, and almost every single one had involved Jane's mom having an extra ticket to something. The first few times it had happened, Victoria's mom or dad had called Jane's mom to thank her, but more recently they just said, "Don't forget to say thank you," and left it at that.

Jane raised an eyebrow. "And in fact you will be . . ."

Victoria smiled wickedly. "At a concert with Jack."

Jane let out a scream and fell back against the pillows. "Oh my god, I am *loving it*!"

Jane's enthusiasm made Victoria feel better about her Valentine's Day plans. It *was* pretty romantic to be sneaking off to a concert with Jack. Maybe dinner at a restaurant was kind of dull.

"So who are you going to hear?" asked Jane, propping herself up on her elbow.

Victoria wrinkled her forehead briefly. "Um, Lost Leaders? Something like that. They're Jack's favorite band."

Jane laughed gently. "Of course they are."

"What?" asked Victoria, not laughing.

"Nothing," said Jane quickly. "I was totally joking. So . . ." She sat up and crossed her legs. "What else happened? Did he sing you a love song like the sensitive rocker guy he is?"

But Victoria wanted to know what Jane had meant. "Jane!" Her voice was mild, but Jane knew Victoria too well not to hear the threat in it.

Jane shrugged. "It's no big deal. I just . . ." She didn't finish.

"You just what?" Victoria prompted.

"I just . . ." Jane glanced briefly at the ceiling, as if the words she wanted to speak might be printed on it, then finally met Victoria's eyes. "Lately it just seems like you do a lot of stuff that Jack likes to do, and, you know, he doesn't do stuff you like to do."

"That's not true!" Victoria said immediately, then added, "Like what?"

"I don't know. Like, since when are you so interested in music?"

"I like music!" Victoria pounded emphatically on the pillow.

"Okay, fine." But Jane's voice clearly said it *wasn't* fine, and a second later she blurted out, "Why isn't Jack coming to Nana's art opening with you?"

Victoria chucked the pillow to the other side of the bed. "I told you when I first asked him. It's Rajiv's birthday party." When Jane didn't say anything, Victoria insisted, "It's not his fault if he has plans for that night."

"Okay, okay," said Jane, holding her hands up in a gesture of surrender.

"What?" asked Victoria.

Jane looked Victoria straight in the eye. "I just think if the situation were reversed and *you* had plans and *Jack* asked you to do something, then, well, maybe you'd cancel your plans and do what he wanted."

Victoria blazed with anger. "When have I *ever* canceled plans to do something with Jack?" She felt a twinge of guilt thinking about how she'd ditched her community service, but told herself they were just talking about plans *with Jane.*

Trying to defuse the situation, Jane said, "Vicks, look, I'm sorry. It's no big deal."

Now it was Victoria's turn to laugh. "No big deal? Jane, you're criticizing my entire relationship."

"No I'm not. I just feel like . . . like, why is it you always seem to go places with his friends, and he never does stuff with us?"

Jane suddenly thought of something. "I bet his friends are going to be at the concert tonight, aren't they?"

"So what if they are?" asked Victoria. She sounded defensive, even to herself. "Is there something *wrong* with that?"

"Vicks, tell me you can see the irony in what's happening here." Jane laughed, slightly incredulous. "You're pretending you're going out with me so you can go out with Jack and his friends."

Victoria's voice quivered. "Why does everyone criticize me all the time?"

Jane was surprised by the effect her words were having on Victoria, and her tone immediately changed to one of concern. "What? Vicks, I'm sorry, okay? I don't want to fight with you."

Victoria lifted her enormous blue eyes to Jane's but didn't say anything.

"Vicks, do *not* give me the puppy dog eyes," Jane pleaded. "I'm *begging* you here."

"I'm not!"

There was a silence, and when Jane spoke, she completely changed the subject. "Hey, do you want to check out this dress I saw in the window of Act Two?" She poked Victoria in the leg with her toes and grinned. "It has *feathers*."

"What?" asked Victoria, but before Jane could repeat the question, Victoria quickly added, "I mean, sure, of course I'll come see it." She would have agreed to anything Jane had asked, if only to make peace with her friend.

They gathered their bags and headed into the hallway. As Jane wrote a note for her mom saying where they were going,

Victoria wondered if maybe her friend had a point. Maybe it *was* bad that she kept doing things Jack wanted to do instead of Jack's doing things that Victoria liked. Maybe it was weird that Victoria had a boyfriend who didn't care about her favorite holiday.

"Okay," said Jane, placing the note in the center of the counter and weighing it down with a saltshaker shaped like a snowman. "Now, get ready to see the dress of the century."

"Great!" Victoria was glad they'd moved on from the subject of Jack. It was one thing when her sister criticized her relationship. Emily had been criticizing Victoria for as long as Victoria could remember. But Jane's pointing to something weird going on was different.

Especially when the thing she was pointing to was exactly the thing Victoria was trying not to see.

# Chapter Twenty

NATALYA STARED AT her computer screen, where several windows were open, each one showing a different document relating to the origins of the current crisis in the Middle East. Just as she read the opening sentence of the Balfour Declaration, her dad popped his head into her room. *"Hotite igrat' v shahmaty?"* He was holding an unlit pipe in one hand and a steaming cup of tea in the other.

Natalya shook her head. "I've got a ton of work. Maybe when I'm done?" She felt a little guilty for lying, but what was she supposed to say—*I'm trying not to think about the boy I like, and chess reminds me of him?*

Besides, it wasn't like she *didn't* have a ton of work.

"*Horosho,*" he agreed, kissing her lightly on the head. "*Uvidimsya pozzhe.*" He gave her a little wave from the doorway.

"Yeah, see you later." She forced herself to smile back at him. After all, it wasn't her dad's fault that he'd taught her to play a game that caused her to be crushed out on a guy who also played the game but who had a girlfriend.

Once her dad had headed down the hallway, Natalya went back to reading the Declaration, but it was hard to focus on the paper she was supposed to be writing when she was so busy trying to imagine what Colin and Alison were doing to celebrate Valentine's Day.

She'd barely been able to look at Alison in school yesterday and today. After Bio on Monday, when she and Alison and Jordan had walked out of class together, Alison had said casually, "Dr. Clover rocks," and Natalya had nearly screamed, "Dr. Clover is *mine! Do you hear me?* She's *mine!*" Instead, she'd made some excuse about having to print up a history paper, and had successfully avoided having lunch with her friends.

Now, sitting in front of the half-written paper she'd supposedly printed up at lunch yesterday, Natalya was actually glad to have such an enormous, impossible essay to write. She was *seriously* busy. Way too busy to even think about having a boyfriend. After all, if she and Colin *had been* going out, it wasn't like she would have been free to do something with him tonight, what with this seven-page paper due tomorrow. So even if Colin were her boyfriend, she'd still be sitting in front of her computer screen all alone on Valentine's Day night.

At the thought of Colin's being her boyfriend, two things happened simultaneously. First, her stomach lurched in a now-familiar way. Second, a new window popped open on the lower-right-hand corner of her screen.

Cbprewitt@thompson: Hey.

Natalya was shocked. Totally and completely shocked. She could not have been more shocked if Colin had suddenly materialized in her room.

Her amazement at seeing his name on her computer made her forget to respond, and a minute later, he wrote again.

Cbprewitt@thompson: Um, hey?

This made no sense. Why was he writing to her if he had a girlfriend?

Cbprewitt@thompson: Hello? Hello? Is this thing on?

Of course, Natalya realized, he'd always already had a girlfriend. It wasn't like Alison was a new discovery for Colin the way she was for Natalya, who'd assumed Colin hadn't contacted her since Saturday because now that she knew he had a girlfriend, there was no point in talking to her anymore.

But why *was* he talking to her? What did he want? Natalya squinted at the words on her screen as if they were a slide and she were one of the girls in her class who didn't know how to use a microscope.

Cbprewitt@thompson: Is this thing on? Testing. 1. 2. 3. Testing.

Deciding without deciding, Natalya typed a response.

Npetrova@gainsford: hi.

Cbprewitt@thompson: Wait, is that a smoke signal on the horizon?

Npetrova@gainsford: Try binary.

Cbprewitt@thompson: I always knew u were cutting edge.

This was, without a doubt, the strangest conversation Natalya had ever had in her life. She'd pretty much given up on ever hearing from Colin, but when she'd let herself imagine their having a conversation, it would have gone more along the lines of, *Hey, sorry for not telling you about the whole girlfriend thing.* Instead, here he was, acting like nothing had changed between them.

And maybe nothing had. Being at Gainsford, she often felt like she was visiting a foreign country, one where the natives had their own language with phrases like *my country house* and *my driver* and *my investments.* Maybe what seemed flirtatious to the rest of the world was just simply friendly banter on Park Avenue.

As if to confirm her theory, Colin asked casually:

Cbprewitt@thompson: what r u up 2?

If Colin *hadn't* been flirting with her, Natalya knew she should feel relieved. It meant he wasn't a total sleazeball like Jane had said. She should be happy that her friend's boyfriend wasn't flirting with her.

But all she felt was a strange emptiness.

She realized she hadn't responded to his question and quickly typed:

Npetrova@gainsford: not much. learning about the roots of the crisis in the middle east.

Cbprewitt@thompson: is there a crisis in the middle east?

Npetrova@gainsford: I guess u don't get out much.

Cbprewitt@thompson: I try not to. that's what I love about chess. u don't have 2 leave the house.

Npetrova@gainsford: u left the house 2 play Saturday.

As soon as she hit RETURN, Natalya inhaled sharply and held her breath. She shouldn't have mentioned Saturday. Saturday had been the day of THE BIG CONFESSION.

But as if to confirm that his telling her he had a girlfriend meant nothing, Colin wrote back:

Cbprewitt@thompson: Speaking of Saturday, want to play a quick game?

She exhaled, not sure if she was relieved or disappointed by his being unaffected at the mention of Saturday.

Npetrova@gainsford: I have a paper to write.

Cbprewitt@thompson: u think I don't?

She smiled. What was it about Colin that made it possible for her to hear his voice even though she was just reading his words? But then she shook her head roughly. He had a *girlfriend*. Why didn't he play chess with Alison if he was so desperate for a game? She imagined Alison sitting in her ginormous bedroom with the private terrace, admiring a bouquet of roses Colin had sent her that morning with a note. *I kind of love you. Colin.* The picture in her head made Natalya feel irritated and guilty.

Npetrova@gainsford: im not playing.

Cbprewitt@thompson: one game.

Npetrova@gainsford: no thanks.

Cbprewitt@thompson: speed chess. ten minutes a move.

Npetrova@gainsford: nope.

Cbprewitt@thompson: five minutes.

Npetrova@gainsford: NO!

Cbprewitt@thompson: Well, Petrova, u drive a hard bargain. I'm afraid we're going to have to have this rematch in person. What about Saturday afternoon @ 3. My house. You, me and our well-matched wits. You game?

Okay, *wait* a minute.

He was inviting her to his house? His *house?*

She gently slid her fingers over the keys on her computer, not typing anything, just thinking. She thought about how much fun she'd had hanging out with Colin. And she thought about how happy she'd been walking through the emptying corridors of Gainsford with Alison and Jordan on Friday afternoon, how comfortable it was to be with them, how glad she'd felt that Alison thought of her as an invite-you-to-my-birthday-party friend.

Did she really have to choose? Couldn't she be friends with Colin *and* with Alison?

There was no reason that just because Colin kind of had a girlfriend (whatever that meant), Natalya couldn't be his friend. And it wasn't like just because she was friends with Alison's kind-of boyfriend Colin, she couldn't be friends with Alison too. That wasn't some kind of a *rule*. There were no *rules*.

That was Natalya's whole problem.

Though it was only three words long, Natalya's response seemed to take forever to type. And even after she hit RETURN, and the sentence was up on the screen, she couldn't believe it was she who had written it.

Npetrova@gainsford: OK. It's on.

# *Chapter*
# Twenty-one

JACK HAD TOLD her it was a nine o'clock concert, but at a quarter of ten, the warm-up band was still going strong. Nobody but Victoria seemed to notice the late hour; Jack, Lily, and Rajiv were debating whether some group Victoria had never heard of had sold out with their latest album. Jack said he liked a bunch of the songs, but Lily kept complaining that it was overproduced, and Rajiv kept saying, "It's the principle of the thing." Actually, he wasn't saying it so much as screaming it, because the club practically pulsated with the warm-up band's (The Crying Babies? The Lying Ladies?) tooth-rattling music.

Victoria kept checking her phone, and not just because she

couldn't believe how much time had passed without the concert's starting; even though her mother thought Jane's mother was sitting at a production of *Hamlet*, Victoria was completely paranoid that any second now she'd get a text from her mom saying, i just talked to Jane's mom & i know u lied!!!!

On her way to Act Two with Jane to see the feathered dress, Victoria had taken a deep breath, then called to ask her mom if she could go to *Hamlet* with Jane and her mother. She'd expected her mother to say something generic like, *That sounds like fun,* or maybe, *Aren't they sweet to invite you,* or even, *Are you sure you want to go? It might be boring.* She'd actually scripted the plea she'd have to fake, all about how she was really getting into Shakespeare.

But her plans to convince her mother she should be allowed to go to the play had proven to be completely unnecessary. As soon as Victoria said Jane's mother had offered her an extra ticket to *Hamlet,* her mom had *gone nuts!*

"*Hamlet* at The Public?"

Victoria wasn't actually sure it *was* at The Public, but she just said, "Um, yeah."

"Oh my god!" her mom cried. "That's incredible."

As her mother went on and on, Victoria gleaned from her enthusiasm that this was the best production of *Hamlet* since, like, the Renaissance, that it was sold out for the entire run, and that somebody's having an extra ticket was luckier for Victoria than if she'd won the lottery. "That is just *soo* generous of Anne," Victoria's mom said, about ten thousand times, and each time she said it, Victoria could practically hear her dialing Jane's mother to say thank you.

"I'll tell her thank you!" Victoria shouted, nearly hysterical. "I'll buy her some flowers to say thanks." Literally sick with anxiety, she pressed her hand against her stomach to quell the nausea. What had she done? Why had she lied? This was insane. Her mother was totally going to say something to Jane's mother. Her parents were never going to trust her again.

She'd just have to go to the play. She'd tell Jack she couldn't go to the show, that her parents wouldn't let her.

But then she remembered she *couldn't* go to the play, that Simon had already taken Jane's extra ticket. So what was she supposed to do? It wasn't like she could tell her mother that Jane's mother had offered her the ticket and then rescinded the offer. If she didn't go to the concert, was she supposed to wander around the city by herself until eleven thirty, at which point she could probably claim the performance had ended?

Her mother's voice broke through the ocean of panic swirling in her brain. "Are you at Jane's now? What about homework?"

"We're running a quick errand, and then we're going back to Jane's to do homework." Uttering the first truth of the entire phone call, Victoria breathed more easily.

"Listen, sweetheart, I'm sorry, only I don't want you going out for dinner with Jack *and* going to this show, okay? That's too much on a school night."

*Dinner with Jack.* Had her conversation about dinner with Jack taken place only that morning? It felt like a million years ago. "Right, Mom. I totally understand. I'm just going to eat with Jane and her mom before the show." Was her mother going to be suspicious that she was acquiescing on the dinner thing too easily? But she couldn't bring herself to start a fight with her mother about an entirely fictitious dinner with Jack.

Her mom was still talking. "And don't wear jeans. It's awful to wear jeans to a play. Borrow something nice from Jane, okay? And you'll take a cab home. Do you have enough cash? Ask Anne for some and then I'll pay her back."

"I've got money!" The idea of getting caught because her mother offered to give Jane's mother twenty dollars for Victoria's imaginary cab ride home from downtown made her stomachache return a million times more intense than it had been earlier. She couldn't believe how many ways there were to get tripped up in this lie.

"Okay, sweetheart. I love you. Have a wonderful time tonight."

At her mother's gentle, generous good wishes, Victoria felt her eyes swimming with tears. What kind of horrible daughter was she? How could she reward her mother's trust and love with a complete lie?

"I love you too, Mom." As she spoke the words, she hoped her mother could sense that they were true, even if every other sentence Victoria had uttered over the course of their phone call had been a complete lie.

She hung up and looked at Jane, who was standing next to her in front of Act Two, her eyes full of sympathy. "That sounded kind of brutal."

Victoria nodded, then added, "Do you have anything I can wear to a rock concert that will look like I could have worn it to go see *Hamlet*?"

Jane gave her friend a tight hug. "Totally." Then she pulled away and smiled encouragingly at Victoria. "And listen, forget everything I said before, okay? Tonight is going to be *awesome!*"

"God, they so totally stole this melody!" Rajiv yelled, and Jack and Lily laughed.

"What melody?" asked Victoria, who could barely hear a melody. But she'd asked her question too quietly for anyone to hear, and besides, Rajiv had just said, "They're here!" and pointed at a tall, curly-haired guy standing over by the bar.

By the time the opening band had left the stage and Lost Leaders had finished tuning their instruments, it was ten thirty. Victoria put her hand on Jack's arm. "I've gotta go."

Jack cupped his hand around his ear and leaned down toward her. "What?"

She pointed at her wrist, though she wasn't wearing a watch, and said again, louder this time, "I. Have. To. Go."

Jack's face was concerned. "Are you sure? They're just starting."

As if to underline his point, the curly-haired guy stepped up to the mike and said, "Hey, everybody!"

Should she tell Jack the entire story? Explain how she'd lied to her mom and how if she got home even a second later than she was expected, her mom would be on the phone to Jane's mom and the jig would be up?

The crowded room erupted into enthusiastic cheers; even if she'd wanted to explain to Jack, she didn't have the energy to shout the entire story into his ear.

"I wish you didn't have to go." He gave her a hug, then said in her ear, "You didn't have a very good time, did you?"

For a second, Victoria considered admitting he was right, but it was crazy to try to discuss their night when they couldn't even hear each other. So she just said, "I had a *great* time." She held up the single, long-stemmed white rose Jack had given her when she walked into the club. "And I love my flower."

Jack squinted and gave her a look that said, *Are you telling me the truth?* but Victoria stared him down. "Okay," he said finally. "You had a great time." He kissed her and said quietly, "Happy Valentine's Day, Vicks. I love you."

"I love you too," she said, glad she could at least be honest about that. Then she quickly made her way to the door of the club and onto the street.

Victoria was sure she'd arrive home to a lengthy interrogation, so she was amazed to find a note from her mother on the kitchen table apologizing for her being too tired to stay up and hear how the show went. At first she was relieved, but as she lay in bed watching the numbers on her clock count down the hours until she had to lie to her mother's face about the play she hadn't seen the night before, she wished she'd just been able to get their conversation over with.

She finally dozed off just as it was getting light out, then dragged herself out of bed to her blaring alarm after hitting snooze several times, and stood, bleary-eyed, under a scalding shower in an attempt to wake up.

"Good morning!" Her mother, a morning person, came

159

into the kitchen practically singing her greeting, and Victoria felt a welcome surge of adrenaline rush through her veins at the thought of all the lies she was about to have to utter. "So, tell me everything! Was it as wonderful as everyone's saying?"

"Oh, it was," Victoria said. She shook her head in amazement, as if the memory of the acting she'd enjoyed the previous night was more than she could find the words for.

Her mom poured herself a cup of coffee. "And did you understand the story? It can be hard when you haven't read the play."

The question threw Victoria into a complete panic. She didn't have the faintest idea what *Hamlet* was about, and she cursed herself for not having read at least a plot summary when she was at Jane's yesterday. "It was a little confusing," she admitted.

Her mother suddenly furrowed her brow and stared at Victoria. "Honey?"

*I'll never lie to you again. Please, please, please, this one time, please, don't catch me.*

Victoria's mouth was dry. She couldn't part her lips to speak.

Her mother looked at the wall behind Victoria. "Aren't you going to be late for school?"

Victoria could have cried with relief. "Yeah, I should go." She kissed her mother and flew to the front closet. She felt awful and guilty, and for a split second, as she was zipping up her coat, she felt furious with Jack. Why had he put her in this position? Why had he made it so she had to lie to her parents?

But then she stopped herself. Jack hadn't *made* her lie to her mother. She remembered how in the fall she'd claimed to her parents that she'd only lied to them about sneaking out to a party

160

because Natalya and Jane had pressured her to go.

Well, Jack certainly hadn't pressured her into going to the concert. In fact, it had almost seemed like he barely wanted her there.

First period, Victoria and Jack had Bio together, but Jack wasn't there. Either his parents had let him sleep in or they'd left too early to know he wasn't at school in time for his first class. Victoria handed in the lab she'd finished at Jane's, trying not to think about how unfair it was that Jack was probably sleeping in *and* would have an extra night to work on the lab. She couldn't decide which she was more jealous of: his getting to hand in the homework tomorrow or his being asleep. The thought of sleep made her head feel even heavier than it had before; she had to jerk herself upright more than once during the period to stop herself from dozing off.

When Victoria came out of class, Georgia was waiting for her by her locker. "So where should we meet later?"

"Wait, what?" Victoria did a quick mental check. It wasn't time to go to the community center again.

"We have to write up that summary of our work. Tomorrow's the deadline, remember?" Georgia smiled. "I know, payback sucks."

*Was that today?* All Victoria wanted to do after school was sleep. How could she possibly write up a report?

Georgia gave her a funny look. "You're not going to bail on us, right?"

The word *again* wasn't spoken, but it was definitely implied.

Quickly, Victoria shook her head. "No. No. Of course not." She gave Georgia's arm a quick, reassuring squeeze. "I'll meet you in the library after school."

"Cool. I'll see you then." Georgia was clearly relieved, and Victoria felt bad at the idea that someone who counted on her might think of her as the kind of person who couldn't be counted on.

She gave a little wave and headed down the hall, so bleary-eyed she almost didn't see Jack, who was walking toward her with Rajiv and Lily. They were all eating egg sandwiches and laughing about something.

"Hey!" called Jack, stopping in front of Victoria.

"Hi, Victoria," said Rajiv and Lily. "Great show, right? Sorry you couldn't stay."

"Oh, totally!" Victoria was glad to hear how enthusiastic her voice sounded.

"See you later!" said Lily.

"Later!" Victoria smiled as Rajiv and Lily turned to go.

When they were alone, Jack held out his sandwich to Victoria. "Bite?"

Victoria was so tired that the thought of eating anything made her stomach turn over. She shook her head.

He nodded, then put his arm around her, walking along in the direction she'd been heading. "Listen, Rajiv and Lily are going to come over after school, and we're going to listen to the final mix of the album. Want to come?"

*Did these people do anything but listen to music?!* She shook her head, glad to have an honest excuse for why she couldn't join

162

them. "Can't. I have to work on a report with Maeve."

"Got it," said Jack. "In that case, any interest in a *Twilight Zone* marathon Saturday night? A bunch of us are going to Rajiv's."

Victoria wrinkled her nose. She could fake an interest in music, but not science fiction. Years ago she and Emily had watched *Alien*, and the memory of it still grossed her out. But luckily, she didn't have to tell Jack she hated something he apparently liked. "I can't. I'm going to see *Casablanca* with Jane and Natalya." Suddenly she had an idea. "Do you want to come, instead of going to see *The Twilight Zone*? I think Jane's boyfriend is coming."

Jack briefly made a face that gave Victoria the impression he liked *Casablanca* about as much as she liked *The Twilight Zone*. Then he shook his head. "I'm kind of cohosting the *Twilight Zone* thing, so I don't want to bail." He posed like a bodybuilder and made his voice deep and dramatic like a sports announcer's. "You're looking at the official popcorn maker of this year's marathon." Then he dropped his arms and his voice went back to normal. "Besides, I'm not that into old movies."

"*Twilight Zone*'s old, isn't it?" Was she nagging? This was starting to sound a little like nagging.

He considered her question, then said, "Okay, let me qualify that as old *romantic* movies."

Victoria didn't know what to say. She wanted to be with Jack, but she didn't want to watch *The Twilight Zone*. And he had said he wanted to be with her, just not enough to bail on his friends or to get over the fact that he wasn't into old *romantic* movies.

The warning bell rang.

"Well, maybe you'll come by before you go to the movie?" Jack suggested, squeezing Victoria's hand.

Remembering her conversation with Jane, Victoria squeezed back. "Maybe you'll take a break from the marathon and come to the movie." She felt good for having said it, proud that she hadn't just caved and agreed to sacrifice her plans to meet Jack.

He laughed, kissed her lightly on the cheek, and said, "Maybe," before heading off to history class.

Part of Victoria wanted to call for him to come back, to ask him why he didn't want to see her enough to go to a movie he might not otherwise have gone to, to remind him that she'd gone to the concert with him for no other reason than that it was important to him.

But what if he said, *Well, Victoria, maybe I'm not as into you as you're into me?*

Just thinking about Jack's loving her less than she loved him made her feel awful and empty, as if she'd gone without food for a week. Besides, he hadn't said no. He hadn't said he *wouldn't* come to the movies with her. He'd said maybe.

*Maybe* could mean *yes*, Victoria reminded herself.

All the way to class she kept saying, *Maybe could mean yes, Maybe could mean yes*, over and over in her head. But despite having repeated the sentence more than a hundred times, when she sat down and took out her algebra homework, she still hadn't managed to convince herself.

# Chapter
# Twenty-two

JANE NEARLY DROPPED her tall cappuccino when Natalya called and informed her of her plans for Saturday afternoon.

"Okay, first of all, you're *so* not going to Colin's house," Jane said into the phone. She wrapped her fingers more firmly around her drink.

"What?" Natalya sounded genuinely shocked, which surprised Jane. "Of course I'm going. Why shouldn't I go? We're *friends*."

"You're *not* friends," Jane shouted. The barista who'd just made her cappuccino looked startled, and Jane shot her an apologetic look.

"Thanks a lot," Natalya shot back.

Jane stepped outside, and the chilly air calmed her down a little. "Sorry. What I *should* have said was that your friendship is . . . problematic." Then she couldn't resist adding, "In that you *like* him."

"Okay, fine. I like him," Natalya admitted. "And your point is . . . ?"

Jane took a sip of her coffee. "You're going to get hurt."

"No I'm not!" Natalya said firmly. "I know he doesn't like me. And I'm fine with that."

"You seriously expect me to believe that?" asked Jane, wiping a drop of foam from her lip with the back of her hand.

"Yes."

The light changed, and Jane crossed the street, heading back to school for rehearsal. "And you're not hoping anything is going to happen with Colin on Saturday."

"Exactly. Alison's my friend."

Jane stood on the sidewalk in front of school but did not walk up the steps into the building. "So, you're not, like, going to ask me what you should wear to his house."

Natalya didn't answer. She was thinking about how much she wished Victoria had answered her phone earlier. There followed a lengthy silence.

Finally, Jane said, "I want to go on record as saying that your going over to Colin's strikes me as an extremely bad idea."

"Fine," Natalya said curtly. "Duly noted."

As soon as they hung up, Jane replayed their conversation in her head. She couldn't help feeling she'd failed Natalya, that if only she'd said the right thing, she could have convinced her not to go over to Colin's on Saturday.

But no matter how hard she tried, she couldn't figure out the magic words that would have gotten Natalya to change her mind.

When Jane arrived at rehearsal, Simon and Mark were already there, moving extra chairs out of the way. They looked up as she banged through the door. She could not *believe* how stupid Natalya was being.

Despite being irritated, one look at Simon calmed Jane down. No matter how many times she saw him, Jane could never get used to how beautiful he was. He was like a great painting or a Beethoven symphony or a Shakespeare sonnet. Seeing him, even if it happened several times a day, always took her breath away. She made her way over to the center of the room. Simon slipped his arm around her shoulders. Standing there pressed against him, Jane felt . . . complete somehow. Like nothing could be wrong in the world as long as Simon was in it and they had their arms around each other.

"I commend you on your ability to get into character," Mark said as Jane wrapped her arm around Simon's waist. "But let us remember that Jason and Medea have a *sub*textual love."

Jane was about to say something snotty, but before she could, Simon shook his head in mock sadness. "Subtextual. Get your mind out of the gutter, would you, Mark?"

They all laughed as Jane and Simon crossed to their positions and Mark grabbed one of the audience chairs, swung it around, then straddled it.

Once Mark was seated and had indicated they should take it from the top, Simon launched into his lines. "'This is not the first occasion that I have noticed how hopeless it is to deal with a stubborn temper. For, with reasonable submission to our ruler's will, you might have lived in this land and kept your home.'" As Mark had told him to be, Simon was in a deep rage. When he said, *This is not the first occasion*, he really sounded as if he'd said the same thing so many times before that he was barely able to find the patience to utter it again.

Jane and Simon circled each other, speaking their lines and glaring at one another. Medea accused Jason of having betrayed her. Jason responded that Medea had brought exile on herself by cursing the king's family. Medea told Jason that she'd only cursed the king's family because it was *Jason's* family.

Jane knew her lines, and she knew her blocking, but she still didn't know how to do what Mark kept telling her to do. Simon seemed to be okay. Mark had told him to act impatient with Medea, and he was looking at Jane as if he just wanted her to shut up already. Mark's direction to Jane, however, was completely useless. She *tried* to yell without yelling, but you were either yelling at someone or you weren't.

Round and round they went, growing angrier and angrier, until they were definitely screaming at each other. Finally, Jane shouted the final line of the scene at Simon: "'Your marriage will be one of regret and horror!'" Her voice was hoarse from all the yelling she'd done. Though she was trying to stay in character, she made a mental note to drink a lot of tea with honey on the night of the performance. If she didn't, her voice was never going to hold out for the entire scene.

Simon stormed offstage. There was a long moment of silence.

Mark sighed and shook his head. "Jane, I just feel like you're not . . ." He pulled at his hair in frustration. Was he annoyed by her performance, or by his own inability to find the words he wanted? "It's like . . . you're just yelling. It's too much."

Jane was embarrassed. She knew she was doing a bad job, but she couldn't figure out how to do a better one. And how dare Mark criticize her when *he* was the one who was giving her the meaningless directions that were causing her to humiliate herself?

Before she could stop herself, Jane snapped at Mark, "Or maybe I have no idea what you're talking about." She gestured from herself to Simon. "Maybe *we* have no idea what you're talking about."

Simon opened his mouth to say something, but before he could, Mark asked Jane, "I'm sorry, who nominated you to be the official spokesperson for this cast, again?"

"Simon's just too polite to tell you that everything you're saying is ridiculous." She imitated his slightly ponderous way of giving directions. "Keep the love subtextual. Yell, but don't yell. This is a subtle manifestation of a complex theme. Blah blah blah blah blah. This isn't an English essay, okay? Give me something I can *use*."

Mark got to his feet. "I'm *trying* to give you something you can use. But you're not *using* it."

"Um, guys . . ." Simon said hesitantly.

"Directors have to direct." Jane raised her voice, speaking over Simon. "They need to say things that translate into practical suggestions. For example . . ." She began to count off sentences on her fingers. "Look at this person like you want to kill him. Look at this person like you want to kiss him. Shout this line. Whisper *this* line." Now she looked at Mark, five fingers held up in the air for him to see. "These are directions that are helpful. On the other hand . . ." She held up her other hand and extended her index finger. "Yell but do not yell? Yell at this person in a loving way? That's a cool idea, Mark, and I can totally see why you're psyched about it. But if you want to be a director someday, you should probably know the truth, okay? And I'm sorry I have to be the one to tell you, but here it is. All that crap you've been spewing? It's not called directing. It's called wasting everybody's time."

There was a deadly silence in the black box. Both Simon and Mark were staring at her—Mark furious, Simon with a horrified expression on his face.

Jane knew she'd gone too far, which only made her angrier. "What?" she demanded, her voice defensive. Okay, maybe she hadn't said it as gently as she might have, but she'd only been telling the truth. Couldn't they see that?

"Jane, sometimes you're a real bitch, you know that?" Mark said finally. And with that, he stormed out of the theater.

There was a long silence.

"Um, you're gonna call him, right?" Simon asked Jane finally. He'd dropped into a chair when Mark left, and now he toyed with a strip of loose rubber on the sole of his shoe. "You're planning on working this out?"

"Oh, come on, Simon. What would I say if I called him? You know I didn't tell him anything that wasn't true. I'm the one who has to be onstage looking like a total idiot. Am I just supposed to accept that? Am I supposed to set myself up to be embarrassed?"

Simon gave her a sad smile, then stood up, walked over to her, put his arms around her, and gently kissed the top of her head. "Just call him, okay?" he whispered into her hair.

Jane pulled away and looked into Simon's eyes. "For me, okay? Talk to him before Saturday," he said. The next time they'd been able to reserve the black box was Saturday morning at seven a.m. No surprise, it wasn't exactly a popular hour to rehearse.

"Simon . . ." Jane began to object, but he put his finger to her lips and just kept staring down at her. She began to smile. "You know I can't resist when you look at me like that."

"I know. Why do you think I'm looking at you like this?" Simon asked, smiling back at her.

*God. Could he be any cuter?*

"Fine. I'll talk to him." She wagged her finger at Simon. "But I don't regret saying what I said."

"Okay." Still smiling that same smile, Simon said, "You know, it's a delicate balance."

"What?" Jane had no idea what Simon was talking about.

"Being honest and being kind," he answered.

Jane didn't hesitate. "It's more important to be honest. There's nothing kind about lying."

"I think there's a difference between being kind but honest and lying." Simon spoke slowly, as if he were developing the theory while articulating it.

Jane made a face. "You just want me to be nicer to Mark."

Simon made a face back at her. "I just want you to remember that nobody's perfect."

"You're perfect." Jane held out her hand to Simon. "Or at least, *extremely* close."

He took her hand and held it tightly. "No, I'm not." His voice was sad, and Jane felt guilty. She hadn't meant to make Simon feel bad. Just evil Mark.

She closed the distance between them and pressed her head against his shoulder. "Buy you a latte?" she offered.

"Sure," said Simon.

She hoped that leaving the theater would put Simon in a better mood, but for the whole time they were at Starbucks, he was sad and distracted. She couldn't understand his feeling that bad about what she'd said to Mark, but she didn't see what else he could have had to be upset about.

# Chapter
# Twenty-three

ON WEDNESDAY NIGHT Natalya lay awake until nearly dawn. For part of that time, she was thinking about her annoying phone call with Jane, but mostly she was thinking about Alison. Specifically, she was trying to figure out if she should have said something to Alison about being friends with Colin.

That morning Natalya had gotten to first-period English early. Extremely early. So early, she was the first person to arrive, and she took her seat in an empty classroom. She told herself she wasn't waiting for Alison, but every time the door opened and another blond head crossed the threshold, Natalya's heart beat a little faster until the discovery that it wasn't Alison made it return to its normal pace. When Alison's familiar face did appear, Natalya was so worked up she half expected her friend to cross the room, shove her finger in Natalya's chest, and announce, *I know what you're planning on doing Saturday afternoon, so don't even* think *about going over to Colin's house.*

But Alison just smiled at Natalya, gave a little wave, and sat down. When class ended, they fell into step beside each other as they often did when they had Bio right after English.

"You missed a *killer* soccer game yesterday. We kicked serious butt." Barely breaking stride, Alison demonstrated a quick shot on goal.

"I was working on a paper!" Natalya almost shouted. "Pretty much all night."

Alison sighed. "I'd rather have a paper than a test. I *know* Dr. Brixton's going to give us a map, and I totally suck at maps. All that spatial-relational stuff—" She gestured in the air before her, as if sliding pieces of something together and apart. "I'm a lost cause."

"Yeah," said Natalya, sympathetically. She was finding it hard to concentrate on what Alison was saying.

Was it weird that she hadn't told Alison she and Colin were friends? *Hey, I played chess with your boyfriend Saturday in Washington Square Park. I mean, I didn't know he was your boyfriend at the time. But then he told me. Because I asked him out on a date, only he already had plans with you. Because you're his girlfriend. And now I'm going over to his house this weekend.*

Maybe Colin had already *told* Alison that Natalya was coming over. Maybe he'd been like, *I have this dorky, ugly, poor girl I like to play chess with, and she's coming over Saturday. You don't mind, do you? Her name's Natalya Petrova.* And Alison had said, *Oh my god, I love Natalya. She's so nice. But also dorky and ugly and poor, like you said. Of course I don't mind.*

"You too?" asked Alison hopefully.

"Me too?" Natalya had absolutely no idea what they were talking about.

"Maps?" Alison reminded her.

"Right!" Natalya laughed with relief at having regained the thread of their conversation. "No, actually, I'm pretty good with maps."

"So's my boyfriend," said Alison, chuckling and shaking her head with amazement. "You guys are so lucky."

Natalya thought she might drop dead from shock right there in the hallway. Literally. She could imagine the feel of the cold floor as her head slammed against it, could see the students in the hallway gathered around her body in a distraught mass. For the first time in her life, she understood what it meant to have an out-of-body experience.

"Um . . ." Natalya groped for a response.

Okay, Alison had never, *ever* mentioned having a boyfriend. She'd mentioned her younger brother, her older sister, her dog (dead), her cat (alive), her grandparents, and her parents. She'd told Natalya about a cousin she had at Brown (where she hoped to go) and a girl from her summer camp whose parents were Russian.

But never, not once, had she uttered the phrase *my boyfriend* in Natalya's presence.

Was this a test? Was this Alison's way of informing Natalya that Colin had mentioned Natalya to Alison and that Alison was now waiting to hear Natalya acknowledge that she and Colin did, in fact, know each other? Was this a hint? A gentle warning from Alison that while she may not in the past have referred to him as such, she did consider Colin her boyfriend, and Natalya should, therefore, be warned against thinking it was okay to spend a Saturday afternoon lounging around Colin Prewitt's home as if he were some random unattached guy?

Or was it none of these things? Was it possible that Alison had mentioned her boyfriend, not once but *millions* of times, only Natalya had never noticed her mentioning him because the words had no significance for her? Was it conceivable Colin and Alison had referred to each other regularly, in front of Natalya, *as* boyfriend or girlfriend, only Natalya hadn't noticed?

Besides, why did it matter? So Alison was Colin's girlfriend. Well, Natalya was Colin's friend. They were friends. And there was no reason one friend couldn't go over to another friend's house on a Saturday afternoon.

They'd arrived at the bio lab, and Alison pulled open the door and held it for Natalya. Now was the time for her to follow up on Alison's mentioning her boyfriend. Natalya should ask who it was, or say, *Isn't your boyfriend Morgan Prewitt's brother?* Or did that sound completely obvious? Maybe she should just ask *who* Alison's boyfriend was? But she *knew* who Alison's boyfriend was. So if Alison was trying to catch Natalya in a lie, Natalya's asking the name of Alison's boyfriend was like her admitting she had a secret relationship with Colin.

Which she didn't.

Or did she?

For a second, Natalya didn't move, not even when a student heading into the lab jostled her shoulder.

"You okay?" Alison's face wore a look of confusion bordering on concern.

"Um . . ." Natalya said for the second time.

"Seriously," said Alison. "Are you okay? You look really pale all of a sudden."

*What is happening? What do you mean? WHAT DOES ALL OF THIS MEAN?* Natalya wanted to shout.

Instead, she took a deep breath and plastered a smile on her face. "I'm fine. Just hungry."

"Lunch next," said Alison cheerfully. "Right after our favorite class of the day."

Jordan arrived behind Natalya in time to hear what Alison said. "Okay, can you *please* not say that? I completely cannot deal with the two of you and your little lovefest."

Alison shrugged and winked at Natalya. "What can we say? Great minds think alike. Right?"

Still wearing her bizarrely forced smile, Natalya echoed what Alison had just said. "Right! Great minds think alike."

As she followed Alison into the bio lab, Natalya tried not to think about just how surprised Alison would be to discover what Natalya's "great mind" was really thinking.

# Chapter
# Twenty-four

ON HER WAY home from school on Friday, Victoria stopped at the supermarket and picked up some butterscotch chips for the cookies she'd decided to bake. But she was having trouble concentrating. Even though she'd been shopping at the same local market since she was old enough to cross the street by herself, she walked by the aisle with the baking ingredients twice, then found herself at the register holding a bag of chocolate chips, not butterscotch chips. When she realized what she'd done, she told the cashier, who was nice enough to wait while Victoria went back and switched the bags.

But still, Victoria couldn't get her mind off her last interaction with Jack.

He'd come by her locker at the end of the day.

"Okay, I don't want to be annoying, but I'm going to ask one last time. *Twilight Zone?*" He'd given her a broad smile and ruffled her hair.

The scene in *Alien* where the monster flies out of the guy's stomach materialized in her brain, and she shook her head. "*Casablanca*," she countered. "Humphrey Bogart. Ingrid Bergman. It's a classic."

Jack laughed and shook his head, just like he had the last time she'd made the offer.

"So," she suggested, "do you want to come over and help me bake cookies?" She'd promised Jane and Natalya she'd bring butterscotch-chip cookies to the movie.

"As much as I love eating cookies, I'm not much of a baker," he answered. She was about to offer to give him a baking lesson when he said, "Anyway, I've got to go home and meet my folks. We're driving to Jersey for my grandfather's birthday dinner."

"Oh, right. That's tonight." Suddenly Victoria was overwhelmed by the realization that Jack was saying they weren't going to be seeing each other until Monday.

She could have cried, but Jack didn't seem to notice. Or maybe he noticed but didn't care.

Either way, he just kissed her good-bye gently and said, "I'll call you." Then he headed out the door, leaving Victoria slumped against her locker, feeling so far away from him it was as if the afternoon they'd said they loved each other had been a dream.

Normally, no matter what was bothering her, Victoria could completely lose herself in a recipe, but today it was work to focus on measuring and stirring each ingredient. She had to keep reading and rereading the recipe, and after she cracked the eggs into the batter, she couldn't remember if she'd cracked two or three and had to go back to the egg carton and count.

Victoria felt as if there was nothing holding her and Jack together. Their relationship was like a piecrust without enough Crisco—in danger of crumbling at any second.

Supposedly they loved each other. So why didn't Jack care that they couldn't see each other this weekend? Was he tired of her? Tired of hanging out with a girl who didn't like the things he liked?

But she'd *tried* to like the things he liked. She replayed her hours at the recording studio and the Lost Leaders concert. Jack had clearly guessed she was having a bad time. If only she were as good an actress as Jane.

Only, she didn't want to be a good actress. She didn't want to have to pretend she was having a good time with Jack, she just wanted to have a good time with him.

Was it normal, what she was feeling? Did other people have these problems? She thought of other couples she knew. Simon and Jane—they were both into theater and old movies. And her parents had *tons* in common—they were always talking about politics and social justice, history and law . . . They seemed to have an endless supply of subjects to debate and discuss.

Victoria tried to imagine having a discussion with Jack about politics, but it was impossible. She hated talking about politics. In fact, one of the things she most liked about Jack was that, unlike the rest of her family, he *didn't* talk about politics.

Two people who didn't talk about politics.

It didn't exactly sound like a match made in heaven.

She spent a lonely afternoon baking, then watched what felt like a thousand hours of the Cooking Channel. Her parents were out for dinner; they'd invited her to join them, but she'd gotten the feeling that they wanted an evening alone after being apart for the whole week. Plus, whenever she was with her mother lately, she felt hyperconscious of having lied to her, like any second her mom might turn to her and say, *Quick, what happens in the opening scene of* Hamlet*?!*

Everyone had plans. Jane's dad had come to New York at the last minute for a medical conference and had taken Jane out for dinner. Natalya's neighbor's daughter was having a birthday party, and the whole family had gone. A little after ten, Victoria almost called Jack, but she didn't want to bother him if he was still having dinner with his family.

Luckily, just as she was sure she was going to go completely insane with boredom and loneliness, Natalya IM'd her.

RUSKIGIRLNAT: Vicks?

Victoria leaped off the bed, where she'd been reading an old issue of *Martha Stewart Living*, and sat down at her desk.

QV210024: Hey, how was the party?

RUSKIGIRLNAT: twenty ten year olds. that's like 200 years of fun.

QV210024: At least.

RUSKIGIRLNAT: what time is the movie Saturday?

QV210024: 6. y?

RUSKIGIRLNAT: idk how long the chess game will last. but 6 will b ok.

Natalya had told Victoria about her plans with Colin, and Victoria had told Natalya she was worried about her spending an afternoon with a boy she had a crush on who had a girlfriend. She'd made her point, and unlike Jane, she knew better than to say more than she already had.

QV210024: we can buy u a ticket and save u a seat.

RUSKIGIRLNAT: is Jack coming?

Victoria considered telling Natalya what was going on with her and Jack, but mentioning it felt disloyal, like complaining about him behind his back.

QV210024: he can't.

Victoria found herself hoping Natalya would ask why not. If that happened, Victoria would just tell her everything and ask what Natalya thought was going on.

But Natalya didn't ask. Instead, she wrote: Jane thinks I m crazy for going over there.

QV210024: I know.

RUSKIGIRLNAT: do u think so 2?

Victoria didn't know what to say. She'd thought she and Jack were the perfect couple, but clearly they weren't. Maybe Colin and Natalya, even with the deck seeming to be totally stacked against them, were the ones who were actually destined to be together.

After all, what did she know?

As she was trying to decide how to respond, a line of type appeared on her screen.

RUSKIGIRLNAT: if u say im crazy, I won't go.

**Victoria hesitated. Finally she wrote:** u know what I think?

RUSKIGIRLNAT: what?

QV210024: when it comes to boys, we're all crazy.

# Chapter
# Twenty-five

JANE HAD TOTALLY meant to call Mark before their rehearsal Saturday.

It *kind of* wasn't her fault that she'd never gotten around to doing it. Between dealing with a math test *and* an unexpected dinner with her dad, who was in from L.A. for a medical conference, *and* trying to convince Natalya that going over to Colin's house to play chess with him was a *majorly* bad idea, Jane had had her busiest week since *Midsummer* ended. It was like every time she thought she was going to be able to catch her breath for a second, she got dumped in the dunking tank again. Simon kept telling her not to forget to talk to Mark, and she kept swearing to remember. But remembering to do something and actually doing it were apparently two different things.

Now, as she pushed open the door to Black Box B, she was definitely feeling a little guilty. Not so much because of what she'd said to Mark, but because she felt bad about breaking her promise to Simon. Jane liked to think of herself as someone who kept her word, and this time she hadn't.

As soon as she stepped into the theater, she could see that Mark was there and Simon wasn't. Of *course* Simon wasn't. Ugh. She'd been hoping to sort of . . . well, not avoid Mark exactly, since they were going to be in the same space all morning, but just kind of . . . not deal directly with him. Only, she needed Simon there to do that. And Simon was late.

Simon was never late.

She looked at her phone—five after seven. Just seeing the time made her want to crawl back into bed. And she had a text from Simon that she'd somehow failed to notice when it first came in. Maybe his train was delayed or something. She opened it.

text me after u talk 2 mark.

That *bastard*!

She raised her eyes from the screen of her phone. Mark was sitting against the wall with the light switches, his elbow on his knee. In his hand was a script, which he was either reading or pretending to read to avoid looking at Jane.

She cleared her throat. "Hi."

Mark grunted.

Okay, could he act *more* like a Neanderthal? At least she was trying to be civil.

"Um, I just got a text from Simon. He's, uh, running a little late."

"Mmmm," Mark non-answered.

She put her stuff on a random chair, then wasn't sure what to do with herself. She knew if she texted Simon, he'd just text back, talk 2 mark or something equally annoying. She started composing a text to Victoria and Natalya, but then she remembered it was only seven o'clock on a Saturday morning.

Probably not an ideal time to text anyone.

She fiddled with her necklace, let it go, sat down, leaned back, then leaned forward. The whole time, Mark didn't take his eyes off his script.

"So," she said finally.

Mark didn't respond.

Now she was getting annoyed. "So, what, are you just going to *ignore* me? Oh, that's really mature."

Still looking at his script, Mark said, "Yeah, well, I'm sorry we can't all be as mature as you, Jane."

Jane crossed her arms. "Do you think we could at least *try* to have a civil conversation about this?" She was proud of how calm she sounded.

"Oh, are we being civil now?" Mark finally dropped *Medea* and looked at Jane. "I'm sorry, I guess I never got the memo."

Jane snorted. "Look, Mark, if you can't handle a little *dialogue* about your direction, I don't see how you expect to—"

"Dialogue!" Mark leaped to his feet and jabbed his index finger in her direction. "You call reaming me out *dialogue*?! I've been working my *ass* off trying to do something exciting and new with

186

a play that's been around for a few thousand years, and when it's not perfect after a few rehearsals, all you can do is insult me. Do you know how hard it is to direct? To try and hear a scene in your head when nobody's acting it? Do you have any idea how stupid I feel when I tell you to do something and it doesn't work? How about saying, *You know, Mark, I think maybe it could be a little more X or a little more Y.* Because that's *dialogue*, honey. What you did? That's a *drive-by.*"

No one, not even her mom during one of their monster fights, had ever yelled at Jane like that. For a minute after Mark stopped talking, Jane couldn't find her voice. All she could do was stare at him.

Was that what had happened? The exact words she'd used had faded, but she definitely remembered telling him he didn't know how to direct. She tried to imagine how she would have felt if she had done a crap reading of a scene and Mr. Robbins or Mark had told her she didn't know how to act.

*Ouch.*

"Well, I'm sorry," she said finally.

It was weirdly hard to say.

She expected Mark to say something sarcastic, but what he said was, "I accept your apology." Then he sat down on the floor and opened his script again, adding, "I have a feeling Simon's waiting for us to resolve this before he comes. Do you mind texting him that the coast is clear? You have his number, right?"

Jane laughed as she took out her phone. "I would hope so. He's my boyfriend."

Mark jerked his head up. "I'm sorry, what did you say?"

Jane had thought it was pretty obvious that she and Simon were going out, considering they basically couldn't keep their hands off each other. But apparently Mark was too distracted by his directorial responsibilities to realize what was going on. "I said he's my boyfriend."

"But—" Mark was still staring at her; his jaw had literally dropped.

Jane hardened her gaze. "If you're about to say he's too hot to go out with me, I'm going to kill you."

"No, I . . ." Mark shook his head, then went back to studying his script. "Nothing."

*Whatever.*

Jane sent Simon a message: we talked. About half a second later, Simon pushed open the door to Black Box B.

"Hey." He smiled a question at Jane, and she nodded a response. Looking relieved, he dropped his bag on a chair and came to stand in the center of the space. Mark didn't say anything to acknowledge his arrival, and Jane and Simon just stood, not holding hands or touching in any way, waiting silently.

"Okay," Mark said finally, and he dropped his script to the floor and looked up at them. "Here's what I think."

Jane continued to stand in silence, looking back at him.

"Like we talked about, Medea"—he gestured at Jane—"is never free of the effects of Cupid's arrow, right? I mean, this is a lifelong spell, as far as I know. Agreed?"

Jane nodded. "Okay."

"Okay." Mark's smile had a touch of gratitude in it. He stood up. "I think this scene is about her trying to get out of a box."

He moved his hands around him, miming striking the walls of an invisible box. "And she's *frustrated*. She wants to punish Jason, but she wants to be with him too."

Jane thought about how hard it had been to apologize to Mark. She'd *wanted* to apologize, but she'd barely been able to speak the words. "I think I know what you mean," she said, hesitantly.

"Great!" Mark nodded and turned to Simon. "And here's what I'm thinking about Jason. He's *always* been able to manipulate Medea, right? Because he knows she loves him."

Simon nodded.

"But this time, he's not *going to* be able to manipulate her. She's going to kill their kids to punish him, even though it punishes her, too. Only, Jason doesn't realize just how enraged she is. So he's just trying his old tricks. He's—"

"Confident!" Jane almost shouted, seeing where Mark was going. "He's confident that she's going to accept his version of things."

Mark snapped his fingers. "Exactly. Simon, I've been telling you to play him angry, but why would he be angry? He's got it all—babelicious new wife, two sons. The king's totally on his side."

"Medea's just annoying to him," Simon realized. "He's, like, *What's your problem, honey?*"

"Yes!" agreed Mark, nodding enthusiastically. He crossed to the edge of the performance area, talking all the while. "So try this. When Jason says, 'Try understanding: it was not for lust I climbed into my present royal bed. I did it, as I said before, to keep you safe . . .' I want you, Jane, to get a . . . like, a pained look on your face, okay? I want the audience to see you want to believe him, and then I want them to see you wipe that look *off* your face and get . . . hard. Cold. But it's a conscious choice, okay? Because you're literally powerless *not* to love him."

Jane nodded.

Mark went on. "And, Simon, I want you to see that moment, okay? You see her fighting with herself, and you feel like it's only a matter of time before she loses and does what you want."

"Got it," said Simon.

"Good," said Mark. "Let's take it from the top."

As they went through the scene, Jane played up Medea's attraction to Jason. Rather than screaming her lines, she imagined she was saying them *to Simon*, to someone she was completely in love with. Just thinking about being in love with Simon if he wasn't in love with her made her voice quiver, and a couple of times she actually thought it might break.

Toward the end of the scene, Mark called out from where he was pacing in the shadows at the edge of the performance space, "Keep going, but, Simon, I don't want you to yell your final lines; I want you to speak them. Be confident. Almost cocky. And right at the end, I want you to put your hand on Jane's shoulder."

Following Mark's new direction without missing a line, Simon walked toward Jane, reached out his hand, and rested it on her shoulder. "'Well, then, I ask the gods to be my witness: I only wish to serve you and the children in every way; but you do not like kindness; you willfully push the help of friends away. Because of this you are going to suffer more.'"

"Okay, hold it there," called Mark from offstage. "Stay just like that."

Simon and Jane stood there, Simon's hand on her shoulder, his smile condescending, like he *knew* Jane was going to fall for whatever crap he dished out to her. They stayed that way for what felt like an eternal moment.

"And . . . now!" Mark shouted. "Jane, get rid of this bastard!"

Jane stepped away from Simon, speaking sadly to him, "'Go, go: I see you've been so long away from her. You're itching with desire for your new-broken girl. Get on with being married while you still can. Because I prophecy: Your marriage will be one of horror and regret.'"

Slowly, Simon walked offstage. Jane watched him go as Mark applauded. "We're really getting somewhere now. Let's try it again. But Jane, I want you a little bit angrier, not quite so sad."

They took the scene from the top, and this time, Jane tried to imagine she was furious at Simon. She made her words clipped, and furrowed her brow, but it felt awkward.

When they got to the end, Mark told her she was doing better. To Simon he said, "Don't be *quite* so cocky. You're sure of yourself, but you're not a total idiot, and you know how dangerous Medea is when she's mad."

They ran through the scene three more times. Each time Mark said something complimentary, but Jane felt like she was speaking her lines more and more awkwardly, as if she was getting worse with every attempt, not better.

Finally, Simon glanced at his phone. "I hate to do this, but I've gotta run. I'm meeting my mom for brunch."

"No problem," said Mark. "I'll let you know when we can have the space again. Probably not till Thursday."

Simon waved good-bye to both of them, then left the theater.

Alone with Mark, Jane finally blurted out what she'd been thinking more intensely with each run-through. "I suck, don't I?" As soon as the words were out of her mouth, Jane dreaded Mark's reply. She thought of how mean she'd been to him about his directing. What if he took advantage of this moment and got back at her by saying something brutal about her acting?

Mark had been carrying two chairs across the stage, but he stopped and put them down. "What? No. Why would you say that?" He sounded genuinely surprised.

"It just . . ." She groped for the words. "It feels pretty forced."

"It's new," Mark said calmly. "But we're on the right track. I can feel it."

Jane gave a slightly bitter laugh. "Maybe you and Simon are on the right track. I'm, like, not even on a train."

Letting go of the chairs, Mark studied Jane carefully. "You're on a train."

Jane shrugged. "If you say so."

"You know what I think?" Mark sat down in one of the chairs.

"You're not going to say, *If at first you don't succeed, try, try again*, are you?" she demanded. "Because if you do, I may have to pummel you."

He chuckled and shook his head, but then turned serious. "Have you ever wanted someone really, really badly? I mean so badly you thought you would die if you couldn't have the person?"

"I . . . I don't know." She'd liked Mr. Robbins so much. But had she thought she would *die* if he didn't like her back? Now it was hard to remember.

Mark held up a finger, indicating he wasn't done. Then he continued. "Well, you need to imagine it. And then you have to imagine wanting someone *that* badly, only *hating* yourself for wanting it. And hating the person you *want* for it."

Jane was enthralled by what Mark was saying and by how quietly and passionately he was saying it. He sounded so . . . real. More than anything, she wanted to be able to act what he was describing.

"Come here," Mark said. Out of habit, Jane found herself following his direction. When she was standing in front of him, he took her hands in his.

"You're doing great." His voice was still quiet, but it had an intensity about it, and he squeezed her fingers gently on *great*. "You'll find the right tone for this scene. I know you will."

For a second, Jane remembered that when she'd first met Mark, she'd thought he was cute. So much had happened since then that she rarely thought about that. But suddenly, just for an instant, she saw him again the way she'd seen him then. The memory was almost a physical sensation, and it surprised her.

"Anyway," Mark said teasingly, letting go of her, "you have to get it right."

"Oh, yeah, why's that?" As she matched his teasing with her own, the feeling faded and he was just Mark again.

"Too late to recast the scene," he said simply. Then he gave her a wicked smile. "See you at rehearsal."

"See you at rehearsal." Walking out of the theater, Jane felt a million times better. It was amazing how much confidence she had, all because of *his* confidence in *her*. She played over their morning, how little she'd improved, how clear his direction had been, how poorly she'd translated it into action.

The more she thought about it, the more she realized how wrong she'd been. Mark had *all* the qualities a good director needed to have: He had ideas. He had patience. He wasn't petty or mean. And he had the ability to make his actors feel like they were doing a good job even when they really weren't.

Halfway down the block she had a realization so intense it literally stopped her in her tracks. All this time, she'd felt like Mark was lucky to be working with her.

But really, *she* was lucky to be working with *him*.

# Chapter
# Twenty-six

NATALYA COULDN'T BELIEVE she was standing in front of the Prewitt mansion again. It seemed as if a lifetime had passed since she'd rung this bell the night of Morgan's party. All she had wanted that night was for Morgan to like her, to find her acceptable and cool.

Now all she wanted was for Morgan not to be home.

She wasn't actually sure what she would do if Morgan *were* home. The idea was disconcerting enough that it distracted her a little from her nervousness about Colin. What would she do if Morgan opened the door, scowled at her and sneered, *What are you doing here?*

But if she did that, wouldn't Colin march down, take her by the hand, and say, *Back off, Morgan!* It was cool to imagine Colin defending her, almost cool enough that for a second she found herself hoping Morgan might actually be there. The image gave her the courage she needed to finally ring the bell.

She listened to the melodious chimes of the Prewitt bell and waited for what seemed like a long time before Colin opened the door. He was wearing a pair of jeans and a faded gray long-sleeved T-shirt with THE BLACK DOG written on the front. His hair was wet. Natalya wondered if he'd just taken a shower, and, if so, had he done it because she was coming over?

"Hey." He smiled.

"Hey." She couldn't admit to Victoria or Jane that she cared what she wore to Colin's, so she'd had to put her outfit together herself, and she thought she'd done a decent job. She was wearing her second-favorite pants—vintage green corduroys that Jane had picked for her at a store on lower Broadway a few months ago. She'd paired them with a pale yellow sweater that she thought looked good with her hair.

It was a good outfit, but objectively, it was nothing you wouldn't normally wear to hang out with your friend for the afternoon.

Which was what she was doing.

She followed Colin up the wide staircase. It looked radically different from the way it had looked the night of the party, when dozens of people had been clustered there as if it were yet another room in the Prewitts' enormous mansion. The house was empty, but Natalya imagined she could hear the ghosts of guests laughing and chatting.

"Hungry?" asked Colin as they passed the kitchen.

"Oh, no," said Natalya quickly. She was exceedingly nervous all of a sudden. Was there really no one else in the house? She hadn't expected that.

As they climbed the second flight of stairs, Colin answered her unasked question. "Everyone's up at our country house."

"Got it." Natalya had been introduced to the concept of The Country House during her first weeks at Gainsford, when she'd heard the phrase as often as she'd heard, *Take out your notebooks, please.*

*I'm going to my country house this weekend.*

*I'm sorry, Ms. MacFaddon, I did the homework, but I left it at my country house.*

*We got home from my country house really late last night.*

*Natalya Petrova, you don't have a country house?! Wow, you really* are *poor.*

When they reached the top floor, Colin turned down the hallway, and Natalya followed him to his room, remembering how she'd gone exploring the night of Morgan's party. She'd been so embarrassed when Colin had discovered her after she'd crept in to study the screen of his computer with its online chess game.

And here it was, just a few months later, and she was walking in as an invited guest.

His room looked the same as it had that night, only now

there was an actual chessboard, as opposed to a virtual one. And it was on his bed, not the desk.

On his bed. They were going to be playing on his bed.

Colin walked to the bed and sat down at the pillow end. Clearly Natalya was supposed to sit down on the bed, too. She'd never sat on a bed with a boy before. It seemed so . . . intimate.

Hoping her awkwardness wasn't obvious, she made her way over and sat down on the very edge, reaching over to set up her pieces.

"You can put your feet up, it's cool," Colin assured her, apparently misunderstanding the reason for her awkward position.

"Oh, I'm fine."

"Suit yourself," said Colin.

It was a long game. It had been clear from their previous games that they were well matched, but it seemed to Natalya that they were both playing more fiercely than they had before. Every piece was sacrificed reluctantly; not even pawns were surrendered without a fight. There was none of the casual banter they'd exchanged during past games. At some point, the words *fight to the death* popped into Natalya's head, and after that, she couldn't stop thinking of the phrase.

Neither of them suggested taking a break, not even when the game moved into its second hour. To Natalya, it felt as if there were nothing in the world but her, Colin, and the chessboard on the bed between them.

There was a moment when Colin was taking such an especially long time to make a move that Natalya found herself wondering what would happen if she just leaned forward and kissed him. They were sitting so close, separated only by a foot of space, or at most two. His chin was in his hand, and he was hunched over, studying his options. She would barely have had to move to place her lips against his. It was scary how powerful the idea was; the more she thought about doing it, the less she felt able to fight the urge. She stood up without saying anything and walked down the hall until she found a bathroom. Then she stood, washing her hands in cold water for a long time.

What did she owe Alison? She leaned her hip against the sink, toying with her necklace.

Natalya thought of herself as a good friend. The one time she had lied to Victoria, she'd felt awful about it, and she'd promised herself she'd never again do anything to hurt her friend. But were she and Alison really friend*s*? They were friend*ly*. Okay, Alison had invited her to her birthday party. But for all Natalya knew, she'd invited hundreds of people. The invitation didn't necessarily make Natalya special to Alison. True, they hung out at school. But they'd never hung out at each other's houses or anything. She thought of the study session she'd had at Alison's. But that hadn't been like hanging out at a friend's house. It had been a random choice; if Jordan lived as close to Gainsford as Alison did, they might have had the study session at her house, and Natalya would, therefore, truly never have been to Alison's. So it was almost *as if* she had never been to Alison's.

Even though she had.

And did any of that even matter? What if Alison were someone she'd never met, a faceless girl who lived in . . . Nebraska or China? Would that make it okay for her to want to kiss that girl's boyfriend? Was it different to steal something from a friend rather than from a stranger? Or was stealing from anyone wrong, simply because it was stealing?

*Grrrr.* It was all so confusing. And she liked Colin so much. And Colin seemed to like her. They were so perfect for each other.

But what if he was perfect for Alison too? What if he was *more* perfect for Alison? In which case, Natalya was plotting to steal Alison's *soul mate.*

Natalya was developing a headache. She splashed some cold water on her face and headed back into the hallway.

The bedroom had grown darker in her absence, or maybe the bright light of the bathroom had just made her more sensitive to how dimly Colin's bedside lamp lit the room. As if he could read her thoughts, Colin stretched out his arm to turn on a row of overhead lights. Then he hunched back over the board and moved his queen several spaces to the right.

Whether it was the room's getting lighter or Colin's move, Natalya didn't know, but she suddenly saw what she had to do to win. She was so shocked she almost gasped, and she continued to study the board, not quite believing what she knew was true. She worked out every countermove Colin could make, then the moves she would make to counter him. As far as she could see, if she did what she planned, nothing could prevent her from winning in fewer than three moves. Four at the most. Not wanting to reveal her confidence that victory was hers, she slid her rook forward to its vulnerable position reluctantly, as if she weren't convinced it was a good idea. Colin was clearly puzzled by what she'd done, but it wasn't until he'd swiped her castle that he realized how thoroughly he'd fallen into her trap.

The game moved swiftly after that. Colin was beaten, and they both knew it. The final moves took almost no time, and then Natalya spoke the first word either of them had spoken in hours.

"Checkmate."

"Damn, you're a good chess player." In Colin's voice was a mixture of awe and frustration. He looked at the board for a long time, then stood up. Natalya heard his knees crack.

All her life Natalya's father had drilled into her the importance of being a gracious winner, and her response to Colin's praising her was almost automatic: "I think I play better when I play with you." The words sounded suggestive somehow, and she wondered if she shouldn't have spoken them. But he didn't seem to think her compliment was weird.

"Thanks." He crossed the room and stood by the door, waiting for her. "Come on. Let's get some grub."

They sat in the kitchen, Natalya at the enormous glass table, Colin sitting on the equally enormous white marble counter, eating reheated Chinese takeout and talking over the game they'd just played. Natalya felt better now that they were no longer sitting together on his bed. The impulse to kiss him had passed, and she really did feel as if she were just hanging out with a friend who happened to be a boy.

It made her wish there were a way for her to e-mail Jane a video of this portion of the afternoon with the subject line I TOLD U WE WERE JUST FRIENDS!

"My mistake was falling for your rook." Colin studied the open carton of lo mein on his lap as if it contained an instant replay of the game they had just played, rather than an afternoon snack.

"I can't believe you don't mind talking about this," said Natalya, swallowing a bite of General Tso's chicken. It was decent, she decided, but nowhere near as good as Ga Ga Noodle's.

Colin hesitated, his chopsticks, laden with lo mein, hovering just before his lips. "What do you mean?"

"I just . . . I hate talking about a game if I didn't win." Natalya didn't mean to rub in the fact that Colin had lost, and as soon as the sentence was out of her mouth, she realized she was kind of doing that.

He chewed thoughtfully, swallowed. "But, I mean, isn't that how you get to be a better player?"

Natalya made a face. "I guess. The truth is, I'm *kind of* a sore loser."

Colin threw back his head and laughed. "Yeah, I *kind of* noticed that, last week in the park." His phone buzzed and he checked the message, then typed back, speaking the words out loud as he wrote them. "Yes. Mom. I. Did. Remember. To. Go. To. My. Fitting." He pressed one last button and said, "Send."

Natalya thought she'd heard wrong. "Fitting? Isn't that, like, a wedding thing?" When her cousin had gotten married, Natalya had gone with her for the final fitting.

"Tuxedo," Colin lobbed his empty carton into the garbage. "Got my grandparents' wedding anniversary next Friday. I guess I'm finally going to put all those years of dance class to good use."

"You take dance classes?" Natalya was shocked. She knew objectively that boys studied dance—Nana had taken the Darlings to *The Nutcracker* when they were in fifth grade, and there had been guys dancing in it. But Natalya had never met an actual live boy who'd taken dance classes.

"Five years of ballroom dancing with Mrs. Hanover." He put his arms around an invisible partner and swayed briefly.

"Oh." Natalya laughed at her erroneous assumption that he'd been talking about ballet. Obviously, he wasn't going to be ballet dancing at his grandparents' anniversary party. Still, teenage ballroom dancers weren't exactly a dime a dozen. "I didn't think anyone our age knew how to dance." At that same cousin's wedding, Natalya had noticed that everyone her parents' age or older seemed to know how to do real dance steps, but all the couples younger than her parents just kind of put their arms around each other and swayed whenever there was a slow song. "It looks hard."

"Nah, it's not that hard." Colin slid off the counter where he'd been sitting and headed out of the kitchen.

Natalya didn't know if she was supposed to follow or if he was just going to the bathroom or something, so she stayed put. But a minute later, he called, "Come on," so she pushed her chair back and followed the trail of lights Colin had turned on, ending up in the room with the enormous chandelier and the huge white sofas. He was by the window, facing a wall of built-in bookcases. Suddenly a burst of classical music, heavy on the strings, filled the room. He turned to face her.

"Strauss," he called over the music.

She cupped her hand over her ear. "What?"

Colin crossed the room to where she was standing, then pulled her into the middle of the floor, where there was a large rug between the two enormous sofas.

The second his hand touched hers, she didn't feel like she was spending the afternoon with a friend who just happened to be a guy anymore.

"Strauss," he repeated. "*The Blue Danube*. Cheesy, but for our purposes, effective. Now—"

"I'm not really too coordinated." If she'd been videotaping their time together to send to Jane as proof of how casual it was for her to be hanging with Colin, she would definitely have turned the camera off now.

He ignored her protest. "We're going to do a basic waltz, which is just a simple box step, okay?" He looked at her, but it definitely was *not* a lovey-dovey look. It was the kind of look you might give someone you were tutoring right after you identified the basic concept you were going to be working on together. *When you cross peas with different traits, you begin to see how dominant and recessive genes operate.*

Okay. So. All that worrying about Alison had been for nothing. She'd been right the other day—Colin thought of her as . . . well, maybe not as not the weird ugly girl he played chess with, but definitely as a . . . buddy. A guy. Or not a guy, exactly, but someone he could teach how to dance without feeling weird or guilty or even remotely aware that standing with your arms around a girl was any different from facing her across a chessboard.

Really, when you thought about it, this was a fabulous opportunity. When else would she have the chance to learn how to waltz? Colin was about to teach her a life skill, one she would use at social gatherings for years to come.

So if this was such a great opportunity, why was she feeling like any second she might start bawling?

"Okay, ready?" Again that friendly, open look.

She nodded, not trusting herself to speak.

"Great. All you have to remember is that waltzing is one-two-three, one-two-three." He moved as he counted, sliding alone across the floor. Even his socks, she noticed, were elegant. Pale gray, they looked thick and soft, nothing like the stained tube socks she had on under her boots. "So . . ." He came back to stand beside Natalya, hesitated for a second, then took a step. "You're going to take your right foot. No, wait." He turned to face her, moved his foot forward and back, then jumped to stand next to her again. "Okay, got it. You're going to take your *left foot* and move it back." He demonstrated. "And then you're going to take your right foot and move *it* back. And then you take your left foot and step like this. So that's *one*-two-three, *one*-two-three." It sounded complicated. She looked down at his feet and awkwardly imitated the steps he was taking.

"Awesome!" Colin encouraged her. "You're doing great. Now . . ." He turned and faced her, slipping his arm around her waist and holding his other hand in the air.

At his touch, Natalya stumbled.

"Don't let me throw you off," he assured her. "I'm just going to . . ." He took her left hand and placed it on his shoulder, then took her right hand and held it firmly in his. The fabric of his T-shirt was soft, but the muscles beneath it weren't. She could smell something slightly spicy, but she didn't know what it was. Soap? Shampoo? Laundry detergent? Whatever it was, it smelled great. At the thought that he didn't care what she smelled like, that he only liked her as a friend, she felt as though her heart were literally breaking.

"Okay. Now, you want to hold your arm a little stiff, but not *too* stiff; got it?"

Natalya nodded, even though his instructions were practically inaudible, drowned out by the music and the pounding of her own sadness in her ears. She couldn't believe she was standing there, Colin's arms around her, his hand holding her hand, but none of it meaning anything.

Jane was right: she should never have come.

"And I'll count us in, okay?"

"Okay," she managed to whisper, thinking, *This is torture.*

"And *one*-two-three. *One*-two-three." She risked a glance at his face. His chin was just at the level of her forehead. She saw the smooth ruddy skin.

Colin took a step. For a second she had no idea what he was doing; it was like she'd completely forgotten they were supposed to be dancing. And then the clear pulse of the music took over, and she automatically took a step back. A beat later, she stepped forward. Back. Forward. Back. Forward. The steps were simple, no sudden moves or unexpected twists or turns. Each time she moved, Colin moved, too; each time he moved, so did she.

Natalya had never liked sports. Soccer balls and Frisbees always seemed to come out of nowhere and slam her in the head. Running laps felt pointless and exhausting. She hated climbing ropes and having to duck over and under things and through obstacle courses.

But dancing. Dancing was the physical manifestation of a chess game. It felt orderly and rhythmic. It made sense. It was beautiful. Despite her sadness, she laughed.

If Colin thought it was weird that Natalya was laughing as she danced, he didn't say anything. He just kept steering her around the room. When the movement came to an end, they stayed where they'd stopped. They didn't start dancing when the music began again, but neither of them made a move to sit down.

They didn't speak. Natalya kept her eyes on the opposite wall. Her heart was racing, whether from exertion or exhilaration, she didn't know.

"So, that's about it," Colin said finally. "You can waltz to pretty much any song. It's like the lingua franca of dancing."

She risked raising her eyes and found him looking down at her, his face just inches from hers.

And then, before she could tell herself not to do it, Natalya moved her head and lightly touched her lips to his.

She had kissed a boy only once before. It was at Lily Martin's twelfth birthday party, when they'd played spin the bottle, and Danny McGill had mashed his mouth against hers while everyone in the group cheered and whistled, and in her head Natalya had counted to five, which was how long she'd had to endure Danny's kiss for it to count.

But she wasn't counting to five now. She felt Colin's lips, soft against her own, and then his hand pressing on her back. The kiss became more intense, and she slipped her hand around his shoulder to the back of his neck. There was nothing about the way he pulled her toward him that said he thought of her as merely a chess partner.

Maybe he had a girlfriend. Maybe until now he'd only thought of Natalya as a friend. But at this moment, with his lips tracing a line down her neck and his hands buried in her hair, there was only one way Colin was thinking of her.

And it wasn't as a friend.

His lips traveled back up to hers, and he wrapped his arms around her waist.

Natalya wanted their kiss to last forever.

# Chapter
# Twenty-seven

JANE LOVED *CASABLANCA*. Nana had first taken her to see it when she was ten, and after that they'd gone to see the movie whenever it was playing anywhere in New York on the big screen. Standing on line at the Paris theater, Jane felt the familiar thrill she always felt before going to see the most romantic, heartbreaking film ever made.

"I can't believe you've never seen this before. How have I not taken you? I blame myself," said Jane, putting her arm around Victoria. Just as she did so, Victoria reached into her bag for her buzzing phone. Jane's phone began to buzz also.

"Nat," said Victoria, looking at hers.

"Don't tell me," said Jane, taking hers out of her bag. "She's not coming."

"She's not coming," echoed Victoria. Then she read aloud. "'i m so sorry. can't make movie. don't be mad. i will tell u everything when i come 2nite. r we still sleeping @ jane's? i will meet u there. xoxo n.'"

"Okay, *what* is going on?!" Jane was about to respond to Natalya's text with exactly that question when she felt a hand on her back and heard Simon say her name. She hugged him, then introduced him to Victoria. Seeing Victoria register how handsome Simon looked in his skinny jeans and linen button-down shirt, Jane couldn't help feeling a small flutter of pride. Not that she'd done anything to make Simon so great looking. It was just kind of cool to have a boyfriend beautiful enough to make people do a double take.

"My friends Roman and Jenny are here," said Simon. "I just ran into them, and I invited them to sit with us. I hope that's cool."

"Totally," said Jane, thinking how awesome it was to have a boyfriend who not only wanted to see *Casablanca* but who had *friends* who wanted to see *Casablanca*. A second later, a tall boy with spiky black hair and an extremely thin, pale girl in a fabulous vintage T-shirt featuring Madonna in her *Like a Virgin* period appeared next to them. Simon introduced everyone, and a second later the line started moving forward.

"How do you guys know each other?" asked Jane.

"Summer program at Playwrights Horizons," said Roman, who gave out a superfriendly vibe. He glanced at Simon and added, "Um, Todd's coming, too. We told him we'd save him a seat."

Simon looked startled, and he took a second to respond. "Oh," he said casually.

"Who's Todd?" asked Jane.

At the same time, Victoria said to her, "Why can't Nat come? Do you think something's going on?"

"Um, *yeah*," answered Jane, without hesitating. They entered the theater, and Jane was about to ask Simon again who Todd was, but then Victoria blurted out, "Oh, hey, there's Lily!" She pointed across the theater and waved, but Lily didn't see her.

Jane turned back to Simon, but Simon was talking quietly with Roman and Jenny. A moment later, they waved good-bye to Victoria and Jane. "Nice meeting you," said Roman, planting a brief kiss on Jane's and then Victoria's cheek before heading back up the aisle they'd all just walked down together.

"Wait, aren't they going to sit with us?" asked Jane.

"What?" asked Simon, scanning the enormous room. "Oh, they said there probably won't be six seats together."

Jane thought that was a good point. The theater was getting surprisingly crowded for a movie that had been out for over sixty years.

She thought she saw three seats together, but just as she began to move toward them, someone snagged one. Damn.

Jane liked to be close to the screen but not *too* close, and she realized she had no idea where Simon liked to sit. She turned to him, but he was looking over his shoulder toward the back of the theater.

*Uh-oh*. Jane's mother's favorite place to see a movie was the very last row. "You don't like to sit all the way in the back, do you?" she asked Simon.

"What?" he asked, whipping his head around to look at her. His face was flushed, and she reached over and unwrapped his scarf from around his neck.

"I said—"

"There," said Victoria, pointing to the short row of seats along the wall nearest them.

"Grab them!" Jane ordered, and a minute later she and Victoria were sliding into seats that were a little too far to the side to be perfect, but were exactly the right distance from the screen to be acceptable.

Jane turned to ask Simon if they were sitting too close, but he wasn't next to her. She looked up and saw him, lingering at the end of the row. "We forgot popcorn," he said.

"Not to mention peanut M&M's," Jane replied.

"I brought cookies," Victoria remembered, holding up her overnight bag with the box of butterscotch cookies in it.

"Yum," said Simon. "Still, there's no substitute for peanut M&M's and popcorn. I'll get them."

"You sure you don't mind?" asked Jane. She half rose, but he gestured for her to sit down.

"I'll be right back," he said.

Simon was gone forever. As the first preview began, she finally texted him. where r u? if the line is super long, we can just eat v's cookies. She kept her phone on her lap, but there was no answer, and it wasn't until the screen filled with the Warner

Brothers logo that he slid into the seat next to her.

"Where were you?" she whispered.

"Sorry." He was panting slightly, like he'd just run down the aisle to make it in time for the first scene. As he went to hand the popcorn over to Jane, he spilled some, almost as if his hands were shaking.

"Was it a really long line?" Jane whispered.

"Um . . . yeah, pretty long."

"Sorry you had to wait. Thanks." She took his hand and intertwined their fingers. Normally when they watched a movie at home, Simon put his arm around her or gave her a back rub, but tonight he was completely wrapped up in the movie. Jane had always thought she was a huge *Casablanca* fan, but Simon was even more obsessed with the movie than she was. In fact, he was so into what was happening on the screen that he practically seemed to have forgotten she was sitting there.

Jane was glad to see that a love of *Casablanca* was just one more thing she and Simon had in common. She settled back happily into her seat, feeling glad to be one half of a couple that was clearly destined for a long and beautiful relationship.

# Chapter
## Twenty-eight

VICTORIA HAD HAD to pee for the last twenty minutes of the movie, but she knew Jane would murder her if she got up and left. Whenever they watched movies at home, Jane insisted on pausing if someone had to go to the bathroom. "You can't miss part of a movie! It has to exist as a *whole*. Would you skip part of a book you were reading?" Victoria loved Jane more than anything, but her policy made seeing movies together a little stressful.

Victoria stepped over to the one unoccupied sink. She could not see how Jane could love *Casablanca* as much as she did. The movie was so *depressing*. Humphrey Bogart and Ingrid Bergman loved each other. They were the love of each other's lives. And they didn't end up together. It was the most colossal cheat in the history of movies. Jane was always complaining that they didn't make movies like *Casablanca* anymore, and Victoria was glad. The same thing had happened at the end of *Gone With the Wind*. Victoria had been sure Rhett Butler was going to walk back into the house, sweep Scarlett O'Hara off her feet, and say he'd just been kidding about all that *I don't give a damn* stuff. But then the credits had started rolling.

She was so deep in her thoughts, she didn't see the familiar face appear next to hers in the mirror. It wasn't until Lily said, "Hey!" that she registered her.

"Hey," said Victoria quickly. She wanted to say something interesting about the movie, something that would strike Lily as intelligent and sophisticated. She imagined Lily telling Jack about running into Victoria, Lily saying, *Your girlfriend is so smart and cool.* Instead, she just said, "Hi."

They looked at each other in the mirror rather than turning to face one another.

"Jack's not here, is he?" asked Lily.

Victoria shook her head, then added, "No," as if Lily wouldn't know what a head shake meant. She wished she didn't feel so nervous around Lily all the time.

"Right, he's at Rajiv's." Lily laughed. "I can't exactly see him here." She reached for a paper towel.

Victoria felt a sudden rush of happiness. She and Lily were having a moment. She was standing with Jack's best friend, and they were laughing . . . well, not *at* him, exactly, but at their shared knowledge of him. She giggled with relief. "I know. Can you imagine?"

Lily tossed the paper towel out. Smiling at Victoria—the actual Victoria, not her reflection—she added casually, "Yeah, he was just saying you guys have pretty much zero in common." She laughed, then gave a little shrug. "Well, see you." And then she was gone.

Victoria didn't say good-bye. She didn't say anything. She didn't move from the sink, and her eyes were filled with the sight of her own face in the mirror as she processed the words Lily had just spoken.

*He was just saying you guys have pretty much zero in common.*

Jack had said that?! He had *said that*? And he'd said it not to her but to Lily. Victoria felt a light film of sweat break out on her forehead. How could he have said something like that to Lily?

Victoria pictured the scene. Lily, Rajiv, and Jack grabbing a snack after school on their way to listen to the recording session. Rajiv saying, *Is Victoria coming?* And Jack answering, *Nah. It turns out we have zero in common. I think we're probably going to break up soon.* She saw Rajiv and Lily exchanging a look, silently coming to agreement. Rajiv patting Jack on the back. *Sorry, man. Lily and I knew you were a bad couple, but we didn't want to say anything.* Lily coming up on Jack's other side. Rajiv nodding understandingly. *Totally, man.*

Her face came back into focus as Victoria stared at her reflection. How could Jack do that to her? How could he talk about her behind her back, share his private thoughts about their relationship like it was just so much . . . gossip?

Her phone buzzed. When she saw Jack's name on her screen, she literally snorted. What, was he texting to tell *her* how they had nothing in common?

But all he'd written was: hey, baby. how's the movie?

His calling her baby was usually something she loved, but now it just made her angry. It was like Jack really *did* think she was a baby, like he could just say whatever he wanted about her and she wouldn't understand, even if she heard it repeated.

She wanted to ask him why he'd said that about her—what he'd been thinking. But how could you write that in a text? Just imagining typing the whole story made her want to cry with frustration. She had to talk to him. But what was she supposed to do, call him from the ladies' room of the theater and demand to know what he'd meant by saying that to Lily?

Well, yeah.

She took a deep breath and moved her thumb to press his speed dial, but then she hesitated. He was with his friends. They were all watching *The Twilight Zone*. If she called him now, he'd have to leave the room to talk to her, and when he came back in, they'd be all, *What happened, man?* And what if he *told* them? Worse, what if he answered and she started to tell him what Lily had said, and he just said, *Look, I can't really talk right now. We're at a good part in the show.*

She couldn't say it in a text. She couldn't say it over the phone. They had to talk in person. But Jack didn't seem to want to *see* her in person this weekend. So what was she supposed to do?

Victoria stared at Jack's text for a long time, as if she were trying to decipher an ancient language for which there was no Rosetta Stone. Then, in one swift and decisive motion, she snapped her phone shut and dropped it into her bag without typing anything.

# Chapter
## Twenty-nine

JANE HAD TOLD Victoria and Simon she'd meet them outside, and she made her way through the crowded, stuffy lobby to the street, savoring the memory of Humphrey Bogart's face as he waited for Ingrid Bergman to meet him on the train. Waited and waited until he knew she was never going to show. It was so beautiful how they loved each other, so awful how they didn't end up together. Each time Jane saw the movie, she felt the agony of their separation. And now that she had a boyfriend, the whole story was even sadder than before. She couldn't imagine giving up Simon, not even if it *was* necessary to defeat the Nazis.

She wandered to the edge of the sidewalk, then crossed the

street to lean against the enormous stone fountain. This corner, with the Sherry-Netherland and the Plaza Hotel hovering over it, was one of her favorite spots in all of Manhattan, and she spun around, the chilly air a relief after the stuffy theater. Horse-drawn carriages made their way along Central Park, the clip-clop of hooves echoing through the square. Across the street, people poured out of the theater, one stranger after another, and then Jenny and Roman. A second later, they were joined by a tall red-headed guy wearing cool, rectangular-framed glasses, whom she hadn't met. The three talked briefly before the boy shrugged, took out his phone, and sent a text. Then Roman and Jenny pointed west and started walking. Jane sat on the edge of the fountain waiting for Simon and Victoria, half registering that the boy checked his phone before turning to walk in the direction Jenny and Roman had gone. Just then, somebody called, "Todd," and the boy spun around. Jane followed his eyes and saw Simon standing in front of the theater.

Simon and Todd were at least ten feet apart from each other, and people kept walking between them, but neither of them moved toward the other. They stayed that way for a long, long moment before Todd finally took a step toward Simon. Simon hesitated, and then he took a step toward Todd, and a few seconds later they were standing facing each other. Todd said something, and Simon shook his head, then turned toward the street, across which Jane was waiting. Even though she was only about ten yards away from him, Simon didn't notice Jane beyond the passing cars and crowds of people walking between them.

Jane thought she should raise her hand to catch his attention, but something about how close he and Todd were standing made her hesitate. And then it was too late to wave; he had turned to face Todd again.

Simon spoke. Todd leaned toward him, as though he couldn't quite hear what Simon was saying. As he did, he placed his hand lightly on Simon's hip. Simon spoke again, and whatever he said made Todd laugh, slip his fingers through the belt loops of Simon's jeans, and jokingly shake him. Simon put his hands up as if to say, *What can you do?* Then he slipped his hands into the back pockets of his jeans.

For a long minute they stood there, Todd's hands on Simon's waist, Simon's hands in his own back pockets. Then Todd said something, and Simon took one hand out of his back pocket and briefly ruffled Todd's hair. Todd said something else, and Simon nodded. Then Todd took his hands off Simon's waist and began walking slowly backward, keeping his eyes on Simon. He called out something that Jane couldn't hear, but Simon's response was perfectly audible. "I said I'd think about it!" he called back, laughing.

"Do that," Todd responded. Then, finally, he turned around and headed west down the block.

As Jane watched, Simon stretched his arms up over his head, then dropped them down and shook them. It reminded her of the acting exercises Mr. Robbins had had them do to warm up at the start of rehearsals.

Jane kept watching. Simon interlocked his fingers and again reached his hands up over his head. He took his phone out of his pocket, studied it for a minute, laughed, then put it back without typing anything. Jane, perched precariously on the edge of the fountain, lost her balance, nearly tumbling backward into it. By the time she righted herself, Simon was pulling open the door to the lobby and stepping back into the theater.

What had she just seen?

Her heart pounded against her chest, and she had trouble catching her breath.

Had she seen what she thought she'd seen?

Her phone buzzed. Simon.

where r u?

im outside, she typed, but before she hit SEND, she paused. Should she tell him where she was? She raised her eyes to look at the theater. The crowd had thinned, and she could see Simon inside now, his back to the door, probably scanning the room for her.

What had she seen?

Nothing. She'd seen nothing. She'd seen her boyfriend talking with a friend. Just like a dozen guys standing in front of the theater right this second were talking with *their* friends. Her eyes moved over the people standing across the street from her. Most of the groups were made up of men and women, but there were a few clusters of just guys. She watched them. A twentysomething man said something to another twentysomething man. The second man laughed and said something. The first man laughed.

They did not touch.

They did not stand within a foot of each other.

They did not ruffle each other's hair.

They did not put their hands on each other's waists.

Jane's phone buzzed again.

r u alive?

As she stared at the screen, the phone buzzed once more. Another text from Simon.

feeling kind of beat. might just go home now. is that cool?

Jane felt strangely ill as she read Simon's text, but all she typed back was k.

His response came almost instantly. call u 2morrow. sleep tite.

She didn't respond. A second later, she saw him step out of the theater and walk in the same direction Todd, Roman, and Jenny had headed.

Which was the opposite direction of his house.

# Chapter
## Thirty

NATALYA WAS A little scared she might be going insane.

Standing in the elevator as it ascended to Jane's apartment, she felt elated. Ecstatic. She was the happiest girl in the world. But she also felt awful. And guilty. And more disgusting than something you'd scrape off the bottom of your shoe.

As she pushed open the door to Jane's apartment, her sense of guilt was heightened by the quiet, almost cold, "Come in," with which Jane answered her knock. Were her friends mad at her for bailing on the movie? And if they were mad at her for that, would they be even madder when they found out *why* she'd missed the movie? She really needed her friends to understand what she'd done. But what if they didn't? What if they judged her? The possibility made her stomach clench into a tight ball of defensiveness and fear, but as soon as she stepped into the living room and saw Victoria's tearstained face, she realized she was being paranoid. Maybe her friends were mad that she'd ditched them. But it was hardly the kind of thing Victoria would cry about.

"What happened?" asked Natalya, crossing to sit on the edge of the couch beside Victoria. "Why are you crying?"

Victoria took a deep, shuddering breath. "Nothing. Except that Jack is the biggest jerk *ever*." She blew her nose as if for emphasis.

"Wait, Jack was *there*?" Natalya was confused. Hadn't Victoria said Jack couldn't come?

Victoria took a deep breath. "No," she said angrily. "He wasn't there." She told Natalya what Lily had said to her in the bathroom.

Natalya gasped. "Did you call him? Ask him what he meant?"

Shaking her head, Victoria started to cry again.

"He's at this stupid *Twilight Zone* marathon with his stupid *friends*," Jane explained. "It lasts like, all night long."

"Oh, Vicks." Natalya tucked the blanket Victoria was wrapped in more firmly around her friend's shoulders and pushed the hair out of her damp face. "I'm sure there's been some kind of mistake. Jack loves you."

Victoria just made a quiet mewling sound in response, then whispered, "I don't want to talk about it anymore."

Natalya and Jane exchanged a glance, and Jane shrugged.

"Of course," Natalya said. "Let's talk about something else. I'm just going to get some water." She went into the kitchen and took a long drink, and when she came back, something about the way Jane was looking at her made her stop a few feet from the couch.

"What?" asked Natalya nervously.

"I was just wondering what we could *possibly* find to talk about," said Jane, her voice almost a parody of innocence. She slowly raised an eyebrow at Natalya. "Hmmm . . . What if we talk about what *you've* been doing all afternoon." She gave the clock on the mantel a significant look before adding, "And evening."

"I . . ." Of course Natalya had planned on telling her friends everything, but now that she was standing there, facing them as if they were a jury and she was on trial, she felt self-conscious.

"Hmmm; she hesitates." Jane adopted a German accent. "Verry interesting, vouldn't you say, Herr Doctor?"

Victoria sniffed and blotted her eyes with a damp tissue before nodding.

"Guys, you're being really weird," said Natalya, unconsciously edging backward. She stumbled against an ottoman and plopped down onto it.

"We're just asking about your afternoon with your friend Colin," said Jane, her voice sugary on the word *friend*. "What's weird about that?"

"Nothing," admitted Natalya uneasily.

"Jane!" Victoria said protectively.

"Fine." Jane relented. She folded her hands under her chin as if in prayer. "Pretty please? Brighten our terrible day by telling us about your afternoon!"

Slowly, Natalya rolled the ottoman she was sitting on toward her friends. "I've done a really bad thing," she said, her voice quiet.

"I knew it!" Jane pointed her finger at Natalya. "You guys fooled around, didn't you?"

"Jane!" cried Victoria, tossing her tissue on the floor. "Please! Do you have to be so . . ."

"Direct?" Jane offered.

Victoria had to smile at Jane's accurate assessment of herself. "Exactly."

"There's only one way to shut me up," Jane informed them.

"And that is?" asked Natalya.

"Tell us *everything*." Jane spread her arms wide on the last word. "Tell us everything, and I promise to be quiet for the duration of the tale."

So Natalya told.

After their first kiss, Colin had pulled away briefly, and Natalya had been sure he was going to say he couldn't kiss her again, that she had to go, that he'd made a terrible mistake. Instead, he'd looked at her for a long moment, traced his finger along the side of her face, and then kissed her again even more passionately, wrapping his arms around her so tightly she almost couldn't breathe.

"Oh my god, he loves you!" Victoria stared at Natalya, her eyes wide.

Natalya bit her thumbnail nervously. She wanted to believe Victoria. But did she dare? "Do you know what he said? He said when I blew him off at the Met he basically locked himself in his room for a *month*, he was so bummed out!"

Jane threw herself backward on the couch. "I am literally dying, this is so romantic."

Natalya drew the pattern of the rug with her toe. "He said he never stopped thinking about me from the second we met to the second we ran into each other in Washington Square Park."

"Wait, then: why didn't he answer your e-mails saying you were sorry?" demanded Jane.

Natalya tucked her legs under her and leaned forward. "He thought I just wrote them out of pity. He said he saw me later that night, after I blew him off. I was dancing with Morgan and Katrina, and he said I looked like I was having the time of my life. So he thought I was just saying I made a mistake to be nice."

"You mean he had no idea how much you liked him?" asked Victoria.

It wasn't clear if Natalya had even heard her. She sighed and touched her lips briefly. "It's like I can still feel him kissing me."

"You see me dying, right?" asked Jane, crossing her arms on her chest and lying flat on the couch. "You see that I have died from the perfection of this love story."

"Oh my god," Victoria wailed. "What if you hadn't run into each other that day in the park? What if you'd *never seen each other again*?! You would never have known your true love." She collapsed back against the couch. "This is so incredible. All this time, it's like you were just . . waiting for each other."

"Well, not exactly." Jane sat up and crossed her legs. "Not to be a buzzkill, but what about Alison?"

Victoria rolled her eyes at her own stupidity. "I completely forgot about Alison! How awful is that?!"

Squinting at Natalya, Jane asked, "What *about* Alison? Or, I mean, were you too busy using your mouths for other things to discuss such irrelevant subjects as his sort-of girlfriend?" Jane put air quotes around *sort-of*.

"No, we were *not* too busy doing other things with our mouths to discuss Alison." Natalya closed her eyes briefly, as if to shut out the intrusive reality of Jane's question.

In her head, she saw the fire Colin had built in the fireplace, remembered how they'd kissed and kissed and kissed on the couch until they couldn't kiss anymore, then played a game of speed chess by the light of the flames. Natalya had lost the game so badly even Colin had been surprised.

"Hey," he'd said as she was about to move her queen directly into the path of his bishop, "you see what you're doing there, right?" He drew a line from his piece to hers, and she shook her head once, as if clearing an Etch A Sketch, then slid her queen back to its spot.

"Sorry." She stared at the board without seeing it. "I'm just really fuzzy or something."

Her hair had fallen in front of her face, and he pushed it out of the way so he could see her eyes. "You don't have to apologize." His eyes were enormous, and she watched the fire playing over the dark of his pupils. He smiled at her. "I'm a little fuzzy, too. Hmm . . . wonder why."

"Yeah," she agreed, smiling back at him. "I wonder."

But happy as Natalya was, all afternoon Alison had been flickering at the back of her mind like flames. Twice she'd opened her mouth to ask about her, and twice she'd closed it without saying anything. What was she supposed to ask? *Um, about that whole "girlfriend" thing?*

But then, out of nowhere, Colin finally introduced the subject. "I need to explain about Alison, okay?" They were sitting on the sofa, her back against his chest, studying the shadows playing over the ceiling.

Her whole body had suddenly tensed, and she'd nodded, not trusting her voice to work, and he'd told her the story of their relationship.

He'd met Alison at the dog park not far from their houses. Last spring they would run into each other every once in a while; then this fall they had started purposely meeting up on Saturday mornings to let their dogs (his, a Portuguese water dog; hers, a golden retriever) play together. When she'd invited him to be her date to MoMA's gala in December (their mothers were on the board together), he'd thought they were going just as friends, but by the end of the night, it was clear she'd meant it as more than that.

"I know I should have told you about her," Colin had admitted. "But I didn't know if you even thought about me like . . . you know, like that."

Here Jane interrupted the story. "I don't get it," she objected. "Why did he keep going out with her if he doesn't like her?"

"He *does* like her," Natalya said. "I mean, she's a great person. *I* like her."

"He just doesn't like her the way he likes Natalya," Victoria translated with an air of finality. "And now that he can have Natalya . . ." She trailed off.

Natalya, who was lying with her stomach on the ottoman and her feet and head on the floor, said something incomprehensible.

"What?" asked Jane and Victoria, leaning forward.

Natalya sat up and faced her friends. "I *said*, 'I feel terrible.'"

"What could you have done?" demanded Jane, as if defending Natalya from herself. "You guys really *like* each other."

"It's true," agreed Victoria, and though her voice was calmer than Jane's, she sounded just as definite. "It's not like you *wanted* to hurt Alison. You just fell for someone who happened to have a girlfriend."

"And who fell for you back," Jane added.

"Yeah, but that doesn't mean it's not going to feel really bad to Alison," Natalya reminded them.

In the face of the simple truth of Natalya's statement, the girls were silent.

Finally, Jane reached out and took Natalya's hand. "You're awesome, Nat. You deserve to be happy. It's sad that it has to come at someone else's expense, but there's nothing you can do about it."

Victoria scooched off the couch, squeezed onto the ottoman and slipped her arm around Natalya. "It's true. You're a great friend. And maybe . . . maybe someday you'll get to show Alison that."

Natalya dropped her head onto Victoria's shoulder. She wanted to believe the Darlings. She wanted to believe that someday she could be both Colin's girlfriend *and* Alison's friend.

But she had the feeling that that was like wanting to believe in Santa and unicorns—nice to imagine.

But not real.

# Chapter
## Thirty-one

JANE WISHED VICTORIA and Natalya didn't have to leave. As long as they were there, she was focused on them.

It was way nicer to assure Natalya that she was a good person, or to think of reasons Victoria shouldn't break up with Jack, than it was to think about her own romantic life.

What was the deal with Simon?

She'd thought about telling Victoria and Natalya what she'd seen. In fact, if Victoria hadn't come hurtling out of the theater crying about Jack's text immediately after Simon left, Jane probably would have told her what had just happened with Simon and Todd. But they'd gotten caught up in a discussion of Jack, and then Natalya had arrived with her story about Colin. So there really were a lot of other, more important things to analyze.

But it wasn't just that. It was also *why* she wanted to tell her friends what she'd seen: she wanted them to hear the whole thing and then assure her that she'd misinterpreted it. But each time she'd been about to tell them, she'd had the same thought: What if they didn't tell her that? What if they heard the story and drew the exact same conclusions she had? What was she supposed to do then?

Better to wait and see than have to explain a whole misunderstanding that might lead them to misjudge Simon forever.

*Sleep tite.* Those had been the last words of his e-mail. *Sleep tite.* That was definitely the kind of thing a person said to his girlfriend.

Wasn't it?

Sitting at her desk trying to focus on the United States' entry into World War II, Jane feared she might be losing her mind. She read the column on FDR's lend-lease program half a dozen times, then read the question at the end of the chapter. *What were the pros and cons of the lend-lease program?*

It was like she'd never read the chapter at all. She looked at the words on the page. *Lend-lease. Lend-lease. Lendleaselendlease.*

Was she being paranoid? So he'd been talking to another guy. Talking *intensely* to another guy. Big deal. Wasn't that just one more way Simon was a modern, open-minded metrosexual guy?

But what she'd seen, that hadn't really looked metrosexual. It had just looked . . . sexual.

There was a knock on her door. "Come in."

Her mom stood outlined by the light from the hallway. She

and Richard had slept at his apartment and then spent the day on a hike along some trail north of the city. Jane hadn't seen her since she had left the apartment to go to *Casablanca*.

It seemed like a lifetime ago.

"Hi, honey. How was your day?"

The casual, cheerful way her mom asked made Jane acutely aware of just how little her mother knew about what was happening in Jane's life lately. Normally, Jane told her mom everything— they would have spent hours talking about what was going on with Simon, Jack, and Colin. Maybe because she was a therapist, her mother was a great listener and gave pretty smart advice.

But suddenly Jane couldn't remember the last time she'd really talked to her mother. In the fall, she'd kept the whole Mr. Robbins thing from her because she'd known her mom would have been upset by the feelings Jane had for her teacher. Her mom knew she was going out with Simon and that she really liked him, but that was about all Jane had had a chance to tell her in the few times they'd been alone since she and Simon had gotten together.

Now was the time to tell her mom what was up. She really needed some advice about how to deal with whatever was going on.

"My day was kind of . . ." Jane began.

"Hang on a sec." Her mom called over her shoulder, "Richard, will you take the brie out of the fridge?" She turned back to Jane. "So it was a nice day?"

Had Jane said it was a nice day? Had she said *anything*? And how was she supposed to talk to her mother about whether or not her boyfriend was gay, when Richard was right at this moment standing in the kitchen, waiting for her mother to come back and eat cheese with him?

"Um, yeah," Jane muttered. "It was okay."

Her mom didn't press for more details. "Great. I was thinking about ordering in from Ga Ga Noodle. I know you like that place so much. Maybe Natalya and Victoria could join us for an early dinner. Wouldn't that be fun?"

Jane just stared at her mother, incredulous. Then she said, "Mom, Victoria and Natalya were here all day. They left, like, five minutes before you got home, and we ordered Ga Ga Noodle for lunch."

"Oh," her mom said. "That's right. They slept over." She paused for a moment, and Jane was sure she was going to say something like *Wow, I should probably know a little more about how you spent your day, shouldn't I?*

Instead she gave Jane a big smile. "I guess great minds think alike!"

"Um, I *guess*," answered Jane.

Her mother completely missed the sarcasm in Jane's response. "There's a nice little Italian place that just opened up on Greenwich. Should we try that, since you had Chinese for lunch? Richard and I have been curious about it."

"Sure, Mom." Jane turned back to her history textbook. "Whatever."

Just what she was in the mood for: a romantic dinner.

For three.

# Chapter
## Thirty-two

**VICTORIA DIDN'T KNOW** what she was going to do when she saw Jack.

Saturday night she'd finally replied to his text asking how the movie was with a single word: good. When her phone had rung Sunday at noon and she'd seen his name on the screen, she almost hadn't picked up. But Jane and Natalya had told her she *had* to tell him what Lily had said, that he had a right to explain himself. And she wanted more than anything for there to be an explanation, no matter what that explanation was. *Victoria, I didn't know how to tell you this, but I have a brain tumor. It causes me to say things I don't mean. Only hurtful things. Nice things like "I love you" are always true.*

She sat down at her desk, picked up her ringing phone, and said, "Hi!" in a firm voice.

"Hey!" said Jack.

She heard people talking in the background. Was he *still* with his friends? Did he never spend a second alone?

"Where are you?" she asked, wishing she sounded a little less accusatory.

"I'm at the diner with Rajiv and Sam and those guys," he said. "Want to join us?"

*Why don't* you *want to leave your friends and join* me? *Ever?*

"I've got a lot of homework." Victoria's voice sounded pitifully sad to her own ears, but Jack didn't seem to notice.

"Bummer," he said.

Bummer? *Bummer?!* She was supposed to spill her guts to a guy who said *bummer*? His flip response made her so mad she said, "Actually, I should probably go."

"Oh." He sounded startled by how abruptly she was getting off the phone, and Victoria was glad. "Everything okay?" he asked.

*No, actually, everything is* not *okay.* Victoria *almost* said it. But then in the background she heard Rajiv say, "Could I have another cup of coffee?" She couldn't just launch into her question about what Jack had told Lily with his friends sitting right there. Maybe even *Lily* sitting right there.

"Everything's fine," she answered tersely.

"Okay, then," he said. "Call me later, 'kay?"

"Yeah," she promised automatically. "Sure."

But she didn't call him later. And when he texted her at nine, asking if she was still awake, she didn't respond, just shut her phone and lay there, not sleeping, until way after midnight.

They didn't run into each other all Monday morning. It wasn't until she was walking down the hall on her way to Bio, the only class they had together, that she saw him. He was half leaning, half sitting on the radiator, talking with Lily and Rajiv.

Were they talking about her? What was he saying this time? Probably something like, *You know, after going an entire weekend without spending time with Victoria, I realize how much better my life is without her.*

Jack saw her, hesitated, then said something to Lily and Rajiv and crossed the hallway to Victoria.

"Hey," he said. There was something chilly about his voice, like he was mad or at least annoyed with Victoria. Which was hilarious, considering he had absolutely nothing to be mad about.

Well, two could play at that game.

"Hey," answered Victoria, her voice equally cool.

"You never called me," Jack said. "Did you get my text?"

Victoria shrugged. "I got it." He was wearing the same sweater he'd been wearing the afternoon he'd told her he loved her.

Jack gave her a funny look.

"Did you have a nice day?" Victoria's voice sounded both strange and familiar to her ears, as if she were talking in a way she'd talked before, but not in a long while.

"Yeah," answered Jack. "It was all right." He didn't add anything about having missed her or ask if she'd had a nice day too.

"Great," said Victoria. *Now she knew where she'd talked this* way before. All during the campaign, whenever she'd had to chat with one of her father's supporters, she'd used this robotic voice.

Jack was still looking at her, but he didn't make even the slightest move to embrace her.

The late bell rang and Victoria gestured toward the bio lab. "I have class." She said it like they didn't both have Bio now, like they didn't usually walk into Bio side by side, hands in the back pockets of each other's jeans or arms around one another.

"Oh." Jack shrugged. "Then I guess you should go." And his voice was even chillier and more inflectionless than it had been before.

Victoria turned abruptly and headed into the lab, blinking frantically to keep herself from crying.

Jack left Bio without waiting for her. Victoria walked numbly to history and listened to but did not hear Mr. Mazetti analyze European alliances in the post–World War II era. Then English, where Mrs. Lavinsky assigned an essay on *Julius Caesar*. Had Victoria even read the play? She couldn't remember. At the end of the period, her friend Chloe turned to her.

"Are you okay?"

"What?" The room had emptied out almost completely, but Victoria hadn't even started to put her stuff in her bag. It was as if she were planning to spend lunch sitting in their English classroom.

"You seem a little out of it," Chloe explained.

When Victoria didn't respond and didn't make a move to pack up her books, Chloe said, "Here, why don't I help you?"

Victoria still didn't say anything, just sat silently while Chloe put Victoria's play, notebook, and pen into her bag. Even when everything was packed up, Victoria still didn't move. Chloe eased her out of her seat and hoisted Victoria's bag onto her own shoulder.

"So, do you want to go to Rick's?" asked Chloe. The hallways were crowded, and they joined the current of people heading in the direction of the front doors.

"Sure," said Victoria, even though she hadn't really heard the question.

"I've got a *serious* craving for a Carol Channing," Chloe told her.

"Sure," Victoria repeated.

She turned the corner into the main lobby and literally banged into Jack.

He felt the impact and leaped backward. "Sorry," he said automatically. Only then did he see that it was Victoria he'd bumped into.

They stared into each other's eyes for a long beat.

Victoria felt the now-familiar stinging that signaled tears were about to start. "I've got to go," she muttered. Then she grabbed Chloe by the arm. "Come on."

Still holding on to Chloe, Victoria raced from the lobby as if the school were on fire. She was literally panting by the time they got to the front steps of school.

Chloe turned to her. "Everything isn't okay, is it?"

By way of an answer, Victoria burst into tears.

# Chapter
# Thirty-three

SUNDAY, AS SHE was getting ready for bed, Natalya wondered if Colin was going to call her. He'd said that Alison was at her country house for the weekend and that he couldn't reach her until she was back in New York because her cell service was spotty. Natalya found herself wondering why the house didn't have a landline. Couldn't he reach Alison that way? As soon as she had the thought, that he should have found a way to break up with Alison as quickly as possible, she felt awful. It was like she was some kind of vulture.

She checked her phone one last time right before she went

to sleep, but there was no message from Colin. Why hadn't he called her? Did that mean he hadn't been able to reach Alison? Or had he changed his mind? Had an afternoon with Natalya made him realize she wasn't as great as he'd imagined, that he was happier with his sort-of girlfriend after all?

Natalya lay in bed for a long time not sleeping. She wished she could call Victoria or Jane, but she didn't want to wake them up. Lying in her darkened room, the pale shadows of the streetlamps outside her window playing across the ceiling, Natalya felt full of despair. She remembered how confident she'd been that Dr. Clover was wrong, how life had seemed so totally perfect when Colin had asked her to meet him for a chess game. It had only been a couple of weeks since the lesson about Mendel's peas, but Natalya felt years older than the girl who'd been so sure that her teacher was wrong for saying life was imperfect and messy.

When she turned on her phone Monday morning, there was a missed call from Colin. So he *had* called! Hands shaking, she checked her call log—he'd called right before midnight while she'd been lying in bed trying not to imagine what was happening with him and Alison.

She dialed her voice mail and heard the familiar sound of Colin's voice. "Hey, it's Colin. Sorry to be calling so late, you must be asleep already. Um, I guess, just give me a call, okay? It's all gotten a little . . . complicated."

Puzzled, she played the message over two more times. *It's all gotten a little complicated.* What did that mean? All her fears from the previous night returned. Had he changed his mind? Was he calling to say he liked Alison too much to break up with her?

Immediately, Natalya began to dial Colin's number, but then she looked at the clock. It was way too early to call someone who didn't have to get up at dawn and travel more than an hour to get to school, someone who had obviously gone to bed after midnight. In her mind's eye she pictured Colin asleep in his bed, maybe with his phone on the floor, where he'd dropped it the night before after calling her. She wished he'd left a more detailed message. Today was going to be hard enough to face without knowing exactly what she was up against.

Walking to the train, she couldn't stop thinking about Colin's message and what he might have meant. Complicated. He said things had gotten complicated. It was like she'd never heard the word before, like it was French or Japanese. What could it possibly mean that things were *complicated*? As the Q train lumbered over the Manhattan Bridge, Natalya dialed Colin, but the call went right to voice mail. She watched the sunlight glittering on the surface of the East River, then raised her eyes to study the New York City skyline. Colin was there, in the shower or eating or getting dressed or maybe walking to school already. And so was Alison. Natalya wished she knew what either one of them was thinking right at that moment. Anything she learned would have been better than not knowing.

The Gainsford steps were crowded with uniformed girls, but Natalya kept her head down and didn't pause to say hello to anyone. Instead, she headed into the building and up the stairs, her goal the second-floor girls' bathroom at the end of the hall. There was never anyone in there first thing in the morning, and she wanted a second to be alone and splash some cold water on her face. She had English first period, which meant she was about to have to face Alison. Which would have been *complicated* enough without Colin's message about things being complicated.

But when she pushed open the heavy wooden door of the second-floor bathroom, she found herself looking at Jordan. Jordan was talking to Alison, who was sitting on the wide marble counter beside the sink, a girl whose face was wet with tears, whose nose was red from blowing, and who, at the exact moment Natalya stepped into the room, was saying in a voice made high-pitched by crying, "It just doesn't make any sense."

Alison did not look up at the sound of the door squeaking open, but Jordan did. When she saw who it was, she did not smile or in any way acknowledge that Natalya was someone she was friends with, someone she'd had over to her house, someone she sat with at lunch. Quickly, almost frantically, she waved her hand to indicate that Natalya should leave.

Natalya did not have to be told twice. Heart thumping in her chest, she slipped out the door and pressed herself against the wall beside it.

This was all her fault. Alison crying. Jordan telling her to get out. She was a terrible person. Jane and Victoria had tried to convince her otherwise, but she knew the truth. She was mean and selfish and a sorry excuse for a friend, and now Alison was sitting there crying to Jordan because of what Natalya had done.

The ringing in her bag jerked her out of her thoughts, and she scrambled to extract her phone. Colin. "Hello? Hello?" her voice sounded slightly hysterical.

"Hi," said Colin. "We really need to talk."

Truer words had never been spoken. She told Colin to hang on a minute, and made her way downstairs. She wished more than anything she hadn't seen what she had. It would have made it a whole lot easier for her to be happy if Colin was about to tell her he was free.

# Chapter
# Thirty-four

OUTSIDE, THE CROWD of girls had thinned in anticipation of the first bell ringing. Natalya walked to the corner of the block, the phone still pressed to her ear. The sound of boys' voices in the background from Colin's end made her conscious of the fact that she never heard guys during school hours anymore.

"Hey," she said when she'd turned the corner and was finally alone. "Hi." Her voice was chalky after what she'd just seen, and she hoped Colin would blame it on a bad connection.

"Hang on a sec." She heard someone calling, *Seriously!* and then it was quiet. "I wanted to talk to you. Before school," he said. He sounded surprisingly calm.

There was a long pause, and then Natalya blurted out, "You said things were complicated." She didn't know why she was telling Colin that. He'd left her that message. He knew what he'd said.

"I wanted to tell you as soon as possible that I didn't break up with Alison," said Colin. His words sounded rote, as if he'd rehearsed them.

*But she was just crying in the bathroom.* The sentence formed in Natalya's brain, and once it was there, she couldn't think of anything else. *But she was just crying in the bathroom. She was just crying in the bathroom.* For a second, Natalya had the insane idea that Colin must have broken up with Alison without realizing what he'd done.

She realized how crazy she was being. You don't break up with someone and not know it.

"But . . . I don't understand."

In the same robotic tone, he said simply, "It's not something I'm at liberty to talk about at the moment."

"It's not . . . *what*?" What was he even talking about? He sounded like a lawyer or something.

"I'm sorry, Natalya. I like you a lot, but I behaved badly and I regret it."

He regretted it? He *regretted* it? He'd spent an afternoon fooling around with her behind his girlfriend's back, behind Natalya's friend's back, and now he *regretted* it?

"That's it? That's all you have to say?" Natalya didn't even care that it was obvious from her voice that she'd started to cry.

For the first time that morning, Colin's voice sounded shaky. "I'm sorry, Natalya."

"Yeah, well . . . you know something, Colin? I'm sorry too." She barely managed to choke out the words before a sob broke through. Sick with guilt and disappointment, Natalya snapped her phone shut as sharply as she could. Then she stood alone in the cold morning sunlight for a long time, knowing she had to go inside and face the school day.

# Chapter
# Thirty-five

**SIMON WAS SICK.**

He wasn't in school Monday. Or Tuesday. His throat was sore, and he couldn't really talk on the phone. The one time Jane reached him, he was feverish and out of it.

Wednesday morning when she got his text saying he'd be in school and would see her at rehearsal, enough time had passed that Jane was convinced she had completely misunderstood what she'd seen when she was watching Simon and Todd Saturday night. So Simon had been standing extremely close to a guy he was talking to. So the other guys on the sidewalk *hadn't* been standing extremely close to the guys *they* were talking to.

What did that mean? Nothing. Jane remembered rehearsals for *Midsummer*, how the cast was always giving one another back rubs, playing with one another's hair, sitting practically on one another's laps.

You didn't have to be gay to be a guy who was comfortable touching another guy. You just had to be an actor.

By the time she walked into the dimly lit black box on Wednesday afternoon, Jane was feeling good. She was going to see Simon. They were going to rehearse their scene. And maybe this time it would go all right. Then they'd talk about the fabulous art opening they were going to Saturday night. Years ago, Jane's mom had taught her about a therapeutic concept: the pleasure of anxiety. That was when people who had nothing wrong with their lives came up with things to worry about.

It was totally what Jane was doing.

"Hello?" she called, but she didn't have to wait to not get an answer to know there was no one in the theater.

She crossed to the light switches and flipped a couple more on. It was weird that Mark wasn't there already. He always arrived before she did. She checked her phone. No message. Should she text him?

As if in answer to her question, the door to the theater opened and shut. Without looking up, she said, "Hey, Mark."

"It's me," Simon corrected her.

She spun around. The light was dimmer by the door where Simon was standing, but Jane could see that he looked tired, as if his first day back at school had exhausted him.

She wanted to go over to him and put her arms around him.

They hadn't seen each other in almost a week.

But for some reason, she couldn't make herself take even a single step in his direction.

"Hi," he said.

"Hi," she said.

"So, did you get Mark's text?" Simon took a few steps into the room but didn't cross over to where Jane was standing. It was as if there were an invisible force field separating them.

"What? No." Automatically, Jane reached into her bag and took out her phone, but there was nothing there.

"He's picking up the costumes. He'll be a little late."

"Oh. That's too bad." *That's too bad?*

"So, I guess we just wait," Simon said. He toyed with the strap of his backpack.

Jane fiddled with her phone, sliding it open and shut nervously. It buzzed suddenly, startling her. She checked the screen. "Um, it's Mark's text."

"Oh, yeah," said Simon.

"I finally got it," she explained.

"Good," said Simon.

She read Mark's message. "He says he's getting costumes." She raised her eyes to look at Simon. "But I guess you already know that."

He smiled at her. "Yeah, I guess I do."

This was so weird. Why were things between them so weird? Was it *her?* Maybe *she* was the one being weird, and Simon was being totally normal. After all, he'd been sick for almost a week, and she hadn't even hugged him hello. Maybe he thought she was mad at him or something. She took a step toward him. "Simon, I'm so glad you're—"

"Jane, can I—"

It took a second for each of them to process what the other had said, and then Simon laughed. "Sorry. What did you want to say?"

"No, I interrupted you," said Jane. She was starting to get a funny feeling in her stomach, almost like she was coming down with the flu, too.

"Ladies first," he insisted.

"No, really." She shook her head. This was so dumb. It wasn't as if she had some grand announcement to make. "I just . . . I mean. It's nothing. I was just going to say I'm glad you're better."

"Oh," said Simon. "Well, thanks. I mean, I'm glad, too."

There was a long pause. Jane's stomach was feeling worse with every passing second. She kept waiting for Simon to say whatever it was he'd been about to say, but he remained silent.

"That was a fun movie Saturday night," Jane said abruptly. "I'm sorry you had to leave."

Okay, *why* was she bringing up Saturday night?

"Yeah," Simon agreed. He started chewing on his nail, then seemed to realize he was doing it and dropped his hand to his side.

"Yeah," she echoed.

"Jane!" Simon's voice was bizarrely loud in the silent space.

"Yes?" She didn't meet his eyes.

"I want . . ." Now Simon's voice was extremely quiet. "I mean, I need . . ." He shook his head and muttered, "Wow, this is harder than I thought." He cleared his throat, looked up, and said clearly, "Do you remember when I told you that the person I'd been seriously in like with was a guy?"

Jane's mouth was dry. She tried to say something but settled on a nod.

"Well, Todd . . . that guy, I mean the guy I once liked—he was a friend of Roman's, and he was there Saturday night."

*I know. I saw you.* But she couldn't bring herself to reveal the fact that she'd been watching him. Instead, she just said, "Oh." It wasn't a word so much as an exhalation of breath, as if Simon's statement had been a punch.

Simon took a step toward her. "I think . . . I think you know what I'm going to say, don't you?"

Jane took a ragged breath and gave Simon a pinched smile. "I hope not."

He gave her a smile back. "Jane, I think . . . I mean, I'm pretty sure." He took a deep breath, then said simply, "I'm gay."

"Oh," Jane choked out. She pressed her lips together, terrified that she was going to burst into tears.

"Jane, I'm so sorry I hurt you," said Simon, taking several more steps toward her. "If there were any girl I'd want to be with, it would be you. You're so amazing and talented and funny." Now that he'd gotten his announcement over with, Simon couldn't seem to stop talking. He complimented her all the way across the room, and once he was standing beside her, he continued to list all the things that he liked about her.

But Jane had stopped listening. She was looking at Simon, but she was seeing a double image. Simon Humphrey Bogart.

God, how big a loser was she? She'd spent the movie thinking about her and Simon. And he'd spent the movie thinking about Todd.

Simon must have run out of things that were great about Jane because he finally stopped talking. He started to put a hand on Jane's shoulder, but she stepped away.

"Don't." Suddenly, Jane felt as if she were made of smoke, like if Simon did touch her she would simply . . . dissolve.

"I'm really sorry," he said again.

Jane had no idea what she was supposed to say. She opened her mouth, but for what felt like the first time in her life, she literally could not utter a word.

The door to the black box flew open, and Mark stood framed in it, holding two garment bags, one in each hand.

"Who is about to be the best-dressed cast in the entire universe?!" he cried joyfully.

Neither Jane nor Simon responded, and Mark slung the bags over his shoulders. "Well, don't all thank me at once."

"Thanks, man," said Simon abruptly, crossing to take one of the garment bags from him. "I'm psyched to see these."

Jane took a deep breath and walked over to where Mark was standing. She grabbed the other bag. "Yeah, thanks a lot. I know they're going to be great."

Mark eyed them both suspiciously but didn't say anything. Jane forced herself to smile at him, a grin so wide it hurt her face. She couldn't bring herself to look at Simon.

"I guess you guys should change," Mark said finally.

"Yeah, great!" said Jane, still feigning enthusiasm.

"Awesome!" agreed Simon, heading to the supply closet that had been rigged into a dressing room.

"Hey!" Mark shouted, so loudly Simon literally froze in his tracks. Slowly, he turned to face Mark. Mark looked from Jane to Simon for a long time, but all he said was, "You guys need to change bags. You've got the wrong ones."

"Oh," said Simon, and he laughed a little too hard as he made his way over to where Jane was standing, managing to take his bag from her and give her his without their hands ever touching. Then he turned again and went into the dressing room.

Mark looked at Jane. "Are you okay?"

"Fine," she answered automatically. "I'm fine."

Either she was a better actress than she thought she was, or Mark was a sucker, because after a long pause he just said, "Okay. We'll take it from the top in five."

Dizzy with sadness, Jane took her costume and went to change.

She had been positive she wouldn't even be able to speak, much less act, but as the scene played out, Jane found herself getting into character more deeply than ever before. As she spoke her lines and thought about what Simon had done, she found new meaning in the words. He'd lied to her. Saturday night. He'd lied to her. He'd said he wasn't feeling well, and then he'd gone and hooked up with Todd. Had he even been sick? Or had he just been avoiding her?

She crossed to center stage. "'What arrogance, when you've got a safe retreat and I'm alone and going into exile.'"

Simon shrugged and placed his hand on his hip. "'You chose this course yourself; blame no one else.'"

"'I chose it! How? Did I take a wife and leave you?'" She pointed an accusatory finger at him.

"'You cursed the king, and cursed his royal home,'" he answered simply.

It was all too much. He'd been . . . experimenting with her. Like she was a pair of jeans or a jacket he wasn't sure he liked. *Hmmm, yeah, I thought I wanted these, but it turns out I don't. Is it too late to return them?*

"'Yes, and I'll be a curse to your house too.'" Her voice was angry but not shrill.

Simon was undeterred, a confident, even slightly arrogant Jason. "'I'll not go on with this. There is no point.'"

Had everyone known? She remembered the look his friends had exchanged when they'd met her Saturday night. *Oh, is this that girl you're pretending you're straight with?* What had Simon been thinking every time they kissed? Had he been thinking about Todd? Had he been feeling sorry for Jane, thinking how he couldn't break up with her because she liked him so much?

She answered scathingly, "'I'll make no use of any of your friends, nor will I take your bounty. Give me nothing.'"

Still sure of himself, Simon responded, "'Well then, I ask the gods to be my witness. I only wish to serve you and the children. . . .'"

But he must have liked her at least a little, right? She stood, separated from him by only a few inches, finally looking into his eyes. What she saw there only confused her, because behind the arrogance was something like concern. He had cared. He did care. For a second, she wanted to beg him to reconsider, to remind him of how much fun they'd had as a couple, to insist that no one who really liked boys could have made her feel as good as Simon had made Jane feel.

And against the urge to speak those words, Jane gathered herself up, pushed at the center of Simon's chest, and turned away from him. "'Go, go: I see you've been so long away from her. You're itching with desire for your new-broken girl. Get on with being married while you still can. Because I prophesy: Your marriage will be one of horror and regret.'"

For a long, long minute after Simon walked offstage, there was silence. And then, from just beyond the stage lights, Mark began to clap.

# Chapter
## Thirty-six

NATALYA HAD MANAGED to avoid all but the most superficial interactions with Alison and Jordan for three days; but on Thursday, when Jordan asked if she was busy for lunch *again*, she couldn't think of an excuse fast enough, and she found herself walking down the hall between them.

Alison seemed quieter than usual, but Jordan kept up a steady stream of chatter, mostly focused on how fabulous Alison's birthday party was going to be. "First of all, the birthday girl is going to look *amazing*!" Jordan gestured to Alison like the hostess of a game show presenting the prize. "A shimmering, custom-made dress by none other than Vera Wang. An elegant dinner at the oh-so-chic La Bouche, followed by dancing to the beautiful sounds of a live orchestra at the Park Avenue Armory." Alison's smile was small enough that Natalya was reminded how normal all of this must be to her. How many hundreds of gala events had she been to? How many thousands of limousines had she ridden in? The numbers were staggering to contemplate.

"I cannot *believe* you're busy," Jordan complained to Natalya as the girls entered the cafeteria and made their way to their usual table.

"Yeah," said Natalya.

Jordan paid no attention to Natalya's monosyllabic reply. She continued to rattle off details about Saturday night's party, how much fun it was going to be, how excited she was to be going. When Perry and Catherine joined them, they also talked excitedly about Saturday night, describing the dresses they were considering wearing, wondering if it would be worth bringing pretty wraps in case the recently frigid weather lifted and they wanted to go out onto the patio.

Nobody noticed Natalya's silence, or if they did, they probably chalked it up to her disappointment about not being able to come to the party.

Imagine if she didn't have the opening. If she'd said *yes!* The idea of being at Alison's party and watching Alison lean against Colin as the guests sang "Happy Birthday," or seeing the two of them dance together while she stood with the crowd applauding the happy couple, made her so nauseated she pushed her cheese sandwich violently away. She knew she was getting confused, that in her imagination she'd turned Alison's birthday party into some kind of wedding, but she couldn't stop herself. It was all so unfair. Alison had everything. Everything. Why did she get Colin too?

For a second she remembered Alison's crying in the bathroom. What had that been about? Had her daddy told her she couldn't have a pair of diamond earrings she'd been coveting? Had her mother said, "I'm sorry, dear, but five thousand dollars is just too much to spend on a pair of shoes. I said you could have the pair that costs two thousand, and that's my final offer."

Thinking of the things Alison had to cry about, Natalya had the sudden urge to hurt her, really hurt her, to make Alison feel as bad as she had been feeling ever since Colin called her.

As if on cue, Jordan said, "And we all know how cute Colin Prewitt looks in a tuxedo."

For the first time during lunch, Alison broke into a real smile, one that reached her sparkling blue eyes as well as her lips. The sight only intensified Natalya's urge to draw blood. What would happen to Alison's perfect smile if she knew how her boyfriend had spent his afternoon Saturday? If she found out how he felt about Natalya, how he really felt about Alison? What would happen to Alison's perfect party and perfect birthday and perfect *life* if she knew the truth?

"Did you say Colin Prewitt?" Natalya blurted out.

Though the lunchroom was noisy and everyone at the table had seemed to be talking at once, a sudden silence fell on the table as every eye turned to Natalya.

"Yeah," said Alison, her voice calm. "Do you know him?"

*Do I know him? I made out with him. He told me he can't stop thinking about me, that he only likes you as a friend. Do I know him? Yeah, I know him. But you don't.*

But as Natalya opened her mouth to speak, she realized something. *She* was the one who was an idiot. Colin had said he didn't like Alison, but he hadn't broken up with her. *It's complicated.* What was so complicated? *Alison, I don't want us to go out anymore.* Did he think he was so great Alison was going to kill herself or something just because he dumped her? Or had he just realized he didn't like Natalya all that much, that while she might be fun to play chess with and fool around with on a boring afternoon when there was nothing else to do, she wasn't worth giving up beautiful, perfect, rich Alison Jones for.

Everyone at the table was still staring at her.

"Not really," she said quietly, looking down at her rejected sandwich. "I met him at a party once, but, um, I don't know him."

It was true. She didn't know Colin at all.

"Well, he's nothing like his sister," said Jordan quickly. "She's the worst. And Colin's a great guy."

"Totally," agreed Catherine and Perry.

Natalya forced herself to raise her eyes to meet Alison's across the table. "I'm sure he is," she said.

# Chapter
# Thirty-seven

JANE HAD BARELY made it through their dress rehearsal.

As soon as Mark started clapping, Jane abruptly announced, "I've gotta go," then rushed out of the theater carrying her bag so she could go straight home after she changed. She ran to the bathroom and put on her regular clothes, and only after she'd gotten into her jeans, her shirt, and her jacket did she realize she'd left her shoes under the chair her bag had been on.

"This *sucks!*" she shouted, throwing open the stall door. A girl who had been washing her hands barely raised an eyebrow at Jane's outburst. Drama in the girls' bathroom was hardly new at the Academy for the Performing Arts.

Jane waited, shoeless, in the bathroom for almost twenty minutes—long enough, she hoped, for Simon and Mark to have left. Then she crossed the hall and entered the theater. The lights were on, and Jane thought that she was lucky Mark had forgotten to lock the door.

She was just putting on her left sneaker when the door opened. It was Mark.

He stood just inside the doorway, watching her tie her shoe. "I figured you'd come back for those."

"Yeah," she said quickly, standing up and grabbing her bag. "Sorry I ran off like that."

"It's okay. I'm glad you're not wandering these mean city streets in your socks." As he spoke, he walked toward her slowly, like she was a skittish animal that might bolt at any second.

"Me too," she agreed, though walking around Greenwich Village shoeless seemed like it would have been the least of her problems.

"That was a fantastic performance," Mark said. He was standing a few chairs away from her, and he made no move to come any closer. "I mean, really great. Your best yet. Jane, you are . . . a seriously great actress."

To her utter humiliation, Jane took a deep, halting breath, one that signaled she was about to cry. "Thanks, Mark." The tears she'd been keeping inside all afternoon finally couldn't be held back any longer, and she began to sob. "Oh my god, I'm so embarrassed." She pressed her knuckles to her lips, trying to force herself to stop crying.

Mark crossed the distance between them and put his hands

on her shoulder. "Jane, what is it?" His look was so gentle and worried that Jane had the strange sensation that he knew exactly what had happened.

She wanted to ask him, but when she opened her mouth, she found herself blurting out, "Is there something, like, horribly wrong with me?"

"What?!" Mark gave a brief laugh, then sobered. "Are you serious?"

Her silence indicated that she was, and Mark shook his head slowly from side to side. "Jane, there's nothing wrong with you." He hesitated, then added, "It's kind of the opposite, really."

"There's something right with me?" Jane asked with a snort.

But Mark's reply wasn't the least bit flippant, nor was the look he gave her. "Right."

It seemed to Jane that Mark was about to say something else, but then the door to the theater opened with a bang, and a janitor pushing an enormous garbage can on wheels came in. "You kids just about through in here?"

The moment—if there had even been a moment—passed. Mark turned toward the man. "Yeah," he answered. Then he turned back to Jane. "You gonna be okay?"

Jane thought about how she was going to have to tell everyone what had happened with Simon, to explain over and over again how she'd thought Simon was into her but really he wasn't. She wished there were some magic messenger service that would travel the world informing all your friends and family that your boyfriend had dumped you because he was gay.

All she wanted to do was curl up on the floor of the theater and go to sleep.

Mark seemed to read her thoughts. He gave her shoulder a gentle squeeze. "You're gonna be okay," he promised, answering his own question.

The janitor pulled a broom out of his garbage can and started sweeping the floor. "Thanks, Mark," said Jane. She said it quickly, not looking at him. But when he turned and headed for the door, she called out, "Hey!"

He turned around. "Yeah?"

She gave him a tiny sad smile. "Really. Thank you."

He gave a small bow. "Any time."

And then he was gone.

Jane said good-bye to the janitor, stepped out into the hallway, and zipped up her coat. It felt to her as if Mark had been trying to tell her something, something besides *you're gonna be okay*.

But she was too tired and sad to think about what that something might be.

# Chapter
# Thirty-eight

BEING IN A fight with Jack felt a lot like being physically ill to Victoria, as if she had a headache or a fever. She would wake up in the middle of the night and find she was unable to go back to sleep because of the thoughts gnawing at her. Over Christmas vacation she'd had the flu, and she'd spent the night throwing up. As bad as it had been, when she'd woken up in the morning, she'd felt better, and the relief of not being nauseated anymore erased the horror of the night of being sick.

But now there wasn't any relief. She went to bed thinking about how messed up things were between them, and she woke up thinking about how messed up things were between them.

Then she went to school and thought about it some more.

Were they even in a fight? It wasn't like they'd had an actual argument; more like they were just avoiding each other. Victoria had slipped into Bio simultaneously with the late bell on Tuesday, and Jack was gone almost before the bell ending class rang. They didn't have the same lunch periods, and Jack didn't come find Victoria at the end of school. He didn't text or call her during the day like he usually did, either, and Victoria certainly wasn't going to call him. Why would she? So he could laugh about her with his friends?

When he finally sent her a text, all it said was what's up?

She stared at his message. *What's up?* They'd barely spoken for three days, and all he could think to say was *What's up?*

Well, she wasn't exactly going to bare her soul in response to *What's up.*

not much, she typed back, pressing hard on each letter as if it were a message she was particularly anxious to drive home. Then she added, what's up w/u?

A minute later, he wrote back, not much.

She stared at her phone, openmouthed, then marched over to her computer and logged on to her e-mail.

*Jack,* she typed, *I don't know what's going on, but things with us feel very weird. Lily told me you said we have nothing in common. Why would you talk about us behind my back like that? Do you want to break up? Is that why you're avoiding me? I'm really confused. If you don't love me anymore, I wish you'd just say so. Love, Victoria.*

When she was finished, she reread the entire e-mail. It sounded so . . . pathetic. What if he opened it when he was with Lily and Rajiv and he let them read it, and then they all sat around talking about how lame Victoria was? The thought of anyone, even Jack, reading what she'd just written was suddenly terrifying to her, and she canceled the draft and logged off, then logged back on just to make sure the note wasn't still sitting in her out-box, waiting to be sent.

By Friday she was starting to wonder if she really *was* getting sick. She woke up tired and confused after a terrible night's sleep, and she wandered into school in a daze. She didn't have Bio, so she didn't even get a glimpse of Jack all day, and by the time she was packing up her stuff to go home, she had decided he must not be in school.

And then, as she was double-checking that she had everything she needed for the weekend, he suddenly appeared next to her.

She looked up at him, and it was as if the past week hadn't happened. He was wearing a dark blue, soft-looking, flannel button-down shirt, and she knew how good it would feel to press her face against his chest and be engulfed by his Jack-ness. She missed him so much it was like hunger. She felt starved for him.

"Hey," he said. His voice was chilly.

"Hey." She couldn't possibly put her arms around someone who talked to her like that, someone who sounded like such a cold stranger. Instead, she linked her hands through the strap of her bag and stared at the lockers on the opposite wall.

There was a long pause filled by the eager shouts of hundreds of students who had just been liberated for the weekend. Victoria wondered how it was possible for a moment to be so loud yet feel so silent.

When Jack finally spoke, the accusation seemed to burst from him. "Victoria, I came over here to tell you that Rajiv's parents said I could invite you to his birthday dinner Saturday, but now I feel like . . . I don't know, I feel like, why would I even invite you? You're acting *really* weird."

*Why would you even invite me?!* Victoria couldn't believe Jack had just said that. It wasn't enough that he'd told Lily they had zero in common; now he had to make sure he told her he didn't want her hanging out with him and his friends? In what universe was this the way someone treated the girl he was supposedly in love with?

Victoria was so mad she literally shook with rage. "Well, guess what, Jack? I don't even want to *be invited*, okay? And even if I *did* want to be invited—which I *don't*—I *couldn't* go because I happen to have plans with *my friends* that night. Which you might remember because I *invited you*, but you couldn't come. Only you *don't* remember because all you care about is *your* friends and *your* plans." She turned her back on him, slammed her locker shut, and threw the lock in place.

A girl walking by shouted, "You tell him, sister!" and her friend hooted and whistled.

Jack looked toward the girls as if he wanted to respond to them, but they had passed. Then he took her arm and pulled her around to face him. "Are you seriously saying that you think I don't care about you?" Jack spoke in a furious hiss.

She crossed her arms and stared at him. "You make time for

your friends and your music, Jack. And if I can be a part of those things, great. And if I can't, well, too bad for me."

"I make time for you!" Jack snapped.

"*And* you talk about me behind my back!" Victoria added, pointing at him.

"Okay, that is *crazy!*" Jack pointed back at her. "I do *not* talk about you behind your back."

"Oh, really? So you're saying Lily lied when *she* said that *you* said that we have nothing in common?" Victoria put air quotes around "nothing in common."

"She told you that?!" Jack nearly shouted. A group of guys wearing the Morningside basketball uniform looked toward them, and Jack lowered his voice. "Okay, that comment was taken totally out of context."

"What context could it be *not* awful in?" Victoria's eyes burned with tears. "How can I trust you if you say things like that about me to your friends?"

Jack gave a bitter laugh. "Fine, you don't trust me. You think I don't care about you. Maybe it would be better if we just broke up."

Victoria had heard Jack say that same sentence so many times in her head it was like waking up to find the nightmare you'd been having was real. "Maybe it would." Her voice was soft with hurt.

Jack stood staring at her for a long moment. "Well, fine, then." As soon as he'd said it, he turned and stormed away.

Victoria stood watching him as the tears that had been threatening to fall finally began to roll down her cheeks.

# Chapter
## Thirty-nine

WHEN NATALYA AND Jane got to her apartment on Friday after school, Victoria barely said a word, just let them in and collapsed on the sofa with the roll of toilet paper she'd been using for tissues. After she'd finished telling her friends what had happened, Jane and Natalya curled up next to her on the couch, one on either side of her.

"Love sucks," Jane observed quietly.

"Why are *you* saying that?" asked Natalya. "You're the only one of us with a boyfriend."

Jane took a deep breath. "Not anymore." She pulled away from Victoria and turned to face her friends. "Simon broke up with me."

*"What?"* cried Victoria, dropping her toilet paper roll in shock.

"When?" demanded Natalya.

"Wednesday," Jane confessed.

"Wednesday?!" Victoria and Natalya shrieked.

"But it's *Friday,*" Natalya pointed out. "How could you not have told us until now?"

"I *couldn't* tell you," Jane cried. "It was too . . ." She knotted her fingers together. "Humiliating."

Victoria snorted. "What could possibly be more humiliating than a guy saying he loves you and then talking about you behind your back, telling his friends you have zero in common, and then *dumping you* in front of the entire school?"

Natalya raised her hand. "Um, how about a guy fooling around with you behind his girlfriend's back, telling you he's totally into you, and then saying he regrets it?" She put air quotes around "regrets it."

Jane put her hand in the air too. "Sorry, guys, but I think I've got you *both* out-humiliated. How about a guy telling someone he's totally into her, then fooling around with a *guy* behind his girlfriend's back, and then saying the whole thing was a big mistake and he's breaking up with the girl?"

Both Natalya and Victoria were silent as they worked to translate what had happened to Jane.

Finally, Natalya spoke.

"You're the girlfriend," she offered.

"Right," said Jane.

"And Simon's the guy who fools around with another guy?" asked Victoria gently.

"Bingo!" Jane snapped her fingers and gave a tight smile.

"Oh, Jane," said Victoria, leaning her shoulder against her friend's. "I'm so sorry."

"Thanks."

Natalya pressed up against Jane's other side. Nobody said anything for a few minutes.

"You know," Natalya finally offered, "when you think about it, it's kind of a compliment."

"Okay, this is going to be good." Jane's voice was bitter.

"Well," Natalya continued hesitantly, "I mean, here's Simon and he's, you know, gay, but he likes you so much that you make him think maybe he's *not* gay. I couldn't even get a straight guy to like me enough to break up with another girl. You practically got a guy to change his sexual orientation for you! Which, I will point out, is a biological impossibility."

Despite how sad she was feeling, Jane smiled.

It was silent again. Finally, Jane spoke. "We read a poem in English last semester that said it is better to have loved and lost than never to have loved at all."

Victoria stared at the opposite wall, though she didn't seem to be seeing it. "Whoever said that was an idiot. Or a guy."

Natalya turned and put her hands on Victoria's shoulders. "Vicks, I can't take it if you become cynical about romance."

Eyes still on the empty space before her, Victoria said, "You'll get used to it."

No one could think of anything to say to that. For a long time they just sat together, pressed tightly against one another and feeling sad.

# Chapter Forty

JANE HATED HER DRESS.

Saturday evening, as she looked at herself in the mirror, she could not for the life of her imagine what she had been thinking buying something so dumb. Feathers? *Feathers?!*

At the time, the purchase had seemed so clever; she could totally see Nana clapping her hands together at the sight of her in the short blue dress. When she'd tried on the dress with Victoria at Act Two, they'd agreed that the feathers circling the neckline and the hem made her look like an old-time movie star going to an Oscar-night party, like Elizabeth Taylor, or maybe Ava Gardner. At the last second, Jane had even bought a rhinestone comb to hold her hair up in an elegant French twist.

She hadn't realized the whole look had been contingent on her walking into the party with gorgeous, fabulous Simon. Being with Simon automatically made her look cool. Because if a guy who looked like Simon wanted to go out with you, you had to be pretty awesome.

Only now she wasn't going out with Simon. She wasn't going out with *anyone*. Worse, the guy she *had* been going out with was gay. She could practically hear her mother's friends saying, *So, I hear you have a boyfriend. Where is he?* And she was going to have to say, *He's not here, because he's gay. That's the kind of guy who goes out with me—the gay kind.*

"Jane?" Her mother pushed open the door at the same time as she said Jane's name. "Sweetheart, you look lovely!"

Hunched up in her chair, shoulders sagging, hair in a messy lump instead of an elegant chignon, Jane glared at her mother, who was wearing a sleek, canary yellow silk jacket over a plain black sheath. Around her neck was an elaborate necklace of Nana's, the one from which Jane, Natalya, and Victoria each had a single pearl.

"I don't look lovely, Mom." Jane brushed the feathers along the neckline of the dress with annoyance. "I look like I'm molting."

Her mom laughed. "Honey, you do not." She stepped into the room. "Nana would have loved your dress. Stand up. Let me see."

"Not right now."

Her mother held out her hands and made a slight gesture with her fingers as if to say, *Yes, now.* "Come on, let me see how you look."

Jane's voice grew harsher. "I *said* not now, okay?"

"*Okay,*" said her mother, taking a step back. "Well, Richard should be here any minute, and then we'll go downstairs and get a cab, okay? And Simon's going straight there, right? I'm so looking forward to meeting him."

Her mother's poor choice of words was the last straw.

Straight? *Straight?*

Jane shot out of the chair. "No, Mom, Simon is *not* going straight there, okay? Simon's not going straight *anywhere*. We broke up, okay?"

"What? Why didn't you tell me?" Her mom's face was the picture of concern, and she took a step toward Jane. Jane opened her mouth to explain just as the buzzer rang, signaling that the doorman was sending someone upstairs. "That must be Richard. I'll go let him in and come right back."

Of *course.* "You know what, Mom, don't bother coming back, okay?"

Standing at the threshold of Jane's room, her mom hesitated. "What is that supposed to mean?"

"I'm just . . . Just go and have a glass of wine with your boyfriend and enjoy your evening, and don't even pretend you care about what's going on with me, okay? You're in love." She threw her arms in the air and grinned maniacally in an exaggerated portrait of a happy person. "Wonderful! I'm *thrilled* for you."

Her mom frowned and crossed her arms. "Jane, I'm sorry you and Simon broke up. I wish you had told me about it."

"Oh, really, Mom? You wish I had told you about it? When, exactly? When was I supposed to have a minute of your precious time to tell you what's going on in my life?" As if to prove Jane's point, there was a hesitant knock at the door of the apartment. She watched her mother's internal struggle as she tried not to show how much she wanted to answer it. Finally, her mom called in a loud voice, "Just a minute!"

"Would you *go*, already?" Jane could feel her face contorting into something ugly as her eyes began to sting. "You've made it totally clear that all you care about is Richard, so don't stand there and pretend you want to talk to me when all you want is to be with *him*."

"Jane, that's completely unfair. If something happened with Simon, I want to know about it. But I can't leave Richard standing out there in the hallway."

Now Jane was truly sobbing, but she felt like they were tears not of sadness but of fury. "Just. Leave. Me. Alone!"

Her mom stared at her, a bewildered expression on her face. Finally a second knock on the apartment door decided her. She turned and headed into the hallway. "This conversation isn't over," she said as she left.

Jane didn't bother to correct her. She knew that as soon as her mom was with Richard, she would be too distracted to remember what Jane had said.

# Chapter Forty-one

JUST AS JANE had suspected, when she came out of her room, her mother and Richard were each holding a glass of red wine. Her mother must have just said something funny, because Richard was laughing.

He gave Jane one of his usual greetings: a wave and a nearly whispered hello.

Maybe that had been her mistake. Maybe Jane should have gone out with someone who didn't talk. After all, if you never spoke, how could you utter the sentence, *I'm gay*?

There was a moment of silence, but even though Jane's mom looked at her over her wineglass, she didn't ask if she could talk to Jane privately. Jane could practically hear her mom's thoughts. *It's not polite to have a chat with Jane while Richard's waiting. We'll talk another time.*

*Yeah, like never.*

"Well, shall we go?" asked Jane's mom.

Richard nodded.

"Fine," said Jane.

She tried to find comfort in the fact that she wouldn't be the only one without a date tonight. Now that Colin had turned out to be a sleazeball, and Victoria and Jack had broken up, the Darlings were going to be one another's dates. Which was how she'd always imagined tonight anyway, before all of their stupid boyfriends and almost boyfriends and gay boyfriends had come along. Really, there was something right about the three of them being one another's dates for an evening dedicated to celebrating Nana. After all, it had always been the three of them with Nana when she was alive.

So if there was something right about how tonight was turning out, why was everything feeling so wrong?

Richard hailed a cab and held the door for them, letting Jane and her mom get into the car before he slipped in beside Jane's mother. Jane looked out the window, wishing she were anywhere but where she was: trapped in a cab with her mother and her mother's boyfriend. Not that it would have helped if she could have been someplace else. What she really wanted was to be some*one* else. Like the old lady crossing the street in front of them. Or the man who owned the newsstand on the corner. She pictured him going home to his happy, loving family at the end of a hard day selling papers and candy.

Here's what he'd never had to deal with: a gay guy dumping him.

Her phone buzzed. Simon. It had to be Simon. And he was texting because . . .

Because what, exactly? What did she expect Simon to write?

hey, jane! it's simon. 4 a second there, I thought I wuz gay, but it turns out im not. can u forgive me?

She dug into her bag and took out her phone. One new text message. And it was from . . .

Her *mother*?!

She looked over at her mom sitting beside her, her phone in her lap. Why had her mother texted her instead of just saying whatever she had to say? Jane didn't even know her mom knew how to text.

She opened her phone.

i wish u would tell me what happened.

Jane shook her head. Despite how bewildered she was by her mother's chosen method of communication, she typed back, u wouldn't understand.

They were sitting close enough that Jane could feel the muscles moving in her mother's arm as her mom typed, try me.

Well, it wasn't like she could keep what had happened secret forever.

simon dumped me.

Her mom wasn't nearly as fast a texter as Jane, and it took her a minute or so to enter her answer: i'm really sorry.

Jane didn't type anything back. A moment later, her mother wrote, r u ok?

Jane shrugged, then typed, i guess.

what happened?

Where could she possibly begin? Certainly not in a text.

it's 2 complicated 2 explain.

i wish you'd try.

when? u r always w/richard. As she typed, Jane was practically growling with frustration.

Out of the corner of her eye, Jane could see her mother shaking her head while she wrote her response. whenever i try to make plans w/u, u r always busy. u r either on the phone or w/your friends.

Suddenly Jane remembered the first night she'd hung out with Simon, how her mother had come into her room and tried to talk to her. Jane had been too busy texting to have a conversation. Okay, maybe her mom had a point. But she wasn't *always* busy. Her mom was busy too.

u don't want 2 make time 4 me w/o richard.

For the first time, there was a long pause before her mother started typing. Several minutes passed before her mom's response buzzed in Jane's phone.

i wanted u and richard to get 2 know each other. i m really sorry if i made u feel like i didn't have time 4 u. u r the most important person in the world 2 me. can we spend the day 2gether 2morrow, just u and me?

Jane glanced over at her mom and saw that there was a tear running down her cheek. She felt awful, but it wasn't just because her mother was crying. It was also because of what she was about to write. victoria and natalya are sleeping over 2nite. we r supposed to go out 4 lunch 2morrow.

She heard her mom chuckle as she read Jane's text. Then she wrote, see?

For the first time since Simon had broken up with her, Jane smiled. sorry.

Shaking her head slowly, her mom wrote, u don't have 2 b sorry. i know your friends r important 2 u.

could we have dinner instead? Jane typed back.

There was a moment of silence, and then Jane's mother said, "Richard, I need to reschedule our dinner for tomorrow."

"Sure," answered Richard.

A second later, Jane's phone buzzed. Let's have dinner 2morrow. just the 2 of us. sound good?

sounds great, replied Jane. Then she slipped her phone back into her bag.

Her mom reached over, took Jane's hand, and gave it a squeeze. "It's a date," she whispered.

Jane had to laugh. She'd been planning on a date with her über-hot boyfriend, and instead she was getting a date with her mom. She thought of all the things she had to tell her mother. Her and Simon. Victoria and Jack. Natalya and Colin.

It was going to be a long dinner.

# Chapter
# Forty-two

VICTORIA COULDN'T BELIEVE she was supposed to go out tonight and see people, to have a good time. All she wanted to do was sit in her room in the dark with the covers pulled over her head.

Her mom was being incredibly nice. She'd even tried to cook Victoria, Jane, and Natalya dinner Friday night, an effort that had ended as badly as Victoria's relationship had. Still, it was the thought that counted, and Victoria's mom was trying to think of every way possible to cheer Victoria up. Victoria had completely lied to her, had utterly violated the trust her parents placed in her, and now she was letting her mother take care of her as if she were some kind of Daughter of the Year.

Just one way her life totally sucked.

With less than an hour before she was supposed to meet Jane and Natalya at Barnard, she looked at herself in the mirror. The pink dress that had seemed so cheery when she'd picked it out at Act Two now seemed like an insulting reminder of how happy she'd once been. *When I wore this dress, I was the kind of person who believed in pink.*

She wished there were a color called *sad*. Now, *that* was a fashion statement she could get behind.

Looking in the mirror, she couldn't believe how puffy her eyes were. With her humiliating pink dress and her swollen eyes, she felt like some kind of tragic mix-up of a before-and-after picture from an April Fool's Day issue of *Seventeen*. *The dress says, I am in a relationship, but the face says, I will be alone forever.* Thinking of magazines reminded her of all the times she'd read that cucumbers have antipuffiness qualities. She put down her unused mascara and headed into the kitchen to find a culinary cure for her ugly face.

As she was standing at the kitchen counter slicing the one limp cucumber she'd found in the fridge, she heard the front door to the apartment being opened, and then her sister's enthusiastic voice calling, "Hello! Anyone home?"

Before Victoria could answer, Emily was standing in the kitchen, an overnight bag slung over her shoulder. She saw that Victoria was standing at the counter and clapped her hands in excitement.

"Ooooh, I so clearly picked the right time to come home. What are you baking?"

Victoria looked at the slices of cucumber lying on the cutting board in front of her, then turned to her sister. "My eyes."

"Um, gross." Emily dropped her bag on the floor and grabbed a bottle of seltzer from the fridge. "What's wrong with chocolate-chip cookies? And why are you all dressed up?"

"I'm going to the opening for Jane's grandmother's paintings."

"Right!" Emily nodded, then took a swig of seltzer directly from the bottle.

Victoria wrinkled her nose. "Now who's gross?"

"I'm going to finish it," Emily assured her, pulling a chair out and sitting down. She watched as Victoria sliced two more pieces of cucumber. "Seriously, what are you making?"

"Seriously, these are for my eyes. They're all puffy."

"Let me see." Emily studied Victoria's face for a minute. "They *are* kind of puffy. What happened?"

"Jack and I broke up." Victoria was proud of how matter-of-fact she sounded. Up until now, she hadn't even been able to think, much less say, that sentence without bursting into tears.

Emily literally choked on her seltzer. Leaning forward, she coughed for almost a full minute. Victoria watched her sister without really responding to the fact of her choking. It was as if there were a wall of glass between her and the rest of the world, a fact she noted without really caring about it. Then she picked up two slices of cucumber and, leaning against the counter, pressed one to each of her eyes.

"I'm choking here," Emily informed her once she caught her breath.

"Not anymore," Victoria pointed out, not lowering the

cucumbers. Their silky cool surfaces felt wonderful against her hot, scratchy eyes, and she had no doubt that what she was experiencing was their gentle healing power.

"I'm really sorry," Emily said. "About your breaking up. It seemed like he made you really happy."

At Emily's sincere assessment of how Jack had made Victoria feel, Victoria's eyes immediately brimmed with tears. She flipped the cucumber slices over and pressed them more firmly against her lids.

"So, I mean, can you tell me why?"

Without removing the slices from her face, Victoria launched into the story about everything that had happened between Jack and her. When she got to the part about pretending to go to *Hamlet*, Emily literally gasped.

For the first time since she'd started talking, Victoria lowered the cucumbers from her eyes. "I know," she said solemnly. "And don't tell me, because I already know that I have to tell Mom the truth."

"What?!" Emily's face was the picture of shock. "Are you completely *insane*?"

"No!" Victoria tossed the warm cucumber slices in the trash, then grabbed two fresh ones from the cutting board. "I'm just completely tired of feeling guilty every time I'm with her."

"Listen to me." Emily leaned forward, her elbows on her knees. "I know you never take my advice, but just this once, please. Trust me. You lied. You didn't get caught. Thank your lucky stars and move on."

Victoria couldn't believe it. Her big sister was encouraging her to lie to her parents. Suddenly she remembered something. "Wait a second. How come when I bagged on the community center thing you were all, *What's your problem? Why are you just doing what Jack wants you to do?* And now you're all, *Yeah, go for it. Lie to mom and dad!*"

Emily rolled her eyes. "Vicks, I didn't want you ditching your commitments just to be with some guy. That's completely different from wanting to do something and, you know, bending the truth so you can do it."

When Victoria responded, "Bending the truth?" in an incredulous tone, Emily gave her a somber look. "*This above all: to thine own self be true,*" she recited. Then she pointed her index finger at Victoria. "That's from *Hamlet*, by the way." She paused and smiled archly at her sister. "But I guess you knew that already."

Ignoring her sister's teasing, Victoria placed fresh pieces of cucumber against her eyes, tilted her head back slightly, and continued telling her the story.

"Ouch," said Emily when Victoria got to Lily's repeating what Jack had said about their having nothing in common.

"Thank you!" said Victoria. It felt good to be reminded of what Jack had said behind her back. The anger was a welcome change from sadness.

"So then what happened?" asked Emily.

"I don't know. We had this fight, and then he said, 'Maybe it would be better if we just broke up,' and I said, 'Maybe it would.' And so we did."

"Wow." There was a long pause. Then Emily asked, "Do you

think . . . I mean, I know he did it first, but maybe you didn't need to go straight to DEFCON One?"

"I don't even know what that means," answered Victoria, not removing the cucumbers from her eyes.

"It's . . . just a way of saying 'going nuclear,'" Emily explained. Then, as if she realized her explanation hadn't been particularly illuminating, she said, "I just mean, why did you let him break up with you?"

"Are you kidding?" Victoria pulled the cucumber slices off her eyes and stared at her sister. "I didn't *let him* break up with me. He *broke up* with me. Period. You can't not let someone break up with you if he wants to break up with you! What could I have done when he said, *Maybe it would be better if we just broke up*? Was I supposed to say, *No it wouldn't*?"

"Well . . . yeah," Emily answered slowly. "I just think, you know, you supposedly care about this guy, and then for some reason he floats this thing about breaking up—"

"Floats this thing? For *some reason*?" Victoria echoed, incredulous. "What are you talking about? What reason besides wanting to break up would make a person say, 'I think we should break up'?"

"I don't know!" Emily snapped. "Maybe he was embarrassed. Maybe he thought *you* wanted to break up with *him*. I don't even know the guy. I just know that if you care about someone, you don't break up over some dumb fight. In the *hallway*, no less." She shook her head, as if amazed by nothing so much as Victoria's shabby etiquette. "It sounds like you were kind of harsh."

"Harsh? Harsh!?" Victoria slapped a cucumber slice on the counter. "And it's not harsh to bad-mouth your girlfriend behind her *back*?!"

"Well, I mean, it wasn't nice of him to say something like that," Emily admitted. "But it's not like he said he hated you." She thought for a second. "And anyway, it's kind of true, isn't it? I mean, you guys *don't* seem to have *that much* in common. Do you?"

Victoria pointed at Emily, forgetting in her frustration that she had a cucumber slice in her hand. "I was *trying* to have things in common with him, okay?"

"You can't *try* to have things in common with someone," said Emily. "That's not a relationship; it's . . . I don't know, it's a job interview."

"You make it sound like *I* did something wrong when *he* broke up with *me*. *I'm* the victim here, Emily." She pointed her finger at her chest to illustrate who she was talking about.

"Okay." Emily shrugged. "If you're so invested in being the victim, who am I to take that away from you?"

"Oh!" Victoria cried in frustration. "You are so . . . so . . ." Too mad to find the word she wanted, Victoria threw a cucumber slice at her sister. As Emily shouted in protest, Victoria stormed out of the kitchen. She had a party to go to. Just because she was the victim didn't mean she was going to curl up under the covers in a dark room. She'd bailed on enough things because of Jack.

She wasn't going to bail on Nana.

# Chapter
# Forty-three

JANE HAD SPENT a lot of time on the Barnard campus. Nana loved attending lectures and poetry readings at her alma mater, and Jane had fantasized about going to college there someday, showing Nana her dorm room, taking Nana with her to classes on visiting day. It had always made being on campus exciting, like she was getting a tiny window into her future as an undergraduate.

Tonight was the first time she had been there since Nana died, and it felt wrong, somehow, like the school should have been buried with its alum. Even as she had the thought, Jane knew it was stupid. How many generations of Barnard graduates had died since the school's founding? The idea made her feel depressed. Really, when you thought about it, what was the point of anything? What was the point of going to college, of performing in shows, of falling in love?

In the end, you just died anyway.

As they made their way across the quad and toward a modern building she had never been in before, Jane tried to think less depressing thoughts. Nana. She needed to think about Nana and how much she loved her, how amazing she had been. It was wrong to erase everything important about Nana's life just because Nana had died.

Jane followed her mother and Richard into the elevator. On the fifth floor, the doors opened onto a small, dimly lit corridor with EDGAR VINYARD: THE ELIZABETH RAWLINGS YEARS, A PERMANENT INSTALLATION painted in small red letters along one wall. There was a small bench beneath the words and a coatrack that, even though it was only a few minutes past eight, already had more than a dozen coats hanging on it.

Jane hung up her coat and stepped through a set of double glass doors into the main gallery space. Everywhere were Nana's friends and classmates, people Jane had met over the years at parties at Nana's apartment or at other Barnard events, and they descended on Jane and her mom, hugging them, kissing them, telling them how proud Nana would have been to see them both looking so elegant. It seemed to Jane that no sooner had she extracted herself from one hug than she found herself smothered in another. But even though seeing all these people reminded her of Nana, they didn't make Jane feel closer to her grandmother. Finally, she backed away from the crowd. She wanted to be with Nana.

She needed to see the paintings.

The first one she stopped at was a portrait of Nana standing at a mirror, applying lipstick. She had her lips pursed slightly, and her head was turned to the side, as though she were evaluating her reflection. The angle at which she was studying herself in the mirror made it seem as if she were looking at the viewer, and Jane found herself suddenly looking into her grandmother's eyes. Nana had been much older when Jane was born than she was in this painting, but her eyes hadn't changed. They were the same round shape and green hue as Jane's, and they looked back at her with the same nonjudgmental understanding they'd always had when they looked at her granddaughter.

Jane wished more than anything that she could ask Nana's advice about what had happened with Simon. Nana would have been able to tell if there was something messed up with Jane, if she was destined to spend the rest of her life falling for men who would never love her back.

Jane needed to speak to Nana, to somehow reach out to her across the divide between them. She walked over to the bar, where her mother and Richard were talking to one of Nana's neighbors, an elderly man whose name Jane was never able to recall.

The bartender smiled as she approached. "What can I get you?"

Jane knew exactly what she wanted. "I'd like a piña colada. A *virgin* piña colada," she added quickly.

"I'm sorry," said the bartender, surveying his wares. "I'm afraid I don't have any piña colada mix. Would you like a Shirley Temple?"

Suddenly, as if it had happened seconds and not years before, Jane remembered. She remembered being a little girl, how the waiter had asked her the exact same question, how indignantly she'd responded. And then Nana had stepped in, smoothing things over with the suggestion that Jane, Victoria, and Natalya try the exotic-sounding virgin piña colada. That had been the first time Jane had heard of the drink that she and her friends now thought of as *theirs*. She'd thought she would be toasting her birthday with Nana for decades, but really they'd only had a handful of years left together. Her eyes filled with tears, and she stepped away from the bar abruptly, not even replying to his question.

Her mother was deep in conversation with Nana's neighbor, but Richard looked up as Jane brushed past him. Jane could tell he'd heard the entire exchange. She couldn't see his face, but she could imagine the condescending smile any adult would wear after listening to her and the bartender talk.

Any adult except Nana, who would have understood completely.

Nana. She would never see Nana again. At the thought, at once completely mundane and utterly monstrous, Jane placed her hand over her mouth. She had to get out of here before she started bawling. To her right was a set of French doors leading to a small balcony. She reached for the handle, praying it would move when she pushed it. To her relief, it did. A moment later she was standing in the chilly night air.

The balcony looked out over the campus and south, to midtown and the southern tip of Manhattan. Was there a corner of this crazy island that wasn't wrapped up in her memories of Nana? Rubbing her arms for warmth, Jane leaned against the railing and studied the twinkling lights of the city, thinking about all the concerts, plays, restaurants, cafés, and stores she'd gone to because Nana had taken here there. But Nana was gone. And Simon was as good as gone from her life too.

She didn't think she'd ever felt so alone.

Suddenly the door to the balcony flew open. Jane turned and saw Natalya, her hair a cascade of lush, thick curls. She was wearing the strapless green dress Victoria had chosen for her at Act Two. Over it, she had on a cropped black cardigan sweater.

"Chicken," said Jane, gesturing at the sweater.

"It's *freezing*," countered Natalya defensively. "I couldn't not wear a sweater."

"It hurts to be beautiful," Jane reminded her.

Before Natalya could point out how stupid it was to believe that, the balcony door opened again and Victoria stepped outside. "Okay, it's freezing out here," she observed, in lieu of hello.

"I just needed some air," explained Jane, putting her elbows on the railing. "I miss Nana. It just feels . . . wrong that she's not here."

"I know," Victoria agreed. "I miss her too."

"If she were here, I know just what she'd say," said Natalya.

"What?" asked Jane, curious.

"She'd say, *What are you girls doing outside without a coat?!*"

Jane and Victoria laughed. Natalya was right—Nana had always made them bundle up for their adventures.

"I'd rather be cold than facing people right now," Victoria answered.

"Yeah," agreed Jane. "Freezing to death is a small price to pay for privacy."

Natalya turned around and looked longingly at the warm gallery. "Maybe, only—" but instead of finishing her thought, Natalya let out a yelp. "Hey!"

Jane and Victoria turned to her.

"What?" asked Jane.

"You and Jack broke up, right?" demanded Natalya.

"Nice of you to remind her," said Jane. "I'm sure she would have forgotten otherwise."

"No it's just . . ." Natalya began.

"What?" Victoria insisted.

Even though it was just the three of them on the balcony, Natalya lowered her voice to a whisper. "Vicks, I think . . . I think Jack is here."

Victoria spun around and stared at Natalya. "You what?"

Without saying a word, Natalya pointed to the room beyond the glass doors. Standing there, looking out at the three girls, was Jack.

# Chapter
## Forty-four

VICTORIA STARED AT HIM. He was wearing black jeans and a pale gray sweater over a blue button-down, and he looked so handsome she had to turn away. As if her movement had decided him, Jack strode toward the doors.

"What should we do?" asked Natalya hurriedly.

"Don't leave me," begged Victoria.

"We won't," Jane promised.

Jack pushed open the doors and walked onto the balcony.

Nobody said anything for a long moment, and then Victoria found her voice. "What are you *doing* here, Jack?"

"We need to talk." Jack's voice was firm.

Protectively, Jane and Natalya moved even closer to their friend.

"About what?" asked Victoria. He'd *already* broken up with her. What else was there to say?

Jack looked at Jane. He looked at Natalya. Then he asked Victoria, "Can I talk to you alone for a minute?"

"Maybe it would be a good idea if we, you know . . ." Jane didn't finish her sentence, just whispered in Victoria's ear, "We're only a text away." Victoria hesitated, then squeezed Jane's hand and released it.

The two of them slipped silently through the doors.

Once they were gone, Victoria repeated her question. "What are you doing here?"

"Look, I don't know why Lily told you what I said."

Had Jack seriously come all the way up here just to blame what had happened between them on *Lily*? When Lily had done Victoria a favor! Victoria folded her arms across her chest. "First of all, I really don't see what it matters now. And second of all, I'm *grateful* to her that she told me."

Jack rubbed his forehead. "Yeah, well, that makes one of us. Look . . . I'm sorry that I said that to her, okay? I was kind of joking."

"You were *joking*?!" Victoria started to object.

Quickly, Jack interrupted. "I said *kind of*." He paused. "I guess I said it to Lily as a joke, you know, like, *Oh, well, too bad I love this girl, but we've got nothing in common.* I guess that's why she repeated it, because she thought it was just a joke." He crossed his arms. "But maybe I meant it a little bit, too. I mean, I was bummed you didn't want to come to the *Twilight Zone* marathon."

"I *hate* science fiction!" Victoria wailed. "And I'd already done all those things you wanted me to do."

"What? Wait, what are you talking about?" Jack honestly seemed to have no idea what she meant.

"The concert. The recording session." Victoria counted off items on her fingers as she listed them.

Jack threw up his hands. "You said you wanted to go."

"Because *you* wanted to!" Victoria could have cried with frustration. "I don't care about Lost Leaders. I barely even care about music. I care about *you*, okay? And here I am, trying to make your interests my interests—which you *never* do, by the way—and all you can do is tell your friends we have nothing in common?"

"So why didn't you *say* something?" Jack seemed as frustrated as Victoria felt. "You said you *loved* being at the recording session. I thought you were *psyched* to go to the concert."

Could Jack *seriously* not see why she'd done what she'd done? "It was *Valentine's Day*! I just wanted to be with you. And you didn't even care about being with me." Tears welled up in her eyes and spilled over at the memory. Victoria knew that in a minute or two, it would be as if the cucumbers had never happened.

Jack put his hands on his head, yanking his hair in fury. "I *did* care. I *always* want to be with you. I just don't care that much about Valentine's Day."

"Well, I *do*!" Victoria was almost as angry at herself for crying as she was at Jack for making her cry.

"Then why didn't you tell me? Why didn't you tell me you

were mad? Why didn't you at least yell at me?!"

"Because I *can't yell at people*!" Victoria yelled at the top of her lungs.

As soon as the words were out of her mouth, Victoria realized how stupid they sounded. She could also see that Jack was trying not to smile.

"Fine," she said angrily. "Laugh."

"I'm not laughing," Jack promised. He pressed his lips together.

Neither of them said anything.

When Victoria finally spoke, her voice was quiet. "How could you have said something like that to Lily and not to me? Even as a joke?"

Jack took a step toward her. "Vicks, I am so, so sorry. Please believe me." He reached out to stroke her cheek, but she jerked her head away.

"But you . . . you broke up with me," she reminded him.

"You think I don't know that?" His voice was almost a cry. "I didn't know what else to do. You sounded so mad, and everyone was staring at us and . . . Vicks, please. If I could take back one thing I've ever done in my *life*, it would be breaking up with you." He took another step closer to her. "Please?" His voice was a whisper now.

Victoria's blue eyes shimmered behind their curtain of tears. "I wish you'd said you'd skip Rajiv's birthday when I told you about this show."

"I wish I had too." Jack put his hands on her shoulders. "I wish I'd realized how important it was to you. But I'm here now."

Victoria bit her lip. "It's hard for me to ask for things. It's hard for me to say if I'm upset."

"Yeah, I think I'm getting that now," said Jack.

Victoria put her hands on Jack's waist. "This has been a really bad week," she admitted.

"Uh-huh," he agreed. He pressed his forehead to hers. "Vicks, the last thing I would ever want to do is hurt you, okay? And I'm really sorry. And I don't care if you don't like listening to music or recording music. You are the kindest, most generous, most beautiful girl I've met in my life."

Victoria pulled away slightly so she could look at Jack. "Do you wish I were more like Lily and Rajiv?"

Jack smiled back at her. "Do you wish I were more like Jane and Natalya?"

Victoria laughed. "No! I mean . . . sometimes I guess I wish I were as sure of you as I am of them," she admitted. "But I don't want you to be different than you are."

"Well . . ." said Jack, putting his hands on her waist. "I don't want you to be different either."

"But what if we don't have enough in common?" asked Victoria anxiously.

Jack cocked his head, considering her question. "Maybe what we have in common is less important than how we deal with what we *don't* have in common. Like, I don't like baking, but I like eating all the amazing stuff that you bake. And you don't care about making music, but you don't mind listening to me play for you."

"I *love* listening to you play for me!" Victoria corrected him quickly.

"Okay," said Jack. "So there you have it." For a minute, they just stood there, arms around each other, staring into each other's eyes.

"And I love you," Victoria added firmly.

"And I love you, too," Jack said.

And then Victoria stood on her tiptoes and pressed her lips to his. As Jack wrapped his arms more tightly around her and kissed her back, she remembered the line Jane had quoted to her. Maybe it *was* better to have loved and lost than never to have loved at all.

But it was way better to keep on loving.

# Chapter
## Forty-five

NO SOONER HAD Natalya and Jane stepped back inside than Jane was swept up in a hug by a British woman who had apparently been a friend of Nana's in Zimbabwe, and who began peppering Jane with questions about her life. For a minute, Natalya lingered next to Jane, but then she let the crowd carry her away toward the picture of Nana that had been on the invitation. She was studying the way the artist had made the water look like it was rippling in a light wind when her phone rang.

She couldn't imagine who would be calling her unless it was her parents, wanting to know that she'd arrived at Barnard safely. She slipped her phone out of her bag and saw the one name she never in a million years would have expected to read on the screen.

COLIN.

*Colin?* Why was Colin calling her? It was Saturday night. Wasn't he at Alison's party, laughing and waltzing and having the time of his life with his girlfriend, who he liked so much that he'd fooled around with Natalya behind her back?

Her phone buzzed in her hand like an angry bug. She never wanted to talk to Colin again.

But she had to know why he was calling.

She never wanted to talk to him again.

Why was he calling?

She never wanted to talk to him again.

She had to know.

"What do you want, Colin?" Her voice as she picked up was sharp enough that two or three people turned to look at her, and she ducked her head and quickly crossed the room back to the entryway, empty except for the now overflowing coatrack.

"I want to talk to you."

"Then talk." She was surprised by how angry and sure of herself she sounded. If she were Colin, she didn't know if she would have dared talk to someone who sounded as mad as she did.

But Colin dared. "I want to . . . no, I *need* to explain. Natalya, I didn't mean to be a jerk. I really meant everything I said to you. About liking you and thinking about you all that time. And I planned to break up with Alison on Sunday. That was not a lie."

Yeah, right. It so clearly *was*. "Oh, sure. That's why you said you regretted it." She emphasized the words so he would know she was repeating his.

"Okay, I deserved that," Colin admitted. He hesitated, then went on. "Look, I couldn't explain before, but as of tomorrow's paper, what I'm about to say isn't going to be a secret anymore. It might even be on the Web as early as tonight. So I'm not betraying anyone by telling you what I'm about to tell you, but if I'd told you on Monday, I would have been breaking someone's confidence."

Despite how mad she was, Natalya couldn't help being curious. How could tomorrow's paper and the Internet have anything to do with why Colin had chosen Alison over her?

Colin took a deep breath. "Last weekend, when they were at their country house and you and I were . . . together, Alison's parents told her that her father was being investigated by the federal government—the Securities and Exchange Commission. And this morning, he was arrested by the FBI."

Natalya gasped. *"What?"*

"He's been . . . well, I don't actually understand all the details, but he's been fudging numbers, misleading investors in his hedge fund, and he lost a lot of money and covered it up."

"I don't . . . I don't understand." Natalya's voice was a whisper. "She's having that big party tonight."

"She *was* having a big party tonight. This morning she had to call everyone to cancel it. Her parents didn't expect the story to break so soon; they thought they had more time before the arrest. I guess his lawyers were trying to work out some kind of deal, and then yesterday it all fell apart."

Suddenly, Natalya remembered Alison crying to Jordan in the bathroom, *It just doesn't make any sense.* She pictured her quiet demeanor when they talked about the party, and Jordan's frantic excitement, like she was a cheerleader trying to encourage a despondent team. No wonder Alison hadn't been looking forward to her party—it was a huge lie she was being asked to participate in.

"Oh my god," Natalya whispered. She tried to imagine the humiliation Alison had to be feeling, the fear of what would come next. Had Alison's mother known what her husband was doing? Were Alison's parents going to get divorced?

Colin was still talking. "I'm not trying to excuse what I did, Natalya. And I'm so, so sorry for hurting you. But I couldn't . . . I couldn't respond to her telling me the news about her dad by telling her I was breaking up with her. I just couldn't do that to someone. And I couldn't tell you what she told me, because it just would have been another betrayal."

In spite of herself, Natalya found herself feeling for Colin's predicament. As if he could sense her wavering, Colin said, "Please. Please, Natalya. Put yourself in my shoes."

"I . . ." Natalya began, but she couldn't finish her sentence.

Colin spoke quickly. "Look, I know you're at that art opening with your friends. I know you have to go. And I know you probably think I'm the world's biggest jerk. And I know I deserve that. But I want you to know that I think you're the most amazing girl I've ever met. And maybe I can't do anything about that right now, but my feelings for you aren't going to go away."

"I really like you," whispered Natalya.

"Natalya, I need to see you," Colin said.

Natalya imagined Alison sitting in her room, the list of people she'd just called to cancel her party on the desk in front of her. She remembered how Alison's face had lit up at lunch when talk turned to Colin.

Natalya took a deep breath. "Alison's my friend."

"Please."

What could she say?

"Natalya . . ." Colin's voice was pleading.

She liked him so much. And he liked her. What did it matter if they didn't act on their feelings? Wasn't the betrayal *having* the feelings in the first place?

But she knew the answer. Maybe she had no control over how she felt. But she did have control over what she did.

"I can't, Colin. I'm sorry, but I can't." She took the phone from her ear and pressed END CALL. As she watched his name disappear from her screen, she wondered if she would ever see it there again.

# Chapter
## Forty-six

WHEN JANE AND Victoria finally found her, Natalya was sitting on the floor behind the coatrack, her phone pressed against her chest.

"Oh my god!" cried Victoria. "Nat, what happened?"

Natalya told them. By the time she'd finished, both Jane and Victoria had sunk down to sit beside her on the floor.

"Wow," said Jane.

"Double wow," agreed Victoria.

They were all silent for a long minute.

"Wait!" Natalya cried. She turned to Victoria, suddenly remembering. "What happened with you and Jack?"

Jane waved away the question. "Oh, they love each other; it was all a big misunderstanding; we'll get the wedding announcements in the mail."

Natalya's eyes popped open. "Seriously?"

Victoria laughed happily. "Not the wedding announcement part." But then she grew serious. "Nat, what . . . what are you going to do?"

Before Natalya could answer, the bartender appeared around the corner. If he thought it was weird to find three girls sitting on the floor in what was basically the coat closet, he didn't say so. Perhaps that was one of the things they taught a person in bartending school.

He looked from each of the Darlings to the next, then asked, "Is one of your grandmothers the woman in the painting?"

Jane raised her hand slightly, like she was in school and he was her teacher, and he nodded briefly, as if she'd given just the answer he was hoping for. Then he ducked out of the room. A second later, he reappeared, carrying a tray with three frothy drinks.

The girls gasped.

"Wait, you said you didn't have any piña colada mix," Jane said. Her tone was accusatory, as if she'd caught him in a lie.

"A guy brought me a can of it. He said he got it at the bodega across the street."

"A random *guy*?" asked Natalya suspiciously. She'd had her hand out, ready to accept a drink, but now she pulled it back.

"Well, I guess that all depends on how you look at it." The bartender turned back to Jane. "Is your mother here with a 'random' date or a serious boyfriend?"

"*Richard* gave you the mix?" Jane's eyes were huge with incredulity. "He went out and *bought it*?!" She remembered how he'd overheard her ordering the drinks and given her what she'd assumed was a condescending look.

The bartender handed each girl a napkin, followed by a glass. "Seemed like a nice guy."

"Yeah," said Jane weakly.

"Well, cheers!" And with that, the bartender was gone and the three girls were alone again.

"Richard," said Natalya, shaking her head in amazement. "Who'd have guessed?"

"Seriously," agreed Victoria.

Out of nowhere, Victoria blurted out, "I should have listened to you, Jane." Jane and Natalya both looked at her, and Victoria took Jane's hand in hers. "When you told me to talk to Jack about wanting him to come to the opening."

Jane smiled at her. "Of course you should have."

"And *I* should have listened to you when you told me not to try to be friends with Colin. You knew that wasn't really what I wanted," Natalya told Jane.

"Naturally," Jane agreed. "Because, as we can see from my track record, I know everything about love." They all laughed. "Oh, and by the way," she added, "*I* should have listened to you guys."

"When?" asked Victoria.

"Yeah, when?" asked Natalya.

"Remember when you said it sounded like Simon was gay?" Jane asked Natalya.

"I said it sounded like Simon was gay?" asked Natalya, surprised. "How prescient."

"At Act Two. When I first told you about our night together. Well, specifically I guess you asked me if I was *saying* Simon was gay. Which is, you know, kind of the same thing. And I should have listened to you."

"I probably should have been more forceful," Natalya said. "Next time I'll just come right out and say it if I think your boyfriend sounds like he's into guys."

"I appreciate that," said Jane dryly.

"You guys, I don't think love sucks anymore," Victoria announced.

"Oh, *there's* a surprise," said Jane.

"Seriously," agreed Natalya.

Victoria put a hand on Natalya's shoulder. "Nat, what are you going to do?" she asked for the second time.

Natalya shook her head slowly back and forth. "I'm not going to see him again. I'm going to be a good friend to Alison."

"That's going to be hard," Victoria said gently. "You and Colin really like each other."

"Don't remind me," begged Natalya, dropping her head back against the wall.

"Oh my god!" Jane cried into the silence that Natalya's admission created. "I just remembered something Nana once told me."

"What?" asked Natalya and Victoria.

Jane gazed at the spot where her grandmother's name was painted on the wall. She spoke slowly. "She said she didn't regret any relationship she'd ever had."

For a moment, the girls were silent, and then Natalya confessed, "I don't know if I can say that. I kind of regret what happened with Colin."

Jane looked disappointed. "You really didn't get *anything* out of being with him?"

"Well . . ." Natalya hesitated, then said, "He taught me to waltz. I guess that's a good thing to know how to do."

Victoria smiled at Natalya. "It's so cool that you know how to waltz. I wish *I* knew how to waltz."

"Yeah, well, I wish the guy I liked didn't have a girlfriend," Natalya sighed.

"Oh, Nat," said Victoria. She slipped her arm around Natalya, who turned to Jane. "Okay, what about you? Do you regret going out with Simon?"

"I don't know," Jane said. "Kind of." But then she grew thoughtful. "Well, I guess . . . he got me back onstage. And acting opposite him definitely made me a better actress. And I'm glad I got to work with Mark." Thinking about Mark made her remember their conversation after rehearsal, how he'd said she was a really great actress. She remembered something else, too: how it had seemed like he was on the verge of saying one more thing to her right before the cleaning guy walked in.

And suddenly she realized something.

"Guys, I don't think Nana meant she didn't regret *anything* about her relationships." She leaned forward excitedly. "She just meant that she wouldn't give up the experience of having had them. That she loved who she was, and she wouldn't have *been* who she was without everything that had happened to her. The

310

good *and* the bad." Realizing what her grandmother must have meant by what she'd said made Jane feel closer to Nana than she had in a long time, like they really had somehow crossed the line between the living and the dead to speak to each other.

Victoria put down her drink and wrapped her free arm around Jane. "You guys, I love you so much."

"We love you too!" Jane said, putting her head on Victoria's shoulder.

"Talk about experiences making you who you are," Natalya said. "I feel like I am who I am because of the two of you."

"Oh, I feel that way too!" cried Victoria.

"Me three," agreed Jane. She lifted her glass, and Victoria wiggled free so she could get hers. Then all three of them clinked their drinks together.

"To us!" said Jane. "To love!"

"To us!" echoed Natalya and Victoria.

And with that, they drank happily from their tall, elegant glasses.

They were the Darlings.

The Darlings in love.

## ACKNOWLEDGMENTS

The writer alone in a room of her own is a beautiful image, but it in no way captures my experience of writing *The Darlings in Love*. So a huge thank you to those who sat in the room with me (literally and figuratively): Rachel Cohn, Rebecca Friedman, Ben Gantcher, Jodi Kahn, Bernie Kaplan, E. Lockhart, and Helen Perelman. And my hat is off to the fabulous team at Hyperion—Deborah Bass, Ann Dye, Nellie Kurtzman, Andrew Sansone, Marci Senders, Laura Schreiber, and Dina Sherman. As always, it takes a village (for me) to write a book. Thanks for being my fellow citizens.

MELISSA KANTOR is the author of *The Darlings Are Forever*, a Junior Library Guild selection; the best-selling *Confessions of a Not It Girl*, a *Booklist* Best Romance Novel for Youth; *If I Have a Wicked Stepmother, Where's My Prince?*, a YALSA Teens Top Ten Pick; *The Breakup Bible*, a YALSA Best Books for Young Adults nominee; and *Girlfriend Material*, a Texas Lone Star Reading List Pick. Melissa is a teacher in Brooklyn, New York, where she lives with her husband, the poet Benjamin Gantcher, and their three children. Visit her online at www.melissakantor.com.